IN THE MOUTH OF THE LION

J GUENTHER

DEDICATION

No man is an island, and this is especially true for writers, though they may work alone in garrets or cellars much of the time. My world of writing is surrounded by an ocean of inspiration and connected by isthmuses of encouragement. People who were particularly important to this process include (but are not limited to): Kate Guenther, Edith Battles, Peggy Connelly, Joe Tomasi, Ann and Shelly Lowenkopf, Dave Kenney, Richard Condon, and Dr. Margaret Fate.

Other works by J Guenther
Sail Away on My Silver Dream
(Mischievous Muse Press)

Commendation for *In the Mouth of the Lion:*

"Guenther takes the factual proximity of two historical characters during the height of World War II to create an astonishing what-if novel about the motives for some of Hitler's darker fantasies. An amazing read . . ." —Edna Bay, historian

"J Guenther's thought-provoking WW2 novel, In the Mouth of the Lion, involves the reader in a suspenseful 'could happen?/did happen?' action-packed story. Though fictional, its sound logic led me toward 'did happen.'" —DavId A. Kenney, WW2 OSS Veteran

"An intelligent, original, fast-paced thriller with vivid characterization and a unique plot line." —James Flaherty

"J Guenther's In The Mouth of The Lion takes the reader on an exciting journey into Hitler's Germany during World War II. Historic characters go on a fictional mission cleverly devised by the author. You will be holding your breath as you follow Carl Jung through a long dark tunnel as he heads to a meeting with the world's most dangerous man." —Jean Shriver, author of The Einstein Solution.

"This fast-moving and absorbing novel examines what might have happened had two most remarkable men met-- and how that encounter might have come to pass." —Kathryn McCary

ACKNOWLEDGMENTS

Thanks to: my editor, Cat Spydell; my beta readers, Edna Bay, Paula Reuben, Dave Kenney, Jim Flaherty, Kathryn McCary, Jeanne Gassman, and Jean Shriver; my friends at SMC Writing Group; Tom Mooney; and my screenwriting instructor, Jeff Hoppenstand.

Prologue
Löwensburg, Austria
June 30, 1942

Carl Jung, tall and scholarly, faces a pair of massive brass doors gleaming in morning sunlight. Above them, an oversized Nazi eagle spreads golden wings, clutching a globe in its talons. Jung looks up at it and scowls, thinking, *God forbid that the world should fall into Hitler's claws.*

He signals his readiness to enter with a nod. Two stone-faced SS men swing the doors apart in perfect synchronization to reveal a dark tunnel. The warm sun at Jung's back casts his shadow, a gaunt giant, far into the mountain.

Beside the doors, a guard throws a switch marked *Tunnel Lichter,* and a line of dim ceiling lamps every six meters flickers on. Even so, the far end of the passageway cannot be seen.

Jung stiffens and takes a deep breath and a few tentative steps. Then he strides forward, gradually moving faster and faster, his footsteps echoing as he silently counts off his paces, *One . . . two . . . three . . . four . . .*

Without warning, the outer doors boom shut. Jung looks behind him, then continues a bit slower. *No turning back, now; he waits for me at the end of the tunnel.*

Fifty nine . . . sixty . . . sixty one . . . The lights die, plunging Jung into blackness. He swears and snaps on a flashlight.

As he walks, the beam turns yellow, then fades to orange. Jung reaches out to guide himself along the wall. Soon, he is in total darkness again, wondering whether he will live long enough to complete his journey into the mind of Adolf Hitler.

Chapter 1
OSS Station, Bern, Switzerland
8:00 AM, June 18, 1942

Bern lay peaceful and quiet in bright morning sunshine. Church steeples pierced a green canopy of trees, and in the distance, mountains dominated the horizon.

Shattering the silence, a lone motorcyclist roared along the Zurich-to-Bern road, wearing a leather jacket, goggles and aviator's cap, with a leather dispatch case over one shoulder. A plume of grey exhaust billowed out behind the motorbike.

Upon arriving in Bern, the motorcyclist turned onto the cobblestoned Herrengasse and parked beside a four-story mansion, not far from the *Bundeshaus*. From the street, no one would have suspected the building housed the continental station of the newly-formed American Office of Strategic Services.

Soon the leather case, goggles, helmet, and other discarded apparel lay upon plush carpeting, marking the wake of the motorcyclist all the way to a pair of pink panties abandoned beside a rattan couch.

Supine upon the couch was OSS spymaster Allen Dulles, 50, handsome, intelligent, and terse. The motorcyclist, Mary Bancroft, a fascinating blonde, straddled him. The two spoke fluent German as the couch creaked rhythmically beneath them.

Mary grinned. "I used to think I'd pump enemy agents for secrets when I became a spy."

"Spy? You're no spy, Mary; you're an analyst—a proper job for a proper Bostonian."

She made a face at him. "But I so want to be a spy, Allen. I read all the manuals. You're the station boss. You can make me one of your agents."

"Too dangerous."

"I like dangerous things."

"Like this one?"

"Oh, yes, Allen. Yes! Yes!! Yes!!!"

Later, Dulles, still sitting on the couch, but looking more his usual professorial self in tweeds, reached out and swatted Mary's bottom with a loud *smack* as she put on her bra.

"Shit!" She spun to face him. "What the hell was that for?"

Dulles laughed. "Some spy you'd make. A little surprise, and you swear in English."

"*Scheisskopf!* Is that better, Mr. Dulles?"

Dulles swung with his other hand, but missed as Mary dodged away.

"We've got work to do," she said.

Late that afternoon, Mary looked at the clock. "Damn! It's almost six, Allen. I'm supposed to be in Zurich at seven." She stood and hurriedly put on her motorcycle jacket.

"Big date?"

"Dr. Jung's lecture."

"Thought you already knew all that psychology business."

3

"I still can learn a lot from him."

"Like what?"

"Allen, I think you're jealous."

"Me? 'Course not. Jung's what . . . ? Seventy?"

"He's only sixty-seven. You've seen his psychological profiles of Hitler and Mussolini?"

"Not bad for an article in Cosmopolitan."

"Well, I think he could be useful." Mary opened her center desk drawer and took out a ten inch square of poster board embellished with a complicated symmetrical pattern.

Dulles noticed. "Nice. What is it?"

"It's a mandala. I painted it for Dr. Jung." She slipped it into her shoulder bag.

"How long did that take you?"

"A week or so."

Dulles rolled his eyes and grunted.

Someone knocked on the door. Mary opened it and found Jaffe, Dulles's young chauffeur, bodyguard, and man of all work, standing there, grim-faced. He handed a folded message to Mary. "That just came in. I . . . I think it's important." He turned and left.

She opened the note and stared at it in disbelief for several seconds, then sneezed twice. *Damn! I thought I was over that.* "Allen, you'd better look at this." She sneezed once more and handed the note to Dulles. It read:

17 JUNE 1942. (AUSTRIA): WAFFEN SS TROOPS MACHINE-GUNNING JEWS NEAR TERZENDORF. EST. 10,000 SHOT, SO FAR THIS YEAR. #404

"That can't be right, can it?" Mary said, standing beside Allen. "These are civilians. I can't believe it." She felt a tear run down her cheek.

"We've heard rumors. Worse ones," Dulles said. He put the note on his desk spike, glanced at the clock, then looked at her closely. "You'll never make it to Zurich by seven. Maybe Jaffe should drive you."

"I'd sooner walk." She wiped her eyes and grabbed her goggles, helmet, and dispatch case from her desk.

They kissed. Mary turned and ran down the stairs, sneezing half way down and again as she reached the bottom. Dulles shouted after her, "Be careful on that damn motorbike. Jung won't mind if you're late."

She ran outside, started her motorcycle, and zoomed off toward Zurich.

Chapter 2
Zurich University Lecture Hall
7:00 PM

Mary Bancroft arrived at the University just as the tower clock chimed seven. She parked her motorcycle in front of the psychology lecture hall, snatched off her goggles and cap, then ran up the steps, still wearing the shoulder bag. A sign on the entrance stated in English:

LECTURE 7 PM TONIGHT
DR. PROF. CARL JUNG, M.D.
SPEAKING ON: "THE SHADOW"

As she entered, Mary slipped past a photographer burdened with a camera, tripod, and equipment cases. Twenty meters ahead of her, she saw Carl Jung walking towards the lecture room, holding the hand of a little boy, evidently one of his great-grandsons. The boy, about six, lugged Carl's briefcase in his free hand, looking up at him and talking as they walked together. They stopped at the door to the auditorium, and the boy handed the briefcase up to Carl, before running to a woman standing nearby. Mary grinned.

Jung entered the lecture hall, and the customary form of applause at German-speaking universities greeted him: rapping on the arms of the chairs. Mary hurried to the open doorway and looked for an empty spot inside, but students and faculty already jammed the room.

Jung put his notes on the lectern, and the room went silent. Mary leaned against the door jamb, trying to remain inconspicuous. She felt anxious and put her hand over her nose and mouth to stifle the sneeze she knew was coming. It came, loud enough for Jung to hear. He looked at her standing there, then smiled, and pointed to an empty seat at the far end of the fifth row. Mary rushed in, blushing as she passed him, and sat as directed.

Jung turned to the blackboard and chalked a horizontal line high up. He stood back and, pointing, said, in English, "The human psyche. Up above, on the surface, we have the conscious mind. Below it, the unconscious: the Cave of The Shadow. Notice that I have left more room below the line than above. Like an iceberg, most of the personality lies beneath the surface. Also, it is easier to write down here than up there."

A little laughter followed. Jung labeled the two areas "conscious" and "unconscious," then asked, "We have some Americans here, do we not?"

Many hands went up, including Mary's. Jung stepped closer to her. "Yes, Frau Rufenacht. You are familiar with the opening line of the American radio show called 'The Shadow?'"

"Yes, Dr. Jung. 'Who knows what evil lurks in the hearts of men—?'"

"'—The Shadow knows,'" Jung droned, in a passable imitation of Lamont Cranston.

The Americans laughed. Jung continued, gesturing at the blackboard, "Only, in our case, it is the Shadow who lurks in the hearts of men, and we who want to know what the devil is inside."

Jung added a sun symbol above the dividing line, a square on the line, and, directly below that, a filled-in square tagged "The Shadow." He strode across the front of the room, stopped, and pointed back at the solid square.

"Everyone has his own personal Shadow, his dark repository of rejected and repressed traits, even Carl Jung, hard as that may be to believe."

The audience laughed once again . . .

Notes now covered most of the board. Jung concluded his lecture and put down the chalk. The roomful of students knocked on their chairs with enthusiasm. Mary grinned and rapped, too.

"Are there any questions?" Jung asked. "Here." He pointed at a student in the front row.

"Why is the Shadow so dangerous, Dr. Jung? If it's a complex of rejected evil, isn't it just like a wastebasket?"

Some students laughed. Jung did not. He addressed the assembly at large. "Imagine a semi-intelligent, powerful wastebasket without a conscience and chock full of evil desires. Wouldn't you be a little afraid of it? You should be. Next question?

A forest of hands went up, but Jung acknowledged Mary's. "Yes?"

"Could you go over projection again, Dr. Jung?"

He nodded. Picking up the chalk, he drew an eye on the blackboard to the left of the shadow square, then added a stick figure out to the right. "Roughly speaking, projection occurs when the unconscious perceives other people through the lens of its own Shadow." Jung wrote "projection" beneath the square.

At that same moment, in Terzendorf concentration camp, Dr. Marcus Rosenberg was standing at attention, facing a camp guard. The guard, a malodorous, sneering Neanderthal in a shabby trench coat, spat out,

"Filthy swine! Piece of shit!" and took out his truncheon. Marcus trembled. Sigmund Rosenberg, standing nearby, started to protest, but Marcus swiftly motioned for his son not to interfere.

Jung continued, "The darker our Shadow is, the more evil we are apt to see in others, even when it's not there."

In the camp, Marcus protected his ears with his arms. The guard struck him repeatedly, spewing spittle as he cursed. "We know all about your perversions, Jew! Ape! Animal!" Marcus fell to his knees, bleeding and in pain. Sigmund stood there, his eyes wide, biting his lip and holding his hands over his mouth.

"For this reason, we should be careful when judging others. And even when we are not projecting, even when our judgment is sound, our opinion usually lacks relevance." Jung shaded the stick figure with the chalk, then turned back to the students. Several had their hands raised. "More questions? You, there."

A student asked, "What is your opinion of hypnosis for treating mental conditions?"

"I don't use it anymore. We can too easily violate a client's autonomy by forcing our own characteristics on him in hypnosis, often another instance of projection . . . "

Afterward, the students filed out, but Mary stood near the door and waited for Jung.

To one side of the crush of departing students, the photographer Mary had seen earlier set up his camera. Two academics then posed with Jung, shaking hands beside the lectern, while the photographer squeezed the shutter bulb and pulled the trigger on his flash tray. There was a *bang!* and the flash powder lit the front of the room, releasing a cloud of pungent smoke.

As the last of the audience straggled out, Jung approached Mary. "The usual place?"

"Sure."

The two of them went to a small restaurant nearby that catered to faculty. There, they ordered bad wartime coffee and over-priced rationed pastries and sat talking about the lecture. Afterward, they walked together back towards the psychology building parking lot. Jung lit their way with a hooded blackout flashlight, as required by wartime regulations.

Jung asked, "What are you doing about your marriage, Mary?"

She sighed. "Nothing, really. Jacques and I have decided to continue as we are: married, but living apart. We'll divorce eventually." She didn't add, "If the Allies win the war." That thought pervaded everyone's plans, and she didn't feel it necessary to state. Instead, she said, "I'm going to ride out the war in Bern as a translator."

"You never did say whom you work for."

I can't tell him I work for American Intelligence, Mary thought. *I'll just make up a story.* "A new American company. Very boring. What about you, Carl? Anything up?"

Jung stopped walking and faced her. "I have stopped taking new clients. I intend to let my practice dwindle and eventually stop doing therapy altogether."

Oh, no! Mary's face fell. "You can't retire."

Jung shook his head. "I am almost seventy. I have plumbed the depths of the human psyche for forty years, now. I have seen it all. It is time for me to do something else."

Mary's stomach churned when Jung said this. "But why *now*—" She paused, covered her mouth, and sneezed several times.

"Gesundheit!"

As they stood there on the darkened avenue, a misshapen woman approached, steadying herself on two canes. As she reached them, she attempted to step off the curb, but staggered, on the verge of falling. Mary rushed ahead and steadied her, then she and Carl helped the woman down to the cobblestones. She murmured her thanks, wished them a good night, and crossed the street.

Mary said in a low voice, "That poor woman,"

Jung watched the woman go, then turned to Mary. "Last year, in Germany, they killed hundreds of people like her. They called it 'euthanasia,' and 'mercy death,' but it was murder."

Hundreds, Mary thought. She wondered if she should tell Jung about the thousands #404 had mentioned. *No,* she decided, *he has enough on his mind.* She put her arm through his, and they continued to stroll along the darkened shops that lined both sides of the street. "People need you, Dr. Jung. Can't you take just a few more clients?"

Jung shook his head. "Sorry, Mary, but I am not interested. My students can use the work. Besides, I have to stop sometime."

"But not *now!* Maybe wait till the war is over. Please, Dr. Jung?"

"There is very little challenge in it for me, anymore."

Mary gripped his arm. "I have a friend who needs therapy. Several friends."

"All right, just for you, I will take one new client, only. Your other friends will have to find someone else."

"Thank you, I really appreciate it. But what will you do when you give up therapy?

"I will continue my lectures. I have a book or two in me." He paused, then added, "I would like also to do some painting. These are the things that still excite me."

"Speaking of painting, I made you something." They halted, and Mary pulled the mandala from her shoulder bag. "I thought it might bring you luck," she said, as she handed it to him.

Jung scanned the painting with the aid of his flashlight. "This is quite nice, Mary. A very thoughtful present."

"I hoped you'd like it."

"And I do. I will put it in my office where my clients can look at it instead of my ugly puss. I thank you."

Mary beamed at him and looked into his eyes again. "Can you see me again next week?"

"Alas, my appointment book is already full."

"The sneezing has started again."

"So I have observed. Did it start after a particularly disturbing bit of news about the war?"

Mary shook her head. "No, it started a month ago, out of the blue."

"And stress triggers it, as it did several years ago?"

"Yes."

"How frequent is it?"

"Not as bad as before. Twenty or thirty times a day, maybe."

"That often? It must happen at work, then, yes?"

"Yes."

"That is most interesting. This new American company, this boring place you work, is full of stress, stress severe enough to echo your father's death, which initiated the problem. That doesn't quite add up, does it?" He turned and they began walking again, arm in arm.

Mary wanted to kick herself. He'd caught her lying. "Okay, Dr. Jung, I fibbed. The job is stressful."

"Those translations must be something to behold."

Ouch! Rub it in, Carl, Mary thought. *I deserve it for being careless.* "It's hard to explain."

Jung waved that away. "No need to explain." Mary relaxed, until he added, "You can tell me all about it at our next session."

Damn! I thought I was off the hook. But at least he'll see me. "When?" she asked.

"I will have to work you in after hours. How about eight, next Thursday?"

I'll have to think up a better cover story before then, Mary thought. *But what will I tell him?*

Chapter 3
Oberkommando Wehrmacht (OKW) Building, Berlin
8:00 PM, June 18, 1942

General Friedrich Olbricht, 53, tall and laid-back, roared down Bendlerstrasse in his Opel Admiral, heading for the offices of the German High Command (OKW). His field-grey Opel, its top down, small OKW flags flapping on all four fenders, drew a lot of attention, mostly because it no longer had a fully functioning muffler. Olbricht was secretly quite proud of the car, with its bullet holes in muffler, bodywork, windows, and one headlight. All these scars proclaimed, "This car has been at the Front." And so it had.

Olbricht brought the Opel to a halt in front of the OKW building, got out, and let an attendant drive it to a line of polished Mercedes Benzes parked nearby. The General, in Wehrmacht-uniformed splendor, except for his spectacles, continued on foot towards the main entrance, carrying only a red folder. Two passing privates stared, then came to attention and saluted. Olbricht was early for General Halder's emergency High Command meeting, so he returned the privates' salutes and paused to shake their hands before going inside.

After dusk, spotlights illuminated the High Command buildings and their tall swastika banners. The windows were dark, except for a corner conference room. There, Olbricht had joined Halder, Field Marshal von Witzleben, and six other key members of the OKW, at a conference table now littered with full, smelly ashtrays and empty coffee cups. Tobacco fumes obscured the *Rauchen verboten* sign posted above the blackboard by order of Adolf Hitler, a rabid non-smoker.

Although Halder had called the meeting, he'd asked Olbricht to chair it. The latter sat at the head of the table, the red folder ready at hand. Field Marshal Von Witzleben, eldest member of the OKW, sat to his immediate right, and General Zeitzler, 50, short, bald, and plump, with a Hitler mustache, to his left. Others present included Admiral Canaris and Generals Fellgiebel and Fromm.

Fromm, his voice now hoarse, was finishing his catalogue of Hitler's recent eccentric behavior. " . . . Then two weeks later, he gave us his final decision on Luftwaffe support. By that time, matters had been decided for us by a Russian counterattack. We no longer had the same tactical situation, but Hitler insisted we follow his ill-timed orders nevertheless—"

Halder, fuming, interrupted with, "—Which made the air support practically useless—"

"—Exactly as occurred with the previous decision regarding reserves! Two weeks too late!" Fromm concluded.

Zeitzler flicked ashes off his cigarette and said, "I must admit I have found the Führer's no-withdrawal strategy, however wise it is in theory, to be a tactical obstacle."

Admiral Canaris nodded. "It would appear from all accounts that Hitler has become . . . " He hesitated and looked around the room before completing his sentence, " . . . ineffective."

Zeitzler, without changing expression, said, "Some would consider that an insult to the Führer."

Fromm looked at him. "How would 'some' describe his behavior lately? His tirades? The shrieking and pounding on the table?"

"They might say the Führer is merely distraught over the recent difficulties on the Eastern Front." Zeitzler shrugged and spread his hands.

Halder squeezed the back of his neck and sighed. "Distraught? Zeitzler, I told him our reconnaissance has detected a million more Russian troops northwest of Stalingrad. He called me a lunatic and has ignored the information completely. He is not distraught; he is going off the rails."

Olbricht shot up a hand to forestall a pointless and divisive argument. "Let us not quibble over nuances of terminology, General Halder. Is there anyone who thinks there is not a problem?" He glanced around the room. The generals lowered their eyes or looked at one another. Zeitzler solemnly avoided everyone else's gaze, staring at his hands clasped in front of him.

Olbricht continued: "So something must be done, agreed?"

Halder nodded. "Olbricht is right. We cannot go on like this."

Olbricht noted Zeitzler's reluctance and addressed him. "General? Do you disagree?"

Zeitzler shook his head. "But what can be done without violating our oaths of loyalty to the Führer? That is the question."

No one spoke.

Olbricht picked up the slack, turning to his superior. "Perhaps, General Halder, now would be a good time to hear from Dr. Sauerbrach."

Halder nodded.

Dr. Sauerbrach, 72, wearing a tweed suit and thick spectacles, stood at the end of the table. Olbricht leaned against the wall off to one side, arms folded, one boot sole on the wall. The doctor, trembling as he spoke, said, "I am most reluctant to participate in this . . . this meeting. As the Führer's physician, I'm required to hold in confidence my knowledge of his condition—"

Halder stopped him. "We have seen what we have seen." He indicated the other officers sitting around the table. "And the Führer's symptoms are relevant to our conducting the war and are all too obvious. So you are not telling us any secrets, nor are we asking you to. We promise as German soldiers not to betray your confidence, nor pass any of what transpires here to anyone outside this room. Is that agreed, gentlemen?"

The others held up their right hands and assented with a chorus of *ja* around the room. Halder went on, "Continue please, *Herr Doktor*. What have you observed?"

Sauerbrach pulled out a handkerchief and wiped his brow. "I . . . the following have been seen over the course of recent weeks . . . " Grasping a piece of chalk in a sweaty hand, he wrote on the blackboard as he spoke. " . . . Insomnia . . . depression . . . hysteria . . . nyctophobia . . . neurasthenia . . . exhaustion . . . tremors . . ."

The generals watched in silence as the list grew longer and longer.

Picking up speed, Sauerbrach continued, "The Führer has slept no more than three hours a night since February. He is deteriorating, displaying both melancholia and rage within seconds of each other—"

"As we have indeed all seen," interjected Heusinger, puffing on a cigar.

Nods and grunts of agreement went around the table. Zeitzler lit another cigarette with the butt of the previous one, then slumped in his chair, frowning. Olbricht tossed the red folder onto the conference table. "Dr. Sauerbrach, what do you recommend?"

"In confidence?"

The Generals agreed as before. Halder added, "We are at war, and if the Führer's condition interferes with the execution of military operations, we are bound as German soldiers to do all in our power to improve matters. You are also bound by that same principle, Herr Doktor, both as a German and as a physician."

"Very well. Even so, I speak theoretically, you understand?" The doctor paused, but there was no response. "For a patient with those symptoms, I would in normal circumstances recommend psychiatric evaluation, followed by the appropriate psychotherapy."

Olbricht said, "Who should see him, Doctor?"

Sauerbrach examined the chalk in his hand, then looked at Olbricht and shrugged.

Olbricht said, "That is the conundrum, is it not? What German psychiatrist would dare to offer an honest opinion of the Führer's mental state?"

"Assuming that is necessary, there must be dozens of good German psychiatrists," Zeitzler put in.

Sauerbrach crushed the chalk in his fist.

Halder snorted and grimaced. "Zeitzler, we would get an honest opinion from a German psychiatrist only if he were himself insane. He would end up in a camp."

Zeitzler now nodded along with the others and said, "Ja, if he were fortunate." Another lengthy silence followed.

Olbricht approached the blackboard and ran a finger down the list of symptoms "Forget for a moment who the patient is. Who are the best at treating these individual problems, Doctor?"

Sauerbrach turned and went down the list. "For insomnia? Marcus Rosenberg in Vienna. For depression? Also Rosenberg. For—"

"Rosenberg?" Zeitzler said. "If he's a Jew, he would be

in a camp by now."

Olbricht turned to Zeitzler. "There are many Aryans named Rosenberg, as you should know, General Zeitzler. But if he is a Jew, and if he is already in a camp, he would have little to lose, ja?"

Zeitzler frowned. "Ja, but if he's a Jew, he'd also be a Freudian psychoanalyst. It is well known that psychoanalysis is Marxist-Jewish pseudoscience. Do you seriously think the Führer would consider being examined by such a man? He would have to be—"

"—Crazy," Fromm finished for him.

Zeitzler jumped up. "We are getting nowhere with this talk. I was never here; this meeting never happened." He gathered up his notes and threw them in the wastebasket, saying a hurried, "Heil Hitler" as he left the room.

Olbricht noticed that the others relaxed a bit once Zeitzler was gone. He said, "I will check on Rosenberg's status. Please name someone else, Doctor."

Sauerbrach dropped the remnants of the chalk onto the blackboard tray. "I just had an idea, Herr General, though it is a very remote one. Rosenberg trained under Carl Jung and worked with him for several years. It's unlikely we could get Jung, though. He is the world's leading psychotherapist."

"All the more reason to get him." Olbricht looked at the ceiling. "Wait. Jung is a Swiss citizen, a neutral, is he not? He would be perfect. I say we try to get Dr. Jung."

The others agreed readily. Sauerbrach waved a hand at the blackboard. "If Jung could give us an initial evaluation, that might make it easier to find a German therapist to assist the Führer further."

"All very well." Heusinger ran a hand down the back of his neck and breathed heavily. "But someone will have to approach Hitler and convince him he needs Jung's help."

All eyes fell on Olbricht. *I am about the only OKW member who has not yet offended Hitler in one way or another,* he thought. *I should have expected this.*

After several seconds of silence, Halder grimaced at him. "The honor would seem to be yours, Olbricht."

Olbricht nodded and clicked his heels. "*Jawohl,* General Halder." *I can do this, if anyone can.* He lit a cigarette and sat down next to the red folder.

Fellgiebel sat staring straight ahead, hands flat on the table in front of him. "Who will inform Reichsführer Himmler?"

The room went silent.

Olbricht sighed. "That decision must wait until I have talked to the Führer back at the Wolf's Lair."

They all stood. Little was said as they filed out of the room. Halder and Olbricht waited until the others had left, then put their heads together.

Halder spoke. "If—I say *if*—Dr. Jung's evaluation states that Hitler is insane, that would release us all from our loyalty oaths, would it not?"

This made Olbricht uncomfortable. He put a finger across his lips. "Not here. I will see you at the Wolf's Lair, tomorrow."

Halder nodded and they left by the hallway. As they started down the stairs, Zeitzler stepped out of the darkened office next to the conference room and watched them go.

Chapter 4
Hitler's Quarters, Wolf's Lair
10:00 PM, June 19, 1942

An aide admitted Olbricht to the Führer's bunker and escorted him along the brightly-lit hallways leading to Hitler's quarters. "Please wait here, General," the aide said, then opened a door leading to Hitler's office and disappeared inside.

Olbricht walked back and forth along the red-carpeted corridor, wishing he could smoke. He nodded to the two handsome SS men on guard duty without speaking. After a minute, both doors opened, and the aide came out and motioned for Olbricht to enter. "The Führer will see you now, Herr General."

Olbricht hesitated, letting his eyes grow accustomed to the darkness inside the room. All but two areas were in shadow. His eyes were drawn to a small circle of reddish light where a lamp illuminated the bronze bust of a young girl, a round-faced gamin in her late teens, robust, with wavy hair. Olbricht knew, as did all those close to Hitler, that the bust was of Geli [Gay'-lee] Raubal, Hitler's niece, who died in 1931 of a self-inflicted bullet wound. Everyone also knew that her name was never to be mentioned in

Hitler's presence. Olbricht looked away and focused on the other dimly-lit area.

A larger circle of light surrounded Hitler. He sat in an overstuffed chair, reading a book. *Probably a Western by Karl May,* Olbricht thought. *I hope it has put him in a good mood.* As Olbricht approached, he noticed the Führer had bags under his eyes and a grey pallor. The General came to attention and gave him a stiff, Nazi-style salute.

"Heil, mein Führer."

Hitler looked at him and merely twitched his fingers in response, then went back to the book. "And what do you want, General Olbricht?"

"Führer, the High Command members are most concerned about your health."

Hitler slammed the book closed and faced him. "Bugger the High Command. Their incompetence has put me in this condition."

"Dr. Sauerbrach thinks a small vacation might help."

"That is the best idea that idiot has had in a long time. A week in the mountains, ja, that is what I need." Hitler put aside his glasses, and rubbed his eyes.

"Yes, Führer. A most excellent idea. Your lodge in the mountains near Bludenz might—"

"But I have no time." Hitler donned his glasses again and took up the book.

Olbricht felt his forehead grow sweaty. "Even a couple of days might help, Führer. You deserve the rest."

Hitler looked up at Olbricht. "Well, maybe you are right."

Olbricht seized the opening. Trying not to let his voice quaver, he said, "Dr. Sauerbrach can arrange for a specialist to see you while you are there."

Hitler nodded. "This damned insomnia is killing me."

Olbricht, feeling he had made a breakthrough, pressed forward. "Quite so, Führer. And we hope the specialist could address your . . . low spirits at the same time."

Hitler slammed the book down again and glared, fuming. "Low spirits? What low spirits? I have just been under too much stress."

Olbricht almost caved in and retreated right then, but there was too much at stake. He knew if he didn't continue, another opportunity like this might not arise. "Certainly, Führer, but there are doctors who can help with stress."

"You mean some mind meddler? Ridiculous!"

"Carl Jung, if possible."

Hitler looked at the book and stroked its cover. "Jung? I met him once. He seemed almost . . . German."

"If you took a brief stay at Bludenz, perhaps I could persuade him to visit you and give an unbiased opinion."

Hitler shook his head. "How do we know he may be trusted?"

"He is a Swiss, a neutral. And a medical professional."

"Still, that is not an absolute guarantee he can be relied on, is it?"

Olbricht sensed a moment of danger. *I must, above all, retain Hitler's trust. If he has doubts about Jung, to recommend him might cause Hitler to doubt me as well,* he thought. *Time to retreat.*

"Very well, Führer." Olbricht didn't know what to add, if anything. *Call me if you change your mind?* No, that wouldn't happen. Olbricht considered apologizing for bringing the matter up, but realized that was a coward's tactic. Instead, he said, "Good night, then, mein Führer."

Olbricht saluted and started away, thinking, *He remembers meeting Jung. That may be helpful. There is hope yet.*

Chapter 5
Hitler's Bedroom, Wolf's Lair
11:45 PM, June 19, 1942

After Olbricht left his office, Hitler took the book to his bedroom and changed into pajamas. Then he lay back against his pillows to finish the Western, a story he'd read many times. The familiar words soothed him, and he thought he might sleep, now. He buzzed for his night guard, Lothar Zimms, a heavily-decorated young member of the Leibstandarte SS.

Within seconds, Zimms entered the bedroom, saluted, and turned off the overhead lights before taking his post in a comfortable chair at the far end of the room, beside a well-shaded floor lamp. He had brought along a crossword puzzle; that was permitted. Zimms wasn't there to guard Hitler's person; his presence had become necessary to prevent night terrors from seizing hold of The Führer.

Hitler lay awake in the dimly lit room for a long time that night; how long he wasn't sure, hovering between wakefulness and dozing. He turned over several times before finding a comfortable position. A little later, he heard whispering. *Has someone entered the room? Or is that Zimms speaking?* Hitler raised his head and saw the SS man's place was vacant. *Where is he? Has he gone into the bathroom?* No, the bathroom was dark. The sight of the empty chair angered and terrified Hitler. *Where is Zimms?* The lamp beside the guard's chair flickered, then went out with a faint *pop.* Darkness.

Hitler feared the dark, a black void that his imagination could quickly populate with hideous, malevolent creatures. He sat up, groping for the bedside lamp, but couldn't find it or the bell that was supposed to be beside it. He tried to call for Zimms and found to his horror that his throat was so constricted with fear he could only hiss like a snake.

Hitler jumped up and staggered across the room, hissing. He reached the door without colliding with any of the furnishings, flung it open, and saw that the corridor outside was also dark. *The power has failed,* he thought. *I must find Zimms and have him fix the generator.* He treaded a few meters along the hallway before he heard footsteps behind him. *That must be Zimms!* He turned and put out a hand, encountering something wet. *What is this? It is sticky. With a distinctive odor. It is blood! What has happened to Zimms? Why does he not speak? But what if this is not Zimms? What if it is something terrible?*

Hitler turned and ran until he reached a fireplace blazing blood red in the darkness. *Good,* he thought, *I have light. Zimms has lit a nice fire. But how could he have lit this fire and come back so quickly to where I just met him? And I do not remember any fireplaces in the corridors of the Wolf's Lair. How very strange!*

Then, by the light of the fire, Hitler saw something awful coming, something that wasn't Zimms, something that whispered a word through bony jaws as it approached.

Hitler's throat tightened. He couldn't cry out; he couldn't breathe. His chest seemed confined. He tore open his pajama top, trying to get more air. Then he saw a bump on one of his arms. It grew bigger as he watched. Another bump formed near it. And two more on his chest. Things were growing out of his flesh, awful things, parasites with heads like skulls.

He began tearing them out, surprised that this didn't hurt, but horrified that they kept on appearing, more and more of them. The wounds began to spew blood over the walls and floor. Soon he was wading in it, his feet slipping as he attempted to run from the skeletal thing coming at him out of the dark, rasping as it came.

"Führer," a man said.

Hitler turned, but saw no one, only the grinning skeleton and the fire.

"Führer," the voice persisted. A hand touched his arm.

Hitler opened his eyes and took a deep breath. He was back in his bed. There was no blood, no parasites, no figure stretching out fleshless arms to him. Greatly relieved, he saw Zimms beside him and the guard's chair overturned in the pool of light at the other side of the room.

"You were dreaming, Führer." Zimms' voice was reassuring, solicitous. "A nightmare."

"Yes. Thank you. All a dream. It . . . seemed very real."

"Is there anything I can get you? Some cocoa?"

"Yes. But I am all sweaty. Put out some dry pajamas."

Zimms did as requested, then left the room. No one saw Hitler naked except Eva Braun and a few particularly trusted SS men. Hitler showered and changed, got into bed, then buzzed for Zimms and the cocoa.

Later, as Hitler waited for sleep to come to him, he thought, *It was dreadful! The blood. All so detailed, so lifelike. I must never have another dream like that.* He carefully avoided thinking about the most realistic part of the dream: the skeletal woman in the dark asking over and over, "Why?"

Chapter 6
Hitler's Quarters, Wolf's Lair
2:00 PM, June 20, 1942

The next afternoon, Olbricht was summoned to Hitler's office. The Führer was seated at his oversized desk, leaning on his elbows. It was clear from his appearance that he had not slept well the previous night and had probably just arisen. *He looks terrible,* Olbricht thought. *I wonder if he has changed his mind.*

Olbricht stiffened and saluted. "Heil, mein Führer. You wished to see me?"

"You suggested that Dr. Jung be requested to attend me?" Hitler asked.

"His name was mentioned," Olbricht said noncommittally, choosing what seemed the safest course.

"Yes, but first you mentioned Bludenz."

"I believe I did, Führer."

"It is probably not an accident that Bludenz is closest to Zurich, is it?"

Caught. "There is a connection, Führer. Jung is rather elderly and might be more willing to travel to Bludenz than to Berchtesgaden or Berlin." Olbricht, sensing his intentions being ferreted out, stifled an urge to gush excuses for trying to set Hitler up with a therapist.

"I have decided to see if Jung can help me. We must rely on his professional deportment."

"Yes, Führer." *Success!* Olbricht wanted to leave before Hitler could change his mind. But, of course, there was no reason to fear that. Once decided, the Führer never changed his mind. Olbricht relaxed.

"See to it personally, will you, Olbricht?"

"Certainly, Führer." Olbricht clicked his heels and bowed.

"Do you think he will come?"

"I will convince him. Of course, I will have to guarantee his safety, first."

Hitler waved a hand. "There is no need for him to worry. I will make sure he leaves Germany safe and sound."

Olbricht decided to address the other concern: "And do you think it necessary to inform Reichsführer Himmler?"

"We probably should . . . "

No! We must not! Olbricht thought. He quickly added, "Or do you think he might interfere with Dr. Jung's visit?"

Hitler clasped his hands together. "Himmler pisses his pants over anything he has not got his fingers into. He does not need to know." Hitler sat back in his chair and gave Olbricht a weak smile.

Chapter 7
Jung's Office, Zurich
7:30 PM, June 25, 1942

Jung's temporary wartime office, a convenience for Zurich clients who had no gasoline ration, occupied a modest-sized, ordinary building on a semi-residential street. An inconspicuous brass plaque outside said merely, "C G Jung." The front door opened into a small anteroom for his secretary-receptionist. The area was sparsely furnished: a desk with typewriter extension, file cabinets, a hat rack and chairs for clients, an oriental rug, a water cooler, and a clock. On the wall hung several Swiss landscapes and a dozen or so group photographs taken at various conferences.

To the right, facing the secretary's desk, stood the baize-covered soundproof door to Jung's therapy room. Inside that inner sanctum, the furnishings were somewhat cluttered: several floor lamps provided light. On the walls hung a map of Switzerland and its neighboring countries, a clock placed where clients couldn't see it, and a few sketches and watercolors by former patients. Bookcases with several shelves full of murder mysteries lined another wall. On a large desk stood a globe and an open mystery novel with a magnifying glass atop it. Mary's mandala adorned the wall behind Jung's chair.

Near a small side table, another soundproof door led to a private exit, an arrangement that allowed exiting and entering clients to avoid encountering each other.

Two overstuffed chairs were arranged faced to face. Jung, chin on his left hand, sat in one chair, doodling in a pad on the arm of his chair. Across from him sat a middle-aged woman in black, smelling of rosewater. As she talked, she twisted her handkerchief, saying, " . . . And then, in my dream, I reached into my purse, and you'll never guess what I found inside." Clutching the handkerchief, she looked at Jung earnestly.

Jung raised his head from his hand long enough to say, "A snake?"

Her eyebrows rose. "Yes, a snake! However did you know, Dr. Jung? And what do you suppose it means?"

Jung jiggled his pen between two fingers and sat forward in his chair. "It is your dream. What does a snake suggest to you?"

She hesitated, her eyes on the pen, then said, "Could it . . . could it be a male member?"

"Yes, it is a prick. Given your history of sexual repression, we should be amazed if it were anything else." Jung looked up at the clock behind her. "And on that felicitous note, our time is up." He closed his notepad and stood.

His patient also rose, and as she walked towards the private exit, Jung raised an index finger. "Be sure to bring that male member up again next week."

She tittered and covered her mouth, then hurried out. Jung smiled. As soon as the door closed behind her, he breathed in and blew out, slumping. After a moment, he went out to the anteroom.

His elderly receptionist was covering up the typewriter. Jung flipped his notepad onto her desk, almost missing the edge. "Done, thank heavens."

She indicated his appointment book. "You have one more, Doctor. Eight o'clock."

"Oh, no." Jung put his hand to his head.

The receptionist tightened her lips. "It's that Mrs. Rufenacht."

Jung grinned and stood a little straighter. "Ah, yes, Mary Bancroft. You may go now."

"Are you sure, Doctor?

"Yes, yes. I'll close up."

The receptionist stood, then said, "Oh, Dr. Jung, I almost forgot. A nice man called earlier and wanted an appointment. I told him you had no times open for the next four weeks."

"You should have told him my practice is closed. But no matter. We can deal with him if he calls back."

A few minutes later, Mary Bancroft approached the office on her motorcycle. She parked and went inside carrying her backpack. She heard faint sounds of classical music coming from beneath the therapy room door. A do-not-disturb sign hung on the doorknob. Finding herself alone, she checked the clock: 7:45—plenty of time to change into something more feminine for her session with Carl.

Mary changed into a skirt in the restroom, stowed her aviator's helmet and backpack behind the desk, and neatened her hair. Still only 7:50. She sat for a minute. She shuffled through the dozen magazines in the reading rack: *Paris Match, National Geographic, LIFE, Autocar,* and a lone copy of *Punch*—nothing newer than 1940. Mary yawned and looked for something more interesting.

She began pacing the room again, wondering, w*hat would a spy do in this situation? Snoop, definitely.* She examined the group photographs on one wall, pictures of Jung and various colleagues. The largest photograph was a sepia image of a youthful Carl Jung standing beside two other men, one old, one young. Mary read the names inked below them: Carl Jung, Sigmund Freud, Marcus Rosenberg.

Next, she slipped behind the secretary's desk and peeked in each of the drawers. Watching Jung's door, she opened the appointment book, and bent down to read patients' names.

A male voice to her right said, "*Guten abend.*"

Mary straightened and whirled in surprise, barely stopping herself from blurting the s-word. She saw a tall man in glasses standing in the doorway. He doffed his hat, bowed formally, and smiled warmly at her.

She wondered, *Who the hell is this?* but replied in German, "Guten abend. You are here to see Herr Doktor Jung, ja?"

The man pulled the door closed behind him. "Ja, I am. You are his secretary?"

Mary sized him up intently, noting his clothing, his bearing, his accent. He seemed polite, but there was something else about him. *Authoritative. Dangerous.* "I don't believe you have an appointment," she temporized. She slipped into the role of secretary, leaning down and putting a finger on the open ledger, as if checking it.

"No, but I called earlier. I need to see Herr Doktor Jung on a matter of great urgency."

A military man, she realized, despite his civilian apparel. High-ranking. Swiss? No. His German had no Swiss colloquialisms. With a sudden clenching of her throat, she connected the last dot. *German.* She felt like running away, but managed to say, "Herr Doktor Jung has another client scheduled, but let me see what allows itself to be done." She forced a polite smile.

"That would be most kind of you, indeed." He bowed once again.

"And what is your name?" she asked, thinking, *He'll*

never give his real name. It's probably something very Kraut, like Colonel Fritz von Huggentuggler.

"Albright. Freddie Albright."

The man had switched to British English, without a trace of German accent. This didn't seem unusual to Mary; she was used to people in Switzerland speaking several languages well. Jung, himself, spoke colloquial American English and four other tongues with complete fluency.

Mary followed "Albright's" lead, changing from German to English, but trying not to sound American. "Please do be seated, Mr. Albright." She indicated the chairs against the wall, then knocked on Jung's door and slipped inside without waiting for him to admit her.

Jung sat at his desk, smoking a pipe and reading a murder mystery while listening to music on the radio. He looked up, a puzzled expression on his face, then glanced at the clock.

Mary held a finger to her lips, rushed to his side, and whispered, "There's a man outside who wants to see you. He says it's urgent."

Jung closed his book and sat up straight. "He will just have to wait. It is almost time for your session."

"I think you should talk to him. He says his name is Freddie Albright, but he's German."

"There are lots of Germans in Zurich these days. For good reasons."

Mary shook her head. "He's got a *Wehrmacht* haircut, and I swear he came within a millimeter of clicking his heels when we met."

"I will tell him to go away." Jung put down the book and stood.

"No. You should find out what he wants."

"If he is who you think, I am not sure I want to know what he wants."

"Sure, you do. I'll show him in."

Jung shook his head. "I told you I am taking no new

clients."

"And you said you'd take one more. For me. This is it."

"What about your 'friend' you said needed therapy?"

"The heck with her."

Jung turned off the radio and put down his pipe. Mary grabbed up a pencil from his desk and stuck it behind her ear, adding to her secretarial air. She smoothed her hair and trotted out, back straight.

Seconds later, Mary led the German in to meet Jung. She put his hat on the side table near the patient exit, then introduced the man in English. "This is Mr. Albright, Dr. Jung."

The man bowed and clicked his heels. Mary smirked at the sound as she went out.

Chapter 8
Jung's Therapy Room, Zurich
7:55 PM, June 25, 1942

Jung pointed at a chair, and "Albright" sat across the desk from him. It took Jung only a second to conclude from the man's bearing and his haircut that Mary's assessment of the visitor was correct. Without the least doubt, this man was a German officer. An intelligent, high-ranking one. *What the devil is he doing here in Zurich—and what does he want in my office?*

The German spoke without preamble, continuing to speak in English. "Dr. Jung, I come on the behalf of my employer, Mr. Wolff, who desperately needs the kind of healing you specialize in."

Jung waved the idea away. "My practice is closed. I am taking no new clients."

"You might find this a most fascinating case."

This piqued Jung's curiosity. "Fascinating in what way?"

"Financially. And professionally." The German arced a hand from side to side.

"But I am not fascinated."

The man became less confident. "Perhaps if you heard

some of the details—"

Jung was tempted to ask him to explain, but fear overruled his curiosity. "No, no. I am not interested."

"Please, Dr. Jung. Mr. Wolff has met you and wants you in particular."

"We have met? I don't recall a 'Mr. Wolff.' Who is this Mr. Wolff?"

The German leaned back and folded his arms across his chest. "Adolf Hitler."

Maria in Himmel! This can't be happening. Jung looked at the German over his glasses, his forehead contorted in disbelief. "You are not jesting, by any chance?"

"You are not laughing, are you?"

"I am not."

"Then neither was I jesting. Not in the least, Doctor. The Führer is suffering, and the consequences for Germany could be severe."

Jung replied without hesitation. "I remind you that as a Swiss, I am neutral. I have nothing in common with Germany except the language, and I speak that only when necessary."

The German nodded. "I understand. But the Führer's decisions have consequences for people outside Germany, unfortunately. I am sure you will agree."

Jung's frown deepened. "I agree that it is unfortunate."

"Then we need not argue that particular point. His condition is my concern, and it is interfering with his decisions."

"His evil decisions. What a pity."

The man spread his hands. "Who can distinguish between good and evil in time of war? But he may be making fewer decisions you consider good if his condition worsens."

"That is the most polite threat I have ever heard."

"It was not at all intended as a threat, Herr Doktor, but as a realistic assessment of the situation." The German held out an open hand. "Please, Dr. Jung. I am seeking your help as another human being. Could you not at least provide an evaluation?"

"An evaluation?" Jung picked up his pipe and checked the ash for signs of life. "Can you describe his condition, Herr General?"

The man jerked his head back and blinked, obviously surprised at his title being used.

At the delay, Jung added, "In confidence."

"He cannot sleep—"

"Not astonishing."

"Spells of severe depression, punctuated by intense anger—"

"Depression. With anger." Jung sucked at the pipe. "Any thoughts of suicide?"

"None that he will admit."

"Ah. That is most unfortunate."

Chapter 9
Jung's Reception Room, Zurich
8:15 PM, June 25, 1942

Mary stood with her ear against a tin pencil cup pressed to the wall. Her eyes grew wide at the mention of the prospective client's name. "Hitler? Holy crap!" she whispered.

She darted behind the desk and, talking as softly as she could, placed a phone call to Allen Dulles's private line in Bern. She clutched the telephone receiver with a shaking hand and watched the door to the therapy room as she waited for the call to go through, half expecting the door to open at any second. She tried not to dwell on what might ensue.

At last, from the receiver, she heard the sound of the phone ringing at the Bern OSS station. After the near-eternity of six more rings: "Burns!" Dulles answered in his telephone voice, using his *nom de guerre*.

Mary whispered quickly, "There's a Nazi general here, and he wants Dr. Jung to go to Germany and see Hitler."

There was a pause, then, "Adolf Hitler?"

Mary had a hard time keeping her voice down. "Of course, it's Adolf Hitler," she hissed, "Damn it, I'm not kidding! That Nazi is in there with Carl right now. What do I do?"

Dulles became serious. "Jung has to agree. Right now."

"How the hell do I finesse that?"

"You're the analyst; think of something. And keep Jung there 'til I arrive. Whatever it takes. On my way." The line went dead.

Mary quietly replaced the receiver with sweating hands. *What can I do?* she wondered. She hesitated for a few seconds, then jerked open a desk drawer, took out a prescription pad, and started writing.

Chapter 10
Jung's Therapy Room, Zurich
8:20 PM, June 25, 1942

Olbricht strode back and forth, entreating Jung to come to Germany. Jung sat smoking and listening, then finally shook his head and said, "I am an old man, and it is far too dangerous."

The General hesitated, then said, "My name is Friedrich Olbricht. I am, as you somehow realized, a Wehrmacht General, a member of the High Command. I give you my word as a German soldier, you will leave Germany safely, with no—" A knock at the door interrupted Olbricht. He stopped speaking and watched Mary enter.

"Sorry to interrupt, Doctor," she said, ignoring Olbricht. "Your eight o'clock appointment is here."

Jung took this in stride, following Mary's lead. "Ah, yes. Thanks for reminding me."

"Here's her prescription. For you to endorse, please." She gave him the pad.

What's this? Jung read the note on the top page. It said, in Latin, "*Carpe Rem!*" (Take the case.) He frowned at her over his glasses and tapped the pad with a forefinger. "This may be too much. Tell her I'll only be another minute."

"Yes, Doctor." Mary left the room.

Jung sat back and looked up at Olbricht. "I really must refuse."

"We will pay whatever you ask. Ten thousand Reichsmarks a day."

"It is out of the question."

"Twenty thousand marks."

Jung's voice grew sterner. "Money is not an inducement to me."

Olbricht stood still and glared down at Jung. "Then I will offer one mark, instead."

Jung shrugged, puzzled. "A mark or a million, my answer is the same."

"Do you know Dr. Marcus Rosenberg, formerly of Vienna?"

Jung was taken aback. Marcus had been a close friend and colleague until Jung broke with Freud. Rosenberg, a devout Freudian, had remained cordial, but their relationship had faded over the years. Marcus was an Austrian Jew and had been on Jung's mind often in recent months. Jung greatly feared that Hitler's SS units had swept up the Rosenbergs some time ago. "He and his son were . . . are both friends of mine. But what are you saying?"

Olbricht took a deep breath. "Dr. Rosenberg has been in a work camp for many months, making land mines. The camp is . . . " Olbricht paused, frowning. " . . . It is better than most, but still a very dangerous place. I may be able to deliver him."

Jung stood. "This is extortion."

Olbricht smiled and spread his hands. "I think trying to free him would be a good deed."

"How can you sit there and smile when we are discussing the life of a human being?"

"You're the psychiatrist; suppose you tell me."

Angered beyond his limit, Jung blurted, "Because you

are a heartless Nazi bastard."

Olbricht waved this away. "I am none of those things. If I seem not to care, it is because I have learned that a cheery attitude helps the day go faster. When will you come?"

"I think you have lost your moral compass!"

"I have little need of one. I am a German soldier. I obey orders. But you will come, yes?" Olbricht smiled again.

I do not want to go to Germany. I should refuse right away. Jung leaned on his desk and read Mary's message on the prescription pad again: Carpe rem. *What if Mary is right?* He relented just enough to say, "I will think about it."

Olbricht nodded. "Very well, I require your answer within twelve hours. Will that be sufficient thought?"

"Yes. I'll let you know in the morning." Jung stood up, hoping the interview was over.

"Nine o'clock, shall we say?"

"Fine."

"Good." Olbricht paused, then said, "And no one else must know. No one, you understand?"

"I will tell no one else, you may be sure of that."

Olbricht smiled once more and held out his hand. Jung instinctively started to take it, then instead silently pointed at the private exit. Olbricht picked up his hat and strode out the door with no sign of being offended by Jung's refusal of his hand.

Chapter 11
Jung's Reception Room, Zurich
8:30 PM, June 25, 1942

Mary was still eavesdropping when Jung's door opened. *Uh-oh!* Surprised, she moved away from the wall, hiding her tin cup stethoscope behind her.

Jung came out waving the prescription pad, his forehead knotted. He looked at her, then at the wall beside her. "How much did you hear?"

"Damn near all of it."

"That was highly unethical."

"He's not a client."

"Hitler may be, depending on my decision."

"Hitler has no ethics."

"Well, I do, as you very well know!"

Mary tried to deflect Jung's anger. "Sorry, Dr. Jung. Can I plead insanity?" She rolled her eyes and waggled her head.

"Mary, this is not a matter for humor, and you know it." He shook a finger at her.

"Yes. I know." Mary felt her face grow warm with embarrassment and shame. She considered apologizing again, but instead approached Jung, grabbed his arm and squeezed it. "But the important thing is that you go."

He pulled his arm free. "No, the important thing is that I would be scared to death. I can't possibly go."

"We'll help you."

"We?"

She nodded. "My new employer. The American Office of Strategic Services.

Jung's brows contracted.

Mary added, "American Intelligence."

"Aha! I might have known." He pointed a finger at her. "Your fib about the boring work now makes sense. And the sneezing."

"My boss will be here in an hour and a half. We need to . . . to . . . " Mary sneezed twice.

Jung tossed the prescription pad onto the desk. "Very well. That will give us time for your session. But I am not going to Germany, no matter what your boss has to say."

Mary felt terrible. "Are you still mad at me?"

"Yes, I am. It saddens me that you would violate our friendship, as well as our professional relationship, after . . . how many years, now?"

"Six. No, seven. But, Carl, my job—"

"I understand. But no job is an excuse for bad behavior."

Mary felt her throat ache and her eyes fill with tears.

"Come," Jung said. He slipped an arm around her waist and walked her towards the therapy room. "Let us talk about it."

Chapter 12
Jung's Office, Zurich
10:30 PM, June 25. 1942

Mary Bancroft was still in the therapy room when Jung heard the clatter of a large engine on the street behind his office. "I think your employer is here," he said, putting down his note pad.

A minute later, a knock came at the back door. Jung opened and saw a handsome, rather suave stranger dressed in a tweed suit.

"Allen Dulles," the man said. "You're Dr. Jung, right?"

"I am. Come in." Behind Dulles, outside, Jung saw a long, dark Auburn sedan, gleaming in the faint light of a partly blacked-out street lamp. The driver lounged against the car, wearing a grey chauffeur's cap and uniform, a cigarette in one hand, a hip flask in the other.

Inside Jung's smoke-filled office, the lights low and the blackout curtains pulled, Dulles relaxed in front of Jung's desk. Mary, biting her thumb and frowning, had her chair close beside Dulles's.

Jung, very aware of how close the two sat, paced on the other side of the desk, feeing disheveled, waving a cigarette. "But I am simply not a spy."

Dulles held up a hand and spoke tersely: "No spying. Get that right out of your head. All we want you to do is go and be a therapist."

"Even if by doing so, I may prevent a total breakdown of Hitler's mind?"

Mary nodded. "If he falls apart, they'll just replace him with somebody else."

"Yes," Dulles agreed. "Somebody a lot more savvy in military matters. Hitler's a lousy strategist."

"He seems to have done fairly well, so far," Jung said.

Dulles shook his head. "Pure luck and Allied timidity. He had his war won, then attacked Russia. His luck's run out."

Jung sat at his desk, tired from the strain. "You want me to just evaluate him and come right back?"

"Yes," Dulles replied, "exactly as the General said. Did he give a name?"

Mary shrugged. "He said his name was Freddy Albright, but I don't think there are any German generals named Freddy Albright."

"No," Jung said. "He told me he was General Friedrich Olbricht."

Dulles took a folder from his briefcase. "There is a General Friedrich Olbricht." He sorted through the folder, selected a photograph, and passed it to Jung. "This the guy?"

Jung looked at the photograph. "Yes, this is the one."

Dulles nodded. "Your 'Freddy Albright' is a highly honored member of the German High Command. A soldier's soldier. You move in august company, Dr. Jung."

"I would rather not," Jung replied.

Mary leaned forward, hands on her knees. "If the High Command is behind this, this is the biggest break we've ever had."

"The question is, is Hitler fully on board with it?"

Dulles said.

"If he isn't, it may be a short trip," Jung said.

Mary took the photograph from Jung and nodded, then gave it back to Dulles. "It will be short. Do a diagnosis, maybe give him some pills, and come back."

Jung looked down at his desk. "That might be feasible . . . "

Dulles said, "Of course, after you're back, we may have a few questions."

Jung stiffened. "What sort of questions?"

"What makes Adolf Hitler tick?"

"That would violate professional secrecy."

Dulles shook his head. "We don't need details of his sex life, just—"

Mary silenced Dulles with a small movement of her hand. She approached Jung. "Look, Carl, don't think of it as having Hitler for a patient."

"What do you mean?"

"This. This is your patient." Mary reached over to the globe on Jung's desk and gave it a spin.

He looked at it and then at her, his expression glum. His excuses were fading away, and his resistance with them.

Dulles said, "If Hitler wins the war, he'll be here in Zurich in a heartbeat."

Jung looked at the wall map and saw Switzerland, completely surrounded by Axis powers. His forehead furrowed.

Mary jumped in. "You may be able to keep the Nazis off our doorstep. And save Marcus Rosenberg, to boot."

Poor Marcus, Jung thought. *If I don't go, he'll probably die. And maybe all the rest of us, sooner or later. Perhaps sooner would be no worse than later.* He took a breath and sighed. "All right. I'll go. But no one must ever know that I have violated a client's trust. Not even Hitler's."

"Hitler will never admit seeing a therapist," Dulles said. "And the OSS knows how to keep secrets."

Chapter 13
Behind Jung's Office, Zurich
11:55 PM, June 25, 1942

Jung left for home as soon as Dulles told him how to reach the OSS station in Bern. Mary changed into her motorcycle outfit, locked up, and carried her backpack outside with Dulles. They sat in the back of the dimly-lit Auburn while Jaffe warmed it up. As they talked, Mary began worrying about Jung. She fell silent, and her brow wrinkled.

Dulles leaned closer and looked at her. "He'll do fine," he said. He took her hand and squeezed it.

But maybe he won't, Mary thought. She looked down at the floorboard. "Why didn't you tell him about the massacre at Terzendorf?"

Dulles shrugged. "Why didn't you?"

"I wish I had!"

Dulles got out his pipe and lit it. "You had no reason to. Besides, it might have scared him off."

"I'm wondering if that isn't exactly what we should have done." She paused. "Maybe I should go with him."

Dulles shook his head. "He'll have Jaffe and this car. Twelve cylinders, three hundred horsepower, armor plate, gadgets. If you go along, Olbricht might get suspicious."

"He already thinks I'm Jung's secretary. I could just—"

"Go on pretending? Sure, do that. Cover Jung's office while he's gone, in case the Germans call here for any reason."

"But I'm trained in OSS methods. I could help him."

Dulles took her hand again. "Not trained; you read the manuals. Besides, Germany is at war with America, and you're an American."

"I'm married to a Swiss. I have Swiss citizenship and a Swiss passport, and I speak fluent German."

"Like when you say 'shit' instead of '*scheisse*?' Nope. Far too dangerous."

Too dangerous? "Hey! If it's too dangerous for me, why are you sending Dr. Jung?" She pulled her sweaty hand from Dulles's grasp.

Dulles removed his pipe from his mouth. "Playing the odds. You've seen Einstein's letter to Roosevelt?"

"About the uranium bomb? That's years away."

"The Germans are developing an A-bomb, too. They expect to have it by mid-'45. If we don't beat them by then, they may sail one up the Thames in a U-boat and order England to surrender. Or maybe sail one up the Hudson."

Mary visualized New York smashed flat. "Jeez!"

"Look, Mary, it's like this: every day the war goes on costs ten thousand lives. Cut it short a year, that's four million lives saved, if Dr. Jung comes back with the right information."

"*If* he comes back? You think he might not?"

Dulles looked at her. "He has the chance of a hailstone in Hades."

"What!?" Mary glared at him.

"Playing the odds, Mary. If there's one chance in a hundred he'll succeed, multiply that times London's population. That's fifty thousand lives saved. What's one man's life compared to that?"

"But it's not just one man! It's Carl Jung!"

Dulles's brow furrowed. He looked at Mary and drew on his pipe again. "Won't matter much who he is, if the Germans win, will it?" He rolled down his window to let the smoke out. "Want to ride back to Bern with me?"

"You cold-blooded S.O.B!" She jumped out and slammed the car door. Dulles rapped on the chauffeur's tinted glass partition, and Jaffe drove the Auburn away, leaving Mary standing in the dark, fuming.

By the time she passed Dulles at 120 kph on the road back to Bern, she'd cooled down just enough that she didn't flip him the finger. *Allen's right, damn him! But I still don't like it.* A minute later, she slowed as another thought struck her: *Whatever I do, I'd better not let my attitude affect Carl's morale. That might get him killed. I need—what did Olbricht call it?—a "cheery attitude."*

Chapter 14
Jung's Office, Zurich
8:00 AM, June 26, 1942

The next morning, Carl Jung arrived at the Zurich office early. When his receptionist got there, he met her in the anteroom and told her, "I am taking a week's emergency vacation. You may do the same, and I'll pay you for the week." She left, looking puzzled, but he didn't enlighten her. *The less she knows, the better,* he thought.

Then he sat in a chair by the door, waiting for Olbricht. *I hope he doesn't come. I can still take the week off. But then Marc Rosenberg may die, God help him! But maybe he's already dead.* As the clock ticked towards nine, Jung stood and paced the anteroom. Despite Jung's hopes, Olbricht knocked on the front door right on time.

Jung let him in and ushered him into the therapy room without speaking. Olbricht remained stiff and formal. Jung stood with his hands clasped together and addressed the General in standard German. "I can only be away from my practice for two days at the most. That's enough time for an evaluation, and not much more."

"That is the most we had hoped for." Olbricht walked over to the map and pointed at a spot not far from the

Austria-Liechtenstein border. "'Herr Wolff' has a place here, near Bludenz. Is that acceptable?"

Jung picked up his magnifying glass and looked at the area. It was not terribly far from Zurich. "Yes, under the circumstances, it will do." *I wonder if I may ask him about Marc Rosenberg now . . .*

"We will provide a car and driver—"

Jung held up a hand. "I will be much more comfortable in my own car, with my usual driver. We can take my . . . Auburn." He'd almost said, "Chrysler," but caught himself at the last instant and named the make of Dulles's car instead of his own.

Olbricht seemed reluctant, but acceded. "Of course, if you would prefer. When?"

"Tuesday morning, returning Wednesday afternoon. That will be sufficient time for an afternoon and, if necessary, a morning session with your 'Herr Wolff.'"

"I must ask you to please remain anonymous while you are in Germany. You will be traveling under papers identifying you as Herr Lang and driver. Please also continue to refer to the patient only as "Herr Wolff."

Jung nodded.

Olbricht rubbed his hands together. "All good, then. I will meet you at the Mauren border crossing on Tuesday at zero eight hundred and escort you from there."

"And back."

"And back, of course."

Jung looked closely at Olbricht's face and said, "And Marc Rosenberg . . . ?"

"Wednesday, while you see Herr Wolff, I will pick Dr. Rosenberg up and bring him to Bludenz in time to ride back with you."

"Good." *But how is Marc? Do I dare ask?*

"You will need your passport. I will arrange for visas and so forth to be delivered here as soon as possible. Do not forget them, please. Getting new documents could present a large obstacle."

"I'll remember," Jung said, a bit irritated. "And how is Dr. Rosenberg?"

"I have located him. He is in good health, as far as I know."

As far as he knows? That tells me nothing at all. "But have you seen him personally?"

Olbricht averted his eyes for a second, then met Jung's stare. "No, I regret to say I have not had that opportunity."

I wonder if this man may be trusted. "Is there anything else I should know?"

"No. We are done." Olbricht started to hold out his hand, but glanced down at Jung's hands, clasped together. He pulled back his hand and clicked his heels before going out the private exit.

Chapter 15
Reichsführer SS Himmler's Office,
Prinz Albrechtstrasse, Berlin
11:00 AM, June 26, 1942

Himmler's office, as he reminded himself daily, was a half meter smaller than Hitler's in all dimensions. The furnishings, he felt, were more tasteful than Hitler's heavily upholstered chairs and davenports, and just as expensive. A large map covered the wall behind the desk where Himmler sat, arms folded, looking quite like a schoolmaster, a forbidding pedant, his basilisk eyes peering through gold rimmed spectacles at Genl. Zeitzler. An aide, Capt. Vogel, stood nearby, observing.

Himmler had already gone on the offensive. "A psychiatrist? Whose idea was that, General Zeitzler?"

Rattled, Zeitzler stuttered his reply. "Dr. . . . Dr. Sauerbrach's, Reichsführer. I was against it, of course."

"You've known this for days, not so? And you're just now telling me?"

Zeitzler stumbled over his words again. "I . . . I assumed the Führer would pass on the information—"

These army officers, they must be put in their place, Himmler thought. "So, Herr General, you can read the

Führer's mind."

"Nein. I mean, I thought I should tell you just in case —"

Himmler stood, menace in his eyes. "Imbecile! If you were under my command, I'd have you shipped off to a labor camp."

Zeitzler stiffened.

Himmler pressed the general. "When? Where?"

"I do not know. I did not hear."

"*Dummkopf.* What do you know?"

"The name of the psychiatrist."

"Oh, very good," Himmler said, his voice full of sarcasm. "Who?"

Zeitzler waved his hands as if to protect himself from Himmler's wrath. "First, they talked about a Jew from Vienna, a Marcus Rosenberg—"

Himmler slammed his fists down on the desk. "Surely they were joking."

"Nein. I mean . . . well, maybe they were. They could not imagine anyone who would agree to see the Führer. But the last name I overheard was Jung. General Olbricht was going to contact him."

Really? thought Himmler. "Carl Jung?"

"Ja."

"Scheisse! We'll be reading all about the Führer's mind in fucking *Time Magazine*! If you learn any more, call me at once. Now get out."

Zeitzler hurried away, sweating, his face red.

"What an idiot!" Himmler muttered. *They are all alike, these Army oafs.*

Vogel, his aide said, "Ja. You should have him shot, Reichsführer."

Himmler turned to him, perfectly calm. "Why, Vogel? He did nothing wrong."

"But he did not inform you right away about the OKW plot."

"I wish he had not told me at all. I prefer to keep all my options open. Now that I know about this OKW *plan*, I have fewer options. I have to get involved, when I would really rather not. As for you, find this Dr. Marcus Rosenberg of Vienna. If he is a Jew, he is already behind my barbed wire. Or dead. One may hope, anyway, not so?"

Vogel approached the desk and wrote the name on a pad.

Himmler turned to his map and ran his finger across Switzerland. "Jung is Swiss, not so? He would be somewhere here. Zurich, if I remember rightly. He is an old man and will not want to travel very far. As far as . . . " Himmler's finger crossed Liechtenstein into Austria, then east towards Innsbruck. " . . . Berchtesgaden, perhaps?"

Vogel joined him at the map and pointed at Bludenz, nearer the Liechtensteiner border. "The Führer also has a chalet here, does he not?"

Himmler nodded. "Ja. It is named '*Löwensburg.*' I will make inquiries. You deal with the Jew—Rosenstein or whatever."

Chapter 16
OSS Station, Bern, Switzerland
7:00 AM, June 27, 1942

Early the next day, Jung drove his blood red Chrysler to Bern. The long drive gave him far too much time to think of the dangers ahead. *Why did I agree to do this?* he asked himself over and over. The answer varied from Marc Rosenberg, to Jung's children and grandchildren, to Switzerland, to the world. He felt the weight of the latter on his shoulders and was glad when the drive was over.

Following Dulles's directions, Jung parked south of the OSS office at Herrengasse 23, and walked towards it. As he neared the building, he recognized Dulles's chauffeur coming towards him. The man didn't greet him, but scanned the street behind Jung, watching for anyone following him. This small precaution made Jung feel a little better.

As Dulles had requested, he took a detour that led into a small park, mostly lawn and flower beds, with a rustic garden shed. As he entered the area, Jung noted that it was well concealed by the tall hedge surrounding it; the only windows overlooking it were on the top floor of the OSS building.

A man dressed in gardener's clothing came out of the shed. "You're Dr. Jung?"

"Yes."

"Come this way," the man said, pointing inside the shed. He opened a trapdoor and led Jung down a steep, narrow stairway to a cellar, where he directed him through a concealed door and down a long, well-lit passage that emerged in the basement of the OSS station.

A secretary escorted him upstairs to a large room. It smelled of gun oil, an odor familiar to Jung, who had served in the Swiss Army in WWI. The walls were covered by maps, a projector screen, two blackboards, a gun rack, and several bulletin boards. One of the latter featured a picture of Hitler, his family tree, and a timeline of his life.

Mary and Dulles were already waiting there, sitting facing away from each other, not speaking. Jung sensed tension in the room, thinking, *I wonder what this is about. Have they had a quarrel? And what was it about?* But the two of them quickly stood and greeted him affably, and the secretary returned with coffee and biscuits on a tray.

"What are we going to cover today?" Jung asked after pleasantries over coffee.

"A lot of things," Dulles said. "Are you going to join us, Mary?"

"Sure. I'll just listen in." Mary grimaced at Dulles and sat at the end of a long table near the gun rack. She took down a 10-gauge sawed-off shotgun and started cleaning it.

"Good." Dulles directed Jung to a place halfway down the table and sat across from him, beside a cardboard carton. He took out a copy of *Mein Kampf,* bound in red, with a circled 'x' on the spine. The volume was stuffed with many bookmarks. "You've read this?"

"I have tried."

Dulles said, "Try again," and shoved the book across to Jung, who gave it a sour look.

Mary sighted down the shotgun barrels at Dulles,

saying, "That's the original edition, Dr. Jung. It's rather blatantly anti-Semitic."

Jung opened the book. It was printed in *fraktur*, difficult to read. He flipped through it before stopping and reading aloud a chapter heading. "'*Der Judische Affe.*' The Jewish Monkey. This is the kind of thing that made it unreadable for me."

Dulles leaned back in his chair. "If Chamberlain read *Mein Kampf*, he must have read the English translation, a sanitized version. Hitler embargoed the original edition, to keep it out of the hands of foreigners." Dulles riffled the inserted bookmarks with a forefinger. "I've marked some of the more interesting passages."

Mary said, "There's a place where Hitler refers to himself as a mama's boy. A *Muttersöhnchen*."

Jung made a wry face. "If only a Mother Complex were all we had to deal with."

"Let's do a quick refresher. Come." Dulles stood and led Jung over to the timeline. "Stop me if anything interests you." Dulles's finger moved along the line as he rattled off the major milestones of Hitler's life, starting with his birth in Braunau am Inn.

" . . . A passable artist, but failed the life-drawing entrance exam, Academy of Fine Arts Vienna, 1907. And failed again in 1908 . . . "

Jung raised his eyebrows. "What a lot of trouble we'd have all been saved if he'd been admitted."

"Yeah. German army, 1914 to 1918, two Iron Crosses. Beer hall putsch in '23. Landsberg prison, '24. Geli Raubal's suicide, '31. Named Chancellor, '33. Night of the Long Knives purge, '34—"

Jung stopped him. "Did we ever find out how many people Hitler ordered killed in '34?"

Dulles looked up at the ceiling, then back at Jung. "Best guess, seventy to seven hundred. Maybe more." He paused.

"A reliable source said Hitler shot at least four of them for purely personal reasons. The source disappeared a week later."

"Dead men tell no tales," Mary said, putting away the shotgun and taking a pistol from the rack.

"True." Dulles continued, "Mussolini's visit, 1937—"

Jung indicated the date. "Yes, I was in Berlin during that visit. I had a chance to observe both Mussolini and Hitler from just a few meters away—"

"Yeah, I read your article." Dulles kept going: " . . . Annexing of Austria, '38 . . . "

When Dulles had finished reviewing the timeline, Jung pointed at September of 1931. "Who was this? 'Geli Raubal.'"

"Hitler's girlfriend." Mary said. She'd joined them and was looking over Jung's shoulder. "She shot herself with Hitler's pistol."

"Do we know any more?" Jung asked. "Her death could be significant."

Dulles shook his head. "Or a pointless distraction. A locked room, dozens of witnesses saw Hitler in another town. Open and shut case. She's over here." Dulles pointed at a square in Hitler's family tree on the next bulletin board. "Geli was the daughter of his half-sister, Angela."

Surprised, Jung asked, "She was his niece?"

"Half-niece." Dulles said. "Technically."

"Still, if she was close to Hitler, she could be important," Jung insisted. He moved to the family tree and examined it up close as Dulles recited Hitler's ancestry, pointing at the various relatives.

" . . . Adolf's father: Alois Hitler. Mother: Klara Poelzl —"

Jung reached out and tapped Klara's lineage. "A most interesting family."

Dulles pointed at the chart. "You noticed the connection?"

"Yes." Jung traced a line with his finger from Klara up and then over and back down to Alois. "Hitler's mother and father are cousins."

"Maybe." Dulles continued the recitation. " . . . Hitler's grandmother: Maria Schicklgruber. Hitler's grandfather. . . " He paused with his finger resting on a square containing only a question mark. "Well, he's somewhat of a mystery."

"What's the mystery?"

Mary put down the pistol she was disassembling. "Hitler's father, Alois, was born out of wedlock. Thirty years after Alois's mother, Maria Schicklgruber, died, the family claimed that Alois's step-dad had been his biological father. If true, that meant Alois was Klara's cousin."

"The step-father was named Hitler?"

Dulles shook his head and pointed at another square on the chart. "Hiedler. Johann Hiedler. But rumor has it that Alois's actual father was the son of Maria's employer, a wealthy Graz Jew named Leo Frankenberger."

"Hitler's grandfather was a Jew? How very ironic. But is there any truth in it?" Jung said.

"Nope," Dulles replied. "The story originated with Hitler's lawyer, Hans Frank. Looks like he made it up. No Frankenberger families in Graz at the time."

"Why would Frank lie?" Mary asked.

Dulles shrugged. "Who knows?"

Jung held up a finger. "Perhaps Herr Frank actually *was* a Frankenberger, and hoped to appeal to Hitler as a kinsman if the SS ever shook his family tree."

Dulles looked at Jung. "You may be right." He returned to the pedigree and continued, " . . . Maria's father, Hitler's great-grandfather, Johannes Schicklgruber . . . "

As the day wore on, Dulles stacked more and more information about Hitler in front of him. Jung looked at the stack and said, "All this, Herr Dulles?"

"All this. We'll give you a shopping bag to carry it.

Take it home, read it all before Tuesday morning. Nothing hush-hush, but best to keep it locked up. People might wonder why you're reading it."

If I'm going to violate professional ethics, I might as well face the issue right now, Jung decided. "Is there anything specific you'd like to know?" Jung asked Dulles.

"What will he do next?"

Mary put down a partly disassembled Mauser machine pistol and looked at Jung. "I wish you could find out who his grandfather really was."

Jung held up a hand and shook his head. "Wish all you want, but I wouldn't dare ask, even if I thought he knew the answer. He'll say it was Hiedler, anyway."

Dulles stared out a window, then back at Jung. "Since we're wishing, it would be nice to find out why the hell he invaded Russia. It made no sense, gave him a two-front war."

Mary nodded. "Stalin wasn't about to attack Germany right then; he was too ill-prepared. But that's just one more question you don't dare ask."

I wouldn't ask a question like that for all the money in the world, Jung thought. *And maybe not even for Marc Rosenberg.*

"True," Dulles said. "And then there's Döllersheim."

Jung raised his eyebrows. "Döllersheim?"

Dulles said, "The home town of Hitler's father, Alois. Four years ago, the Nazis threw everybody out, turned the place into a military enclave. Nobody knows why." He shrugged.

"Perhaps he hated his father," Jung said. "And that, unfortunately, *is* a question I may need to explore." He shivered, hoping Mary didn't notice.

"I'd like to know why he hates Jews," Mary said, applying a drop of oil to the pistol.

Jung said, "He seems to blame them for everything, but does that matter enough to risk investigating?"

"Probably not." She wiped the pistol with a cloth, then snapped the action shut and smiled. "Another item for the wish list: rumor has it that Hitler's only got one ball. If you get a chance, check his drawers."

Jung swung a hand like a pendulum. "I doubt that's what makes him go tick-tock, though I could be wrong." He looked at Dulles. "Is that it?"

"Two more items. Serious ones." Dulles pulled out an index card. On it was printed, "OSS Agent #488" in large letters. He handed the card to Jung while Mary looked on. "It's official. This is you. Never put your name on any OSS documents. Just four-eighty-eight. Burn this card."

Jung slipped the card into a pocket. Mary grinned and kissed his cheek. Dulles grimaced at the show of affection.

Jung pretended not to notice Dulles's expression. "You said two items?"

Dulles reached into a drawer and pulled out a pipe, which he shoved towards Jung. "Here's a little present for you."

Mary exclaimed, "Allen!"

Jung thought she sounded upset, but couldn't imagine why. "I have plenty of pipes," he said, puzzled.

"Not like this." Dulles picked it up again and slid the stem back, revealing a slim steel tube within. "It's a single-shot .22-short pistol."

Jung's jaw dropped. "I can't shoot Hitler."

Dulles held up a hand. "It's not for him; it's for you. If Himmler's men—SS or Gestapo—corner you, stick it up a nostril and push the little button. It's faster than cyanide."

Faster than cyanide? Jung took a deep breath and a tremor shook him as whatever optimism he'd had drained away. "You are serious?"

"Yes. You cock it by twisting the bowl forty-five degrees. See?" Dulles demonstrated this, then took out a small tobacco pouch, dropped in four .22-short cartridges, and put it and the pipe in front of Jung. "Safe trip, Dr. Jung.

Go get Hitler's secrets. And whatever you do, don't get him angry."

Jung saw Mary glare at Dulles. *This looks more and more like a suicide mission,* he thought.

Mary quickly turned to Jung, and her lips stretched back in a semblance of a smile. "He's just kidding, Dr. Jung. Aren't you, Allen?"

Dulles smirked. "'Course I am. The chance of falling into Himmler's hands is essentially zero. Be polite to Hitler, Dr. Jung, and you'll be fine."

Jung was not fooled. *Dulles obviously doesn't have high hopes that my mission will succeed, and Mary is trying to hide that.*

Chapter 17
Jung's Residence, Küsnacht
10:00 PM, June 27, 1942

Jung returned to his home outside Zurich, in Küsnacht, late in the day. Tired from the trip, he parked the Chrysler and sat looking at his house for minute before getting out. *What shall I tell Emmy?* he wondered. *As little as possible. The less she knows, the better.*

When he went in, he heard Emmy typing in her office and joined her there, instead of going straight to his own rooms, as he often did.

Emmy, also a psychotherapist, was preparing a monograph on her specialty, the Grail Legend. Surrounded by notes and books, apparently lost in thought, she looked up as Carl entered. "Ah. You are back." She stood.

Jung put down the shopping bag and embraced her.

"You missed me?"

"Today especially, yes."

Emmy put a hand on his arm. "What's wrong, Carl?"

"Nothing, really. I spent all day in Bern. I'm just tired from the drive."

"I wondered."

Carl knew that Emmy had wondered whether Antonia,

Toni Wolff, his closest associate, had gone along on the trip with him. He fumbled for his pipe and said, "I'm taking on a new client. A Mr. Wolff."

"Wolff? Any relation to Toni?"

"None at all." Carl pulled the pipe out of his pocket before realizing it was Dulles's suicide pistol. He put it back and withdrew his empty hand.

"I thought you had stopped taking new clients," Emmy said, wrinkling her brow.

Carl nodded. "Mostly I have. In fact, this may likely be the last." *If I annoy Hitler, it will certainly be the last.*

"He is in Zurich?" Emmy asked.

"No, he is to the east of us, near the Austrian border." Carl omitted the fact that "Mr. Wolff" was on the far side of that border, in Nazi-occupied Austria. "I'll be away Tuesday and Wednesday to see him and make an evaluation."

Emmy narrowed her eyes and looked at him. "What aren't you telling me?"

Carl returned her look and sighed. "What I mustn't. It's a confidential matter. You understand."

She tilted her head and continued to stare at Carl, then looked down at her notes and said, "Have you eaten?"

"Yes, I had something at . . . in Bern." Jung had almost mentioned the OSS station and realized he was too tired to talk safely about the trip anymore. "I'd best get some sleep. It's . . . it's good to be home." He embraced her again, picked up the bag of Hitler material, and left the study.

Chapter 18
Jung's Office, Zurich
9:00 AM, June 29, 1942

On Monday morning, Mary stood beside Jung in his Zurich office, watching him unseal a large manila envelope just delivered by courier. She didn't see anything on the outside to show it had been forwarded from the Zurich German Consulate.

Jung extracted various documents one at a time, and placed them into either his briefcase or a coat pocket. "A letter from Dr. Sauerbrach . . . my visa . . . papers and ration cards for the car and driver . . . "

Mary reached over and appropriated the car documents. "I'll give these to Jaffe in Bern this afternoon. You have your passport?"

Jung patted his jacket pocket. "Yes, yes. And two notepads, a prescription pad, and, for light reading tonight . . . " He held up *Mein Kampf*, then tossed it into the briefcase. He took the magnifying glass from his desk, saying "I'll need this for the fraktur." He slipped the magnifier into his top jacket pocket. "What about these?" He took out Dulles's pipe-pistol and tobacco pouch. "Surely I shouldn't just leave them in my briefcase."

"There are several secret compartments in the Auburn. I'll conceal them in the back seat."

"Where?"

"In the arm-rest. Swivel it down, push it straight back, then pull it straight forward. It opens like a drawer, but you have to push and pull hard." She hesitated. *Should I tell him? Or not?* She finally said, "I'll put a cyanide capsule in there, too. It's just standard operating procedure. I'm sure you won't need it. Or Allen's silly pistol."

"Thanks." Jung grimaced. He handed her the pipe and pouch. "Maybe you'd better load this, anyway. I have a feeling if I need the gun, I'll want it ready to shoot."

"I'll take care of it." She looked at Jung and said with an enthusiasm she didn't feel, "Cheer up, Carl. Jaffe will be there if you need help." *Jaffe, for cripes sake! A moron.*

"Two of us against how many Nazis?"

"You're not a soldier; you're there by invitation. You have a neutral Swiss passport. You have the backing of the German High Command. You only have to deal with one client—"

"Who is Adolf Hitler, a Nazi and a tyrant who shoots his political opponents."

"He's still just one man."

"Technically, you're right. But it's not the numbers I'm afraid of. It's more . . . "

"More what?" Mary felt her stomach churn.

Jung waved his hands in the air. "That I'm afraid my contempt for that posturing, hand-flapping jackanapes will become obvious! That it will show in my face or a word or a gesture. A single momentary lapse, and I won't get a thing out of him. And it will be my own fault for losing control."

"You're not that judgmental, are you? You're sure not that way with me in therapy."

"No, but you haven't started a world war. Remember, Mary, I observed Hitler close up in Berlin in '37. He's barely human; not a shred of warmth."

"Maybe he was just having a bad day. Look, think of Hitler as just another client. A sick person who needs help."

"I am afraid I have already judged him, but I will certainly try."

You'd better do more than try, Mary thought. *Two lapses, and you'll be on your way to a concentration camp.* "Stay focused, suspend judgment, and nothing bad will happen."

But she knew that it could happen. She forced a smile and added, "You need something lucky to take along tomorrow. Here, take this." She unfastened the mandala from the wall and handed it to Jung.

"Thanks." Jung put the painting into his briefcase. Then he opened a desk drawer, pulled out an envelope, and handed it to her. "Hold onto this. If I don't return . . . " She looked at the envelope. The outside was labeled: "To be opened in the event of my death. Carl Gustav Jung."

Mary's sense of danger sank in a little deeper, and her heart fell. *Carl could die. Allen thinks so, and now Carl knows it, too. My phony "cheery attitude" hasn't helped a bit.*

Chapter 19
Hitler's Bedroom, Wolf's Lair
10:00 AM, June 29, 1942

A polite knock sounded on the rustic pine door. "The *Amerika* is ready for boarding, Führer," his SS adjutant said.

"Tell the engineer I will be there in thirty minutes."

"Very good, Führer."

Hitler was alone. He undressed, showered in the adjacent bathroom, and dried his hair. Then he put on the comfortable outfit his aide had laid out for him.

He combed his hair and checked his appearance in a full-length mirror. Satisfied that he looked properly Führer-like, he slipped into his bullet-proof vest. Over it, he wore a Tyrolean jacket with suede trim. It concealed the vest well. He paused at the door, picked up his .30 caliber Walther PPK, and slipped it into a leather pocket in his trousers. All his pants had been altered that way to hold a weapon.

Another quick look in the mirror, then Hitler opened the door and took the first step of his new adventure, wondering, *Will I have to shoot this Dr. Jung when I am finished with him? If so, he would not be the first.*

Chapter 20
Bern
11:00 AM, June 29, 1942

After Mary left Jung's office on Monday morning, she rode her motorcycle to Bern. Before reporting to Dulles, she dashed down to the basement where Augusta Zvendt, the OSS's local documents specialist, did her magic with paper, stamps, and special inks.

"Gussie, I need something," Mary said.

The little wizard looked up from her microscope and put on a pair of Ben Franklin style reading glasses. "Ja, Miss Bancroft? And what is it that you need?"

"I need a Swiss passport."

Augusta took a pad of paper from a roll-top desk. "And this is for whom?"

"For me."

"But do you not have a Swiss passport already? From your husband." Then Augusta grinned. "Aha! I see. You are finally going to divorce that oaf Rufenacht, ja? Excellent!"

Augusta knew the entire story of the emotional and physical abuse that Mary had endured for years before separating from Jacques. But Mary waved the idea away. "No, we're staying married until the war is over."

Augusta rolled her eyes. "But why not just get a new American passport? I could have a genuine one from the Embassy in a week."

Mary thought fast. The answer wasn't pretty, but it would work. "I need a special passport as a contingency, in case we ever get overrun by Germany. Any American connections on my papers might be dangerous."

"I see." Augusta looked at Mary over her glasses. "Does Herr Dulles know about this? I really should get his approval."

"I'm sure he'd approve, but I don't want him to know I'm afraid. Please, Gussie? I'll love you forever!" She beamed at the technician.

Augusta blushed and returned the smile. "Never let Herr Dulles know where you got this, all right?"

"Right. Not a word. Ever."

"Let me see your passport." Taking Mary's little booklet, she peered into it and said, "And you want the new one to be different how . . . ?"

"I was born in Cambridge, Massachusetts. Change that to somewhere in Switzerland. Basel, maybe."

"No. Mittelbrenn would be better. Their town hall burned down twenty years ago." Augusta made a note on her pad.

"Perfect. And get rid of my maiden name, too. Replace Bancroft with something very Germanic."

"Germanic . . . How about . . . Banghart? Maria Banghart." Augusta grinned and wiggled her eyebrows.

"Great. But leave Jacques' surname on it; make me 'Maria Banghart Rufenacht.' Originally of Mittelbrenn. Swiss national, married. And make me thirty years old, too, while you're at it."

Augusta looked up from her notes. "Why so old? You do not look thirty."

"It'll give me an air of maturity."

"Maturity? You?" Augusta laughed. "Very unlikely. But

I will need to keep your old passport, so try to stay out of trouble. I will have the new one ready for you in two weeks."

"Two weeks? I need it tonight."

"What? Tonight? You think we are going to get invaded tonight?"

"No! I just need to have it with me right away. So I'll feel safe." She grabbed the technician and kissed her forehead. "Please . . . ?"

Augusta Zvendt reddened and straightened her spectacles. "Only for you, Miss Bancroft. Only for you. Give me, please, two, no, make it three hours."

Mary's new passport was ready shortly after she returned from lunch. Augusta Zvendt handed it to her and said, "The inks are perhaps a little off, but as long as no one subjects it to chemical analysis, it would fool Himmler, himself."

"Thanks a million, Gussie." Mary leafed through the passport. It was a masterpiece of diplomatic fiction, with a dozen pages of both real and fictitious border-crossings, all stamped and punched. She concealed it in her purse and went back to work.

Later that night, Mary hesitated, then knocked on the door of an apartment in Bern. The door opened, and she saw Jaffe standing there, giving her a quizzical stare. "Miss Bancroft? What is it?"

"I brought your papers for tomorrow. But first . . . " She held up a large bottle of brandy.

Jaffe grinned and stood back to let her in.

Chapter 21
Jung's Residence, Küsnacht
11:00 PM, June 29, 1942

In Küsnacht, Jung slept little that night, going around and around in his mind, thinking of what he must do . . . and what might happen. The more he thought about it, the more certain he was that he would not be coming back.

After an hour of this morbid train of thought, he concluded that perhaps the best outcome would be to disobey Dulles and use his little pipe-pistol to kill Hitler. The world would be a much better place, and despite Dulles's opinion that Hitler's replacement would be a superior military strategist, Jung was certain whoever took command would be less evil. The encounter in Berlin five years before had convinced Jung that the Führer was a demon in human form.

As for himself, he was nearing seventy, definitely past his prime, and already suffering from various maladies of the elderly. Occasionally, he found himself having to root around in his mind for a word, or a name to go with a face. This would only get worse, in time. The major consideration was Emmy and their children and grandchildren. But, as Dulles had emphasized that morning, if Hitler won the war, he'd take care of unfinished business and attack Switzerland. That must never happen. Jung decided he would kill Hitler, if necessary.

Jung mulled over the question of whether he could load and fire another round up his nose within seconds after shooting Hitler. He decided to practice loading the pistol on the way to Mauren in the morning. He fell asleep thinking about what he must do.

Chapter 22
Küsnacht to Mauren
6:00 AM, June 30, 1942

In the morning, the OSS Auburn V-12 waited in heavy fog in front of Jung's home. He walked out slowly, carrying his bag; Emmy followed with his briefcase. The driver, in full chauffeur's uniform and cap, didn't greet them, just opened the Auburn's trunk and loaded Jung's bag therein.

Carl stood back and looked at Emmy. He didn't know what to say. They embraced and said a brief goodbye. *Is this our last farewell?* he wondered. *Will Germany return my body, if I shoot Hitler? Probably not. My body may not be in any condition for viewing after they get through with me.*

Jung knew that even if he didn't assassinate the Führer, there was no certainty he'd return alive, despite Olbricht's assurances. He said, "I will see you tomorrow evening, but if I'm late, don't wait up. And don't worry."

Emmy's brow wrinkled. "I am already worried. You are concealing something."

He shrugged. "You know me too well. Yes, I'm withholding certain details, but it is a matter of professional secrecy. If anything comes up, call Mrs. Rufenacht at the office. She is filling in for my receptionist while I am gone."

"Mrs. Rufenacht? Is she not one of your clients?"

"Yes, but she is also a student and is helping me with this case, for reasons I can't go into."

"I wish you would give this up, whatever it is."

If only . . . "I wish I could, but it is important."

They kissed, then Carl climbed into the back seat, carrying his briefcase. When he rapped on the tinted glass partition, the driver pulled away smoothly. At the last second, Carl turned his head and waved at Emmy as she watched him ride off.

Carl looked back, uneasy, seeing his home fade into the fog. When the driver turned onto the main road, he shivered and sat back.

The Auburn purred along Lake Zurich, going east toward Liechtenstein. Jung pulled the armrest down and slid it to and fro to open the secret compartment with the pistol and pouch inside. In the light of morning, shooting Hitler didn't seem such a good idea, but Jung practiced loading the pipe, as he'd promised himself he would. He could extract one cartridge, drop in another, and cock the weapon in less than five seconds. It would work. The most important thing was not to panic and drop the bullets.

There was, as promised, a small brass cylinder in the armrest. Jung took off the cap and let the cyanide ampule fall into his hand. He looked at the fine white crystals inside it. Only a thin glass layer separated him from death. He put the ampule back into the brass holder and dropped that in with the tobacco.

He slipped the pouch and the gun, loaded but not cocked, into his coat pockets. *I'll put these back before we cross into Germany.* He slammed the compartment shut, leaned back and closed his eyes.

The Auburn came to a gentle stop. Jung awoke and

looked around. Bright sunshine. Ahead stood a tall fence, with barbed wire, machine guns, and steel barriers. *Have we reached Mauren already?* Jung wound down the glass partition. "Jaffe, where are we?"

Mary, Jaffe's cap atop her blonde hair, turned in the driver's seat and looked back at him. "Entering Liechtenstein, Dr. Jung."

"Mary? What the devil are you doing here?" Jung sputtered.

"It's okay, Dr. Jung; Jaffe had a headache. Has a headache."

A Swiss border guard approached the car, and Mary added, "I need your papers."

Flustered, Jung passed his documents to her. The guard checked their papers and returned them, then stepped back, raised a steel barricade, and threw a switch that sent a heavy concrete barrier trundling out of the way.

Jung remembered the tension between Mary and Dulles during his briefing. As she drove across the border, he asked, "Does Allen Dulles know you're here?"

"He will pretty soon. I set Jaffe's alarm clock when he passed out last night." She giggled.

"Allow me to guess. You went to his place with a bottle and got him drunk?"

"Three sheets to the wind, decks awash. I wish I could be there when he shows up at work. Allen will kill him."

"What about you, Mary? Are you in any shape to drive?"

"I poured a lot faster than I drank. I'm fine."

On the Liechtensteiner side, a guard with a clipboard checked them through. While he stamped their papers, Jung got into the front seat with Mary. He wasn't sure whether he should be mad at her or relieved to have her company. *Now she's in danger, too. It was incredibly foolish of her to come. Still, I'm glad to see her.* "You shouldn't have done this, Mary."

"You're doing it."

"I'm an old man."

"A rare and irreplaceable man."

"All the same, we should go back to Zurich," Jung said.

"If we go back, we'll have blown our chance. It was a fluke that the OKW approached you, and even luckier that I was in your office when Olbricht got there. We can't let this slip away from us, Carl. Er, Dr. Jung."

"'Carl' is okay, Mary. But you may be right. There is a synchronicity here that perhaps deserves to be ridden to its conclusion."

The border guard handed back their papers and swung the barrier out of the way.

"It's up to you, Carl. Zurich and safety for a year or two? Or Germany and glory?"

"Germany, Mary. Forgive me if this ends badly."

She held out her hand. "Okay, it's you and me against the Germans from here to the end, whatever it is."

Jung shook her hand. She stamped on the accelerator and they roared into Liechtenstein.

Jung rode with a map in his lap, following their progress as they passed farms and small villages. After a few kilometers, a black BMW sedan approached. As it went by them, Jung saw four ugly men inside wearing black fedoras. *Those men don't look like Liechtensteiners. They emanate evil. It shows in the way they hold their heads, like lizards waiting for butterflies.*

Mary muttered, "Don't stare at them."

Jung glanced down at the map. Mary turned her head and looked in the rear view mirror.

Jung said, "Can you see them? They looked like Gestapo."

"There are active Nazi groups here in Vaduz, so it's possible. But they're not turning around, so we're okay. Look, if anything happens, duck down. This car is bullet-proof, but the windows aren't quite. War-time shortages. . ."

Jung slouched lower in his seat and frowned.

Mary fumbled in one of the chauffeur uniform's pockets. "Look, Carl, I brought along a toy." She held up a lipstick.

Jung looked at it. "Is that another gun?"

"Don't be silly. It's a spy camera. And a telescope. And a lipstick."

"And what happens if you get caught with that in Germany?"

"I won't get caught. Where's your sense of adventure?"

"I left that in Küsnacht. And I don't expect it to be there when I get back."

They soon reached Vaduz, the capital of Liechtenstein, and, a minute or two later, Jung saw a sign reading "Mauren." At the Mauren border station, they showed their passports and the guards waved them through the first gate into Austria, now officially "Ostmark," a part of the Great German Reich.

Jung noticed a definite difference in the attitude of the German guards. Some of them carried full automatic weapons, and they moved with an air of total authority, if not outright arrogance. Jung felt the air fill with invisible menace.

A guard stepped from beneath a shelter and directed them to a parking space near the swastika-embellished second gate. Two others approached the car, and Mary handed over her and Jung's papers. The guards examined them for a long time, pausing occasionally to stare at Jung and Mary. Jung wondered, *Are they talking about us? Or are they just admiring the car?*

Mary muttered under her breath, "Where the hell is Olbricht?"

"I never thought I'd be this anxious to see him."

"Right now, I could kiss him," Mary whispered, still

watching the guards.

"I am not quite that anxious."

One of the guards stalked to the Auburn and addressed Jung in German. "Out of the car. Stand over there." He pointed at a concrete slab and a table nearby, then turned to Mary and ordered, "You! Park the car over there, to your left. Remove all the luggage and leave the keys in the ignition."

It was only then that Jung remembered the little pipe gun was in his pocket, instead of safe inside the secret compartment. *What if they search me? What if they make me empty my pockets? It looks like a pipe, but it's heavy for a pipe. I may be dead or arrested in less than sixty seconds. Where the hell is Olbricht?*

They followed the guard's orders. While Jung stood on the slab, waiting for Mary to unload the bags, he looked down. The concrete sloped to a central drain surrounded by ominous red-stains. *Is that rust? No, definitely not.* His knees trembled and almost buckled.

Mary set their bags and Jung's briefcase on the table, and opened them. A guard probed through their belongings, peering at everything. Another approached and ordered, "Hands high."

Oh, no, here it comes. What can I do? Nothing. I should have left the pipe-pistol in the car.

The second guard frisked the two of them while the third searched the Auburn. Jung thought, *There's no telling what else Dulles may have hidden in the car. I hope he doesn't find anything.* He shivered.

The guard patted Jung down front and back from neck to ankles. *That wasn't too bad. He missed the pipe-pistol.*

But then the frisking started again at his shoulders and down his sides. Jung stiffened as the man reached his side pockets; he felt the pistol beat against his hip.

"*Was ist das?*" The guard looked Jung in the eyes.

"*Ich rauch ein Pfeife.*"

"Ach, so." The man reached into the pocket and took out the pipe. He held it up and turned it over, looking at it from all sides and sniffing the bowl.

Well, it looks like a pipe, Jung thought. *But is it good enough to fool him?*

Dulles's craftsmen had done their work well—the little gun not only looked like a pipe, it smelled like one, evidently having been smoked for several days before being turned over to Jung. He began to relax, then recalled the bag of tobacco in his other pocket. *I'm doomed,* he thought. *If they look in the pouch, they can't miss the bullets . . . and the cyanide. A dead giveaway!*

But the guard just dropped the pipe back into Jung's pocket and walked away.

Jung looked at Mary. She met his eyes and raised her eyebrows. He inhaled and breathed a silent prayer of thanks, thinking, *I may know the human mind, but none of this is in the textbooks. I shouldn't have come here.* He made a mental note to throw the pipe away at the first opportunity.

Chapter 23
OSS Office, Bern
8:00 AM, June 30, 1942

Mary hadn't come in that morning. Allen Dulles had half expected she'd stop in and see him before going to Zurich to cover the desk at Jung's office. He tried to call the number there, but no one answered. *Too early*, he thought, *I'll try later*. He walked around the briefing room, stopping every so often to look at the clock or the telephone. *Where is she? Hope to God she didn't wrap that damned motorcycle around a tree."* He reached for the telephone again.

There was a noise behind him, halfway between a belch and a heave. Great relief flooded over Dulles. *Sounds like she's drunk. If she is, I'll give her the spanking she deserves.*

Dulles spun around and saw not Mary Bancroft, but Jaffe standing in the doorway, pathetically crapulous. He was not wearing his chauffeur's uniform, and he clutched the jamb, apparently trying to stay upright. A light in Dulles's mind began to glimmer, and his stomach clenched into a tight ball. *Oh, no. No, no, no, no, no.* "Jaffe! What the hell . . . ?"

"I've been taken . . . uh . . . ill," Jaffe blurted, followed by another burp.

"You're supposed to be driving Dr. Jung to Germany. What have you done with him? Where is he?"

"Ger-ermany, by now."

"Who's driving . . . ? No, no, don't tell me—"

"It's all her fault. She got me drunk las' nigh'."

"You idiot! You cretin! You may have gotten my best intelligence analyst killed!" Dulles sank into a chair. "You're fired!"

Jaffe's face fell even further. He appeared about to cry, but instead rushed to the nearest wastebasket, drew it to his chin, and noisily dry-heaved into it, producing nothing but tinny echoes: "*Huah! Huah! Huah!*"

"You miserable bastard!" Dulles told him. "Get out of here! If Mary Bancroft doesn't come back, you'll wish you were never born."

Chapter 24
Mauren to Löwensburg
8:05 AM, June 30, 1942

Jung still had his hands up, knees unsteady, when Olbricht's Opel approached from the Austrian gate. The car's top was down, and small OKW flags flapped on each fender. The border guards snapped to attention and saluted as the car stopped. One guard spun to face Jung and Mary. "You there. Put your hands down."

They obeyed. Jung began looking for a place to get rid of the ridiculous pipe-pistol. Olbricht got out of the Opel in full uniform, smiling and waving as he approached them.

"Herr Doktor Jung! Guten Morgen! Willkommen in Deutschland. Sorry, ich bin spät." He strode towards them, saw Mary and gave her a perplexed look. "Ah. We meet again. You are Dr. Jung's chauffeur, as well as his secretary?"

Mary smiled before explaining. "Dr. Jung's driver was taken ill, Herr Albright. I volunteered to fill in. I hope you don't mind."

"This is most unexpected."

Unexpected. Jung felt his stomach sink even deeper. *If only Mary hadn't come.* He jumped into the momentary gap. "I thought it most discreet not to involve another outsider. I've told Mary our destination, nothing else."

Olbricht looked at Jung, then back at Mary. "I am sorry, you are named Mary?"

"Yes. Short for Maria. Frau Maria Rufenacht."

Jung was horror-struck by his blunder. He'd called her "Mary," an American name. Too late, he realized that her passport might have a different name, evidently Maria. If it said, "Mary," this would be a very brief trip.

The General wasn't fazed. "I am Friedrich Olbricht, Frau Rufenacht. I am pleased to meet you again." He bowed and clicked his heels, evoking another amused grin from Mary. Olbricht, obviously thinking the grin was for him, smiled back.

Jung saw the smile and grew less anxious.

The General continued, "But we will not need your services, Frau Rufenacht. I will drive Herr Doktor Jung from here. You may wait back in Mauren." He motioned with a hand.

"I should assist Dr. Jung here in Germany."

"You cannot be allowed in the presence of the patient."

Mary gave Olbricht a coquettish glance. "I wasn't talking about that sort of assistance."

Olbricht's eyes narrowed. "Ah. I see."

Jung stepped in. "Also, Herr General, I'd hoped to talk with you on the way. While Frau Rufenacht drives."

Olbricht addressed Mary. "Your papers, please."

"The guards still have them."

Olbricht held out a hand to a guard, silently demanding their papers. Jung surreptitiously took hold of the pipe, hoping for an another instant's inattention by the General in which to get rid of it somehow.

Olbricht examined Mary's passport. "Swiss." He opened it and read, "Frau Maria Banghart Rufenacht."

Jung's eyebrows rose. *Maria Banghart Rufenacht? That is not her real name! She has planned ahead. A lot farther*

86

ahead than I have.

Olbricht asked her, "And where is Herr Rufenacht, if I may inquire?"

Mary grimaced. "We have an arrangement."

"Aha." Olbricht nodded, then snapped the passport closed and handed it to her. "Help me put the top up, please."

Minutes later, the Opel roared into Austria, Mary at the wheel, Jung and Olbricht in the back seat. The General held a red folder in his lap, and Jung sat as far away as he could, wishing he'd seen an opportunity to pitch the tell-tale pipe into the bushes or atop a roof back at the border station.

"I am glad we have this time to chat, Dr. Jung," Olbricht shouted over the Opel engine, whose muffler needed repair.

"Thank you."

"Relax. You are safe with me." Olbricht handed him the red folder. "This is an authorized copy of Herr Wolff's medical file. Please look it over and let me know if you have any questions, keeping in mind . . . " He gestured at Mary behind the wheel.

"Of course." Jung read through the material as they drove. The most relevant document was a summary of Hitler's medical history prepared in Dr. Sauerbrach's fine German script. Jung had to read parts of it with the aid of his magnifying glass, but it was self-explanatory, so he had few questions to ask Olbricht. After that, they rode along in silence for a while. Jung thought, *I'll just close my eyes to rest them. I won't fall asleep again.*

When Jung awoke, the Opel was beginning a gradual ascent among mountains. It wasn't much longer before they came to an unmarked side road and Olbricht said, loud enough to be heard, "Go left here, Frau Rufenacht. We take that road all the way up to the end."

The road wound uphill among fragrant evergreens for a

kilometer or more until it widened out into a large parking lot. To their left, against the mountainside, stood a granite and bronze portal beneath a large brass National Socialist eagle with the Earth in its claws. *Not if I can help it,* Jung thought. Four blond armed guards came to attention at the sight of the OKW flags on the Opel.

Mary hopped out, ignored the guards, and opened the rear door to let Olbricht out. As soon as the General stepped out, the guards saluted Nazi-style, hands high in the air, with a hearty "Heil Hitler!" He returned the salute more casually, his arm lax. One of the guards opened a cabinet beside the portal, took out a telephone on a long cord, and rushed forward to hand it to the General.

Mary offered her hand to help Jung from the car. He took it and held it longer and tighter than necessary. She leaned towards him, saying, "You'll do fine, Dr. Jung. He's just another client."

"What do I do with the pipe?" he whispered to her.

"Too late now." She shrugged and added, "Just don't shoot anybody." She smiled and winked at him.

The guards now stood beside the car. Mary took out Jung's briefcase. A guard promptly but politely took it from her, opened it, and started examining the contents.

We're going to be searched again! Jung thought. His stomach clenched and he hoped he was wrong.

But the second guard frisked him gently, found his magnifying glass, looked at it, and put it back in Jung's top pocket. He also inspected the blackout flashlight, unscrewing the end and thoroughly checking the batteries inside.

So far, so good.

Then the guard checked Jung's side jacket pockets and found first the pipe, then the tobacco pouch. Jung looked helplessly at Mary, who mouthed, "Don't panic."

The guard held up the two items in front of Jung. "*Diese sind Kontrabande!*" he exclaimed.

I've been caught. Jung wanted to disappear beneath the pavement, but keeping his head about him, he asked, "But what seems to be the problem?" His knees threatened to give way.

The guard pointed at a large *Rauchen verboten* sign near the entrance. "It is forbidden to smoke in the presence of Herr Wolff."

"Oh, I see. Sorry, I didn't know. I wasn't told." Jung forced himself to shut up and avoid making things worse by chattering.

The first guard placed the verboten items in a large clasp envelope and wrote "Herr Lang" on it, then put it into a cabinet beside the telephone enclosure. Jung thought, *What if the guards decide to smoke some of my tobacco and find it contains bullets and cyanide?*

Olbricht was speaking on the phone: "Jawohl . . . Jawohl . . . Jawohl, mein Führer!" He hung up, beads of sweat on his forehead. He turned and saw Mary looking at him. "You heard?"

"I heard nothing, Herr General."

"Good."

Jung had been listening to the exchange. *Well done, Mary!* He held out his hands as the guards returned his briefcase and flashlight. He slipped the latter into the briefcase.

Olbricht addressed him. "He is waiting, Herr Doktor. You are ready, yes?"

Jung straightened and took a deep breath. "Yes. Let's go."

"Ah. I am so sorry, Dr. Jung. I should have said. From here, you must go alone. I will meet you tomorrow afternoon at the *gasthaus.*" Olbricht paused, then added, "And you may need to keep your torch handy. The tunnel lights have been known to fail."

"Lights fail? In the Third Reich?" Hands trembling, Jung got out the flashlight. He looked at Olbricht and Mary, then glanced up at the Nazi emblem above the doors for a second before nodding to the guards. Two of them rushed forward and swung wide both doors in concert, revealing a dark, arched stone passageway leading into the mountain. Ahead of him on the tunnel floor, he saw his shadow, distorted into a giant's silhouette by the morning sun. His mood became darker. *Why did I ever agree to this?*

Another guard threw a switch to light the tunnel. The ceiling lamps all seemed to work, but did little to make Jung feel safe.

He breathed in, exhaled, then took his first, tentative steps into the tunnel. The motion gave him more confidence, and he was soon striding along rapidly. His fear made him automatically count his steps. He'd only reached sixty when the doors behind him boomed shut. Jung spun around. There was no daylight behind him, now, only the subdued light of the tunnel. *It's as if the rest of the world has ceased to exist. Ahead of me lies Hitler's world.* Jung continued into the mountain.

Before he'd gone another ten paces, all the lights went out. *Scheisse!* Jung flipped on the flashlight and kept going, but its beam gradually turned to yellow, then orange. Jung swore again and put out his left hand to guide himself along the rough stone wall just before the batteries failed completely, leaving him in darkness again. He stumbled and groped his way forward.

After another hundred paces, the echo of Jung's footsteps changed subtly and he slowed. *There's something right ahead of me. Carefully, now.* Seconds later, the lights came on, and a pair of doors slid open before him, revealing a modern elevator car, lined with mirror-bright metallic panels.

Jung entered and pushed the up button. The doors closed, and he staggered as the car rocketed upward, air howling around it. Over a minute passed before the car began to slow, then stopped.

The elevator doors opened onto a large room. Visible through the windows beyond lay a stunning Alpine vista where many of the peaks were below eye level. And there stood Hitler, stiff as a statue on the balcony outside, staring down at the mountains. Jung peered at him for long seconds, trying to read Der Führer's attitude. *He's posing*, Jung decided, *trying to make an impression. Well, I guess he has. But is he not holding onto the railing a bit too tightly?*

Hitler turned and entered the room, approaching Jung slowly, almost majestically. His complexion was pallid and his shoulders slouched. He scowled as he asked, "Why have you come here?"

Jung decided, in the fraction of a second available for thought, that the simple truth was the safest course. "General Olbricht informed me that you are suffering. He promised, in return for my visit, the freedom of my colleague, Dr. Rosenberg. He also gave me his word that I, too, would leave Germany safely. Under these circumstances, why would I not come to help you?"

"Good." Hitler pulled himself together with some effort and gave a weak smile, much to Jung's surprise. "I was just wondering what could bring you so far from Zurich, Dr. Jung. I am honored."

Jung thanked him, and they shook hands, which almost made Jung cringe. *If anyone saw me now, they'd never speak to me again. But I have to do this, no matter what.*

Hitler released Jung's hand and said, "Have you eaten, Herr Doktor?"

"No, we got an early start." *He's putting on the Austrian charm. He's like a different person from the man I met in Berlin five years ago. Was that all an act? Or is this the act? Or both?*

"Good," Hitler said. "We can have a little breakfast."

Breakfast seemed much less stressful than small talk with the Führer, or plunging right into the first evaluation session. "That would be most welcome, Herr Hitler." *Should I address him as President Hitler? Or Führer-Chancellor? No, I can't possibly do either.*

Hitler motioned towards a double doorway, and the two of them proceeded through it to a well-furnished, Alpine-style dining room.

Chapter 25
Bludenz, Austria
8:25 AM, June 30, 1942

Outside the tunnel, as soon as the bronze doors had slammed behind Jung, Olbricht turned to Mary. "Come, I have things to do. I will drop you at the gasthaus." He motioned her to slide into the passenger seat and took the wheel himself.

Mary would rather have retained control of the Opel, but now she was in Olbricht's hands. The Opel's tires squealed on every turn, the exhaust roaring as they descended the mountain. *Jeez! He drives worse than Jaffe!* She clutched the armrest with both hands.

But the trip was a short one. Löwensburg was only two kilometers or so from the little town of Bludenz, barely a minute at the General's reckless speed. He parked the Opel across the street from the gasthaus and was opening its trunk before Mary could unclench her white-knuckled hands from the armrest and get out.

"I will get it," he told her, ignoring her hand outstretched to reclaim her bag. "Dr. Jung is registered as 'Herr Lang and driver.' I thought that an appropriate name, given his height. Come! I will help you check in."

Mary tried to regain some autonomy. "That won't be necessary—"

Olbricht looked at her and smiled. "It is no trouble, Frau Rufenacht." He paused in the middle of the street. "You overheard the name of the patient?"

"We call them clients, Herr General. Dr. Jung never told me his name, and I never asked." *Well, technically that's true*, she thought, then said, "But I can keep a secret."

Olbricht nodded. "See that you do. I will be away for a day, fetching another passenger for the return trip. The food is decent here, so there is no need for you to leave the hotel until I return. Also, for your own safety, do not talk to anyone. Understood?"

"Of course, Herr General." *Of course not, Herr General.*

"I'll pick you and Herr Doktor Jung up here tomorrow afternoon." Olbricht led Mary across the street and up the steps into the gasthaus.

Chapter 26
Dining Room, Löwensburg
8:30 AM, June 30, 1942

Simple Tyrolean-style furniture graced the dining room at Löwensburg. Near the large fireplace, a table had been set with flowers and expensive dinnerware and silver. Hitler paused just inside the room and held out a hand towards one of the chairs. "Please seat yourself here."

Jung complied, and the two of them faced each other across the lavishly set table as a waiter served breakfast and poured two small glasses of wine.

They tasted the wine. Hitler set down his wineglass and said, "I have met you before. 1937."

He remembers! That's a surprise. "Yes. The reception for Mussolini. I'm surprised you recall meeting me."

"You were with your colleague, Mathias Goering, Hermann's cousin. I have a good memory for details."

A small opening. One I must use to my advantage. The sooner, the better. "That is well. Your good memory will be most useful in our work together."

Hitler frowned as he reached for his wine again. Jung tried not to stare as he added a spoonful of sugar to the glass.

When breakfast was over and the table cleared, Jung and Hitler sat opposite each other in large chairs beside a window overlooking the mountains. Jung opened the red folder in his lap, put his notepad on the arm of the chair, and got out his pen.

Hitler spoke first. "You know this was not my idea?"

"But you did agree to it, did you not?"

"To shut those OKW bastards up."

Jung pushed to keep the conversation on track. "Yet you have trouble sleeping, yes?"

Hitler paused, then said, "Yes."

"With spells of depression . . . "

"Who would not be depressed if they could not sleep?" Jung noticed Hitler clench a fist.

" . . . And signs of stress . . . "

The Führer's voice rose a bit. "Of course I am stressed! I have a war to run!"

" . . . Signs of stress that sometimes include emotional outbursts—"

Hitler made a loud sniff, and Jung tensed. But Hitler relaxed and exhaled slowly, spreading his open hands wide, as if to trivialize the rage. "That is merely my way of motivating those louts." His voice rose a little as he concluded with, "And make them obey my orders!"

Jung looked down and read again from the folder. " . . . Outbursts followed by profound sadness."

Hitler folded his arms and tightened his lips, glaring in silence.

Jung continued as kindly as he could. "Perhaps not the most effective means of motivation, on some occasions, would you say? Speaking only in general."

"I . . . perhaps."

Trembling, Jung felt tired from just this brief, but risky initial exchange. *This will be a long day.* He closed the red folder and put it aside. "You may be at risk of developing a psychosis, Herr Hitler."

"I have always taken risks."

"Not like this one." Jung paused to think of a way to move the conversation towards cooperation. He couldn't keep this disputation up for long. "A psychotic break would be a disaster. But, if we work together, we may avert it." *God forbid! Let disaster come for Hitler, and soon . . . ! As soon as I leave here!*

Hitler narrowed his eyes and glared at Jung. "You want to get into my mind."

Of course I do. I must. Jung tapped the red folder at his side. "Dr. Sauerbrach has fully explored the physical factors. That leaves only the psychic possibilities to work with."

"You think I have a guilt complex." Hitler shook a finger at Jung.

Taken by surprise, Jung said, "Which is?"

"'An associative web of guilt-related emotions, memories, perceptions and desires in the unconscious.' I have read your book."

"Which one?"

"All of them. Have you read mine?"

Jung was taken aback once more, but managed to respond. "*Mein Kampf*? Of course."

"Then you should know that I have no guilt whatsoever." Hitler flourished a hand in front of him, waving away the idea with total self-assurance.

Jung considered this. *I can't afford to get into an argument, but I can't just let that statement go. Maybe if I phrase my objection as a polite question, I won't appear judgmental.* "Not even for the war?

Hitler leaned forward and assumed the tone and gestures of a reasonable man. "Look, Herr Doktor Jung, this war is merely to recover what was stolen from Germany, to right the wrongs inflicted upon us by England and other nations at Versailles. I seek only justice, nothing more."

This is too much! Jung clenched his pen, barely maintaining control. "And your . . . " He was about to say 'persecutions,' but managed to say instead, " . . . severe restrictions on the Jews? What of them?"

"Those, too, are no more than necessary. I am saving the German people from the Jews' venality and their tainted blood. In my quest for justice and racial purity, guilt can play no part."

This man thinks he's a Messiah, Jung thought. "Freedom from conscious guilt doesn't mean there isn't any."

"Nor do your expectations mean there is."

Touché. I must get back on track right away. "Still, we have your sleep problem, do we not? Shall we address that together?" Jung broke eye contact and opened the notepad.

Chapter 27
Music Room, Löwensburg

"Let us move to another room," Hitler rose and took Jung into a small music room. Jung admired the piano and the collection of antique violins hanging on one wall. Hitler opened a box of chocolate bonbons and offered them to Jung. "They are Swiss."

Jung accepted one for politeness's sake; his client held onto the box. They sat facing each other in identical chairs. Hitler placed his chocolates on the arm of his chair.

"What was your childhood like?" Jung asked, holding the steno pad on his knee with his pen ready.

"I was a very happy child. I was always the little ringleader, deciding what game all the neighborhood children would play."

Jung was skeptical. "At what age was this?"

"Oh, five, six, seven."

Rather vague, possibly lying or an inaccurate memory.
"Very well. How was your health?

"Quite good." Hitler nodded.

"No severe illnesses?"

"The usual childhood things: measles, that kind of malady."

"Measles can be very serious."

"I know. My younger brother had an awful case and died of a brain fever when I was about eleven."

Brain fever? Encephalitis, most likely. Jung scribbled a note on the pad. "And were you sick at the same time?"

"I had a much milder case."

"No complications?"

"I was delirious for several days and nights, and a little fuzzy minded for a while afterward, but eventually recovered completely." Hitler took another bonbon from the box.

"How did the death of your brother affect you? Did you grieve?"

"Yes, I was inconsolable for months."

"Your parents are also deceased, now?"

Hitler nodded. "That is so."

"Do you miss them?"

"Yes."

"And which do you miss most?"

"My mother."

The questions and answers continued along those lines, delving into Hitler's distant past and childhood memories. Jung had filled and turned over several pages of the notepad, and noticed the chocolates disappearing one by one from the box on the arm of the Führer's chair. He looked over his glasses at Hitler and made another note before continuing. "What were you most afraid of as a child? Your mother?"

"Not at all."

"Your father?"

Hitler looked into the distance, then put his index finger to his lips briefly before pointing it at Jung. "My aunt, perhaps."

"And why would that be?"

"I thought she was a witch." Hitler smiled.

"What made you think that?"

"She always arrived dressed in black."

Jung nodded, but thought: *If she was Catholic, and she must have been, black would not have been exceptional attire for a woman of that age, an aunt. Something missing, here, perhaps.* Jung turned a page in his notebook and wrote a single word: *black*. He and Hitler leaned back in their chairs again.

"What was your father like?" Jung continued.

"He was very just." Again the mouth-covering gesture with index and middle finger before answering.

Hiding something. Jung restrained an impulse to tilt his head. "Just, you say?"

"I was only struck when I needed it."

"What age are we speaking of, now?"

Hitler hesitated for several seconds before answering. "The same age. Five, six, seven. I do not remember exactly."

"Did your father hit you often?"

"Just now and then."

He's lying. "How old were you when he died?"

"I was fourteen."

Jung's brow tightened. "That was most unfortunate. A young age to lose a father. What did he die of?"

"A sudden hemorrhage. In his lung. He was sitting at a table in an inn, waiting for a glass of wine."

Aha. "Did he drink a lot?"

Hitler shrugged. "All German men drank."

Jung made a note: *alcoholic father*. "And what was it like after his death?"

"We got by. There were just the two of us, then, me and my mother. We were very happy." A little smile crossed Hitler's lips.

"The two of you were close?"

"She was very dear to me, and I to her. We got on well."

Jung decided not to delve any deeper into the relationship. *This could drift into dangerous territory, and I think I already know enough. Muttersöhnchen fits perfectly. So does Oedipal.* Jung changed the subject and continued the evaluation along safer and more useful lines of inquiry.

Chapter 28
On the Road to Terzendorf
10:05 AM, June 30, 1942

Olbricht's battered grey Opel sped along a deserted country road on the way to Terzendorf. He planned to stay there overnight at an inn, then pick up Rosenberg the following morning at the concentration camp, as arranged by telephone.

I wish this were over with, he thought. *Is it worth the risk? Yes. Should we have told Himmler? No, he's a troublemaker.*

Olbricht wiped his brow with the back of a gloved hand. *Just one more day, and the OKW will have Jung's evaluation and we can get rid of that madman, Hitler. In just one more day, Rosenberg and Jung will be safely back in Switzerland. And Maria, too. She is a remarkable woman. I would hate for anything to happen to her.*

Olbricht frowned and plunged his boot down on the accelerator, letting the roar of the engine help him focus on driving. *I hope she stayed in the gasthaus as I told her to.*

Chapter 29
Bludenz
10:10 AM, June 30, 1942

Mary stood at the window of her room in the gasthaus, scanning the horizon with her lipstick telescope. She saw Löwensburg, perched high among the nearby mountaintops, and snapped a souvenir picture. Checking the street below, she saw a group of young soldiers laughing as they entered a beer garden. She smirked.

Mary took off her chauffeur's uniform and changed into a more feminine outfit consisting of a simple jumper with embroidered trim in the Austrian style. She trotted downstairs and left the gasthaus by a side door after a cautious look-about. Bludenz was a ski resort, with shops along the main street for summer tourists. Mary sauntered along, looking at everything, stopping now and then to admire the mountains above the town. When she reached the *biergarten*, she darted inside and took a table not far from the soldiers she'd seen earlier.

A waiter brought her a stein of beer. As she sat sipping it, trying to look innocent, the soldiers noticed her. One of them, a corporal, ogled her, grinning and waving for her to join them. After a coy hesitation, she picked up her beer, and sat in the vacant chair beside the corporal.

"Hello," he said, in German. "My name is Albert."

"*Ich bin Maria*," she replied. "And who are these other handsome men?" She beamed and put on her best empty-headed blonde look.

The young soldiers introduced themselves with spirit. Albert was a little older than the rest, perhaps in his early twenties. Heinz sat on Mary's other side, followed by Dieter, Klaus, and five others around the table, all looking entranced with her. *A horny bunch of little Krauts!* she thought. *Albert seems nice, though. And rather handsome.*

Dieter topped up Mary's glass from their pitcher and asked, "Where are you from, Maria?"

I hope you never find out, Mary thought, saying with feigned enthusiasm, "Yes, where is everybody from?"

Heinz held up a finger. "Vienna."

Albert said, "I am from here in Bludenz, home on furlough."

"Innsbruck," Dieter said.

Before the others could reply, Mary tested her luck. "Is anyone from Döllersheim?"

After a short pause, Klaus and four others put up their hands.

"So many of you!?" Mary said.

Albert snorted. "They are from here, not from Döllersheim. They just did their basic training there. We all did. It is the largest training camp in all of Germany."

"As a military reservation, it is not supposed to be discussed," Klaus said.

The hell it's not, she thought. *What's the worst that can happen?*

Heinz lowered his voice and leaned towards Mary. "Why the interest in Döllersheim?"

"It's the Führer's family town, isn't it?" Mary said. "I'd love to see it sometime, and know that my feet are treading the same streets the Führer walked as a boy." She gave a little shiver, then wondered if she'd overdone it.

Klaus rolled his eyes. "The Führer never trod in Döllersheim, Maria. He is from Braunau."

"Besides," Albert added, "there are no streets left to tread in Döllersheim. My artillery company blew them up when we got there in thirty-eight."

"But why?"

Klaus held up his hand. "Do not ask questions. It is not a topic for discussion," He drained his glass and went to the men's room.

Albert looked around, and when Klaus was out of sight, put his hand on Mary's arm and said in a low voice, "The Army needed a training ground, and the High Command determined that Döllersheim was the best location. The Führer did not let personal attachments stand in the way of Germany's military needs."

"How very generous of him," Mary said.

Mary wanted to talk more about Döllersheim, but Heinz said, "Let us not talk about that awful place anymore. Maria, you never told us where you are from."

Mary hesitated, not wanting to give herself away if she had the wrong accent for whatever city she named. Instead, she said, "Where do you think?"

Dieter pointed at Mary and blurted, "Danzig! You have a Danziger accent."

Albert quickly said, "I was just going to say that."

"How clever of you! Danzig is right." Mary smiled at both of them. She turned to Albert and asked, "How long were you in Döllersheim?"

As Albert began to speak, Klaus returned and sat down, so Albert clammed up.

A second later, Mary saw a heavy-set, middle-aged man in a black fedora and a leather coat walking straight towards their table. *Jesus*, she thought. *Gestapo. He must have heard me. Can I get away if I run?*

Klaus glanced at the man and quickly looked back at

Mary. "I told you to shut up," he muttered, stiffening.

As the man got closer, everyone except Klaus scattered in various directions. Albert stood, but hesitated, and then sat back down beside Mary.

But the man in black walked right past them and angled off towards the men's room.

Klaus sighed. "Look, Maria, if you are curious about the Führer's youth, you may visit Linz; he considers that his home town. It is much safer than talking about *that other place*. Understand?"

Mary nodded. *That was too close for comfort,* she thought. *But I really must find out more about Döllersheim.*

But Klaus wasn't finished. "I am curious about you, Maria. What are you doing here in Bludenz?" He leaned towards her, squinting into her eyes.

Uh-oh. Klaus is suspicious. I should have shut up when he told me to. I'd better have a good story. Maybe even a true one. She dropped her dumb blonde act altogether and said, "I'm here with my employer. We are attending to some business up at Löwensburg." She gestured in that direction.

The mention of Löwensburg was magic. Klaus sat back, his eyes wide. "What are you doing up there?"

From the awe in his voice, Mary was sure Klaus knew Hitler often visited Löwensburg. "I am sorry, but I am forbidden to discuss Löwensburg." She drank from her stein, still meeting Klaus's eyes.

Klaus looked down for a second, then said, "I hope we are not in any trouble."

"Not at all. I enjoyed our conversation about Linz, Klaus."

While Klaus took a long pull at his beer stein, Mary slipped her hand onto Albert's knee and said softly, "I enjoyed meeting you, too, Albert. I hope I'll see you . . . very soon."

He blushed. "I hope so, too."

Chapter 30
Löwensburg

Hitler had eaten most of the chocolates; Jung had flipped more pages. He dug into the red folder again and made a notation on one of its loose sheets. "Shall we look at the depression?"

Hitler sat with arms folded, silent.

"I cannot help you if you won't open up," Jung said.

Hitler said, tight-lipped, "I cannot open up while you are constantly judging me."

"But I'm not judging you," Jung lied, hoping it didn't show.

"You are. I speak, you frown, look at me over your glasses, then scribble on your pad. What am I supposed to think?"

Jung became more cautious. "I'm just assessing your statements and correlating them with what is already established." He held up the pad.

Hitler shook his finger at Jung. "With established facts. So you are calling me a liar."

"Not at all. I merely need to—"

"To judge me. Am I wrong?

Jung sensed that he'd misspoken, that the way out of

this was through a concession, not argument. "Not entirely. There is always a very small element of evaluation in this process. I'm sorry that makes you feel judged."

Hitler folded his arms. "I thought so."

Jung leaned forward in his chair and put his elbows on his knees. "Please remember, we have an objective: to help you sleep. I shall avoid more carefully seeming to judge, if you'll agree to open up more."

Hitler unfolded his arms and put his left elbow on his right fist, his left fist under his jaw. "Go ahead, then."

He's shutting down. Not at a good time, either. Jung sat back and took a deep breath, but his hand shook as he reached for his pen. "What are your greatest losses?"

"My brother . . . my father . . . my mother . . . Geli . . . "

"Geli. That was your niece?"

"My half niece."

This could be approaching the core, Jung thought. Keeping his voice as neutral as possible, he asked, "And did you have a close relationship with her?"

Hitler held up a hand and inclined his head to that side. "Just good friends. Uncle and niece." Then he stared off into the distance, silent.

Jung looked at him askance. Hitler refocused on Jung.

"Where did you go just then?" Jung asked.

"I have a fine statue of her. Let me show you." Hitler launched himself out of the chair and went to a bookcase.

Jung scribbled furiously, trying to catch up on his notes and put the pad down before Hitler could turn around.

As if carrying a heavy weight, Hitler returned with the small bronze bust of Geli in both hands. He put it reverently into Jung's grasp.

It weighed less than Jung expected. "Very pretty," he said, examining it. The girl had been quite attractive, if the artist's work was accurate.

Jung watched Hitler carefully. Downcast, Hitler nodded, inhaled heavily, then took the bust two-handed and positioned it back on the shelf. As he released it, Jung saw his left hand tremble. Hitler immediately put the shaky hand on his hip to stabilize it. *Parkinson's?* Jung wondered, stroking his chin. *Geli was very close to him, as close as his mother. Perhaps closer. But given Hitler's Oedipal tendencies, more likely not.* "Tell me about Geli."

Chapter 31
Löwensburg

Geli. Hitler leaned back in his chair, took a deep breath, and relaxed, looking up at the ceiling. He considered how to proceed, then continued in a casual tone: "Geli was the daughter of my half-sister Angela. I had, of course, seen her from time to time, you know, whenever I saw Angela. Not often. But when I began my prison sentence at Landsberg in twenty-four, my sister thought it would be a good deed to visit me there. She brought Geli along."

Hitler raised his head a bit to look at Jung. "You know how it is, when you meet someone and something special happens as soon as you look them in their eyes? It was that way with Geli. She was fifteen or so, then, and very much a young woman. Do not misunderstand me, my interest was not one of base instinct. Not at all. But I enjoyed her company. She was lively and had a certain wit. Our first conversation at Landsberg was mutually enjoyable, and we were good friends when we parted that day."

Hitler leaned his head back again and considered where to continue. He was suspicions of Jung, but at the same time, enjoyed having someone to talk to, a disinterested party he could justify himself to . . . if that were what Jung truly was. It felt good to speak of days gone by, to speak of Geli. Hitler let a tear run down a cheek and fall from his jaw, reluctant to call attention to it by blotting it with his handkerchief. He cleared his throat and continued.

"Angela's husband had died, and by 1929, she was running short of money. Naturally, I had her move in with me, giving her a job as my housekeeper for a while." Hitler looked at Jung again. "It was mutually beneficial."

Jung put his fingertips together. "*Natürlich*. And Geli moved in along with your sister?"

"Of course. That began a happy time for me. For us, Geli and me. I took her to Nazi Party events. She was very popular." Hitler thought back to that first luncheon, when he'd walked into the dining room with Geli. *How they stared, all agog at her, arm-in-arm with me! How I gloried in that moment! She turned every head in the place!*

"When she became more comfortable in Party circles, she used to entertain us. She sang and did little amusements that made her welcome wherever she went. She had a bird she had trained to sit on her wrist and do tricks. It was very funny to watch. Even Himmler used to laugh out loud."

Again, Hitler let his mind wander back to those days. He recalled Geli's youthful spirits, her expressions, her voice, the way she held the bird up for all to see, all those little feminine gestures and postures that made him desire her so much. *How happy it was! We all loved her.*

Then Hitler remembered as if it were only the previous night, opening the doors to Geli's darkened room and stepping inside. He remembered the scent of her *Kölnischwasser,* the sofa, the pictures on the wall, the wind-up clock on the table, the bed. And how quickly they were naked and sweaty upon that bed, Geli straddling him, humping him at a full canter.

Hitler felt his heart constrict, miss a beat. *Fool!* he thought. *I should never have lost her.*

Chapter 32
Löwensburg

What happened just then? Jung wondered. "You seem to have left the room, Herr Hitler."

"I have lost my train of thought." Hitler sat up straight, his eyes boring holes into Jung.

Jung wanted to delve further into the relationship, but changed his mind when Hitler's face became an expressionless mask. Instead of inquiring how close Hitler and Geli had been, he asked, "Was there any friction between the two of you?"

Hitler spread his hands wide. "Ah. I was, if anything, perhaps a little too protective."

"In what way?"

"I did not want some lout marrying her for political motives."

Jealousy, more likely. Jung nodded. "You didn't want to marry her yourself?"

"Nein, nein. Geli was only twenty-three, and I . . . " He shrugged. "I was married to Germany."

"You had no prospects of marriage?"

"Oh, ja, well, there were many friendships with women, but not of the marrying sort, nothing that would take my attention away from my duty to Germany. All very *platonisch*."

"And on Geli's part? Did she resent your attentions to these other women?"

Hitler waved this away. "That would have been ridiculous! There was nothing to be jealous about."

"What were her feelings, do you think?"

"I often felt she associated with inappropriate men."

Deflecting, Jung noted. "Inappropriate?"

Hitler held up an index finger and shook it. "That Emil Maurice, to name only one."

"He was . . . ?"

"My driver. I discovered they were having an affair, contrary to my explicit orders."

Was there more to this possessiveness than an uncle's concern? "Oh? And what was the outcome?"

"Well, I had a bit of a fuss with Emil."

"What sort of fuss?"

"I drew my pistol and told him to leave Geli alone and get out!"

"You carried a gun?"

"I am never without one, not since Landsberg. Nothing punctuates an argument like a pistol." Hitler slapped a bulge in his right hand trouser leg.

Jung stared at the bulge, thinking, *I am an enemy spy, sitting across from an armed man responsible for the deaths of thousands, asking him the most sensitive questions. He could shoot me at any second, yet I must continue. And not be judgmental.* He wrote 'gun' on his pad and underlined it. "And how did you 'punctuate' this incident?"

"I didn't shoot at him."

Didn't shoot <u>at</u> him. "But you did shoot, did you not?"

Hitler hesitated.

Jung watched him. *He wonders whether to portray himself as a man of action or a man of sanity. Which will*

114

win?

"I aimed wide."

I can't imagine this man failing to empty the gun at Maurice. Let me see if I can get him to admit shooting more than once. "Each time?"

Hitler frowned and batted a hand, dismissing the incident. "Ja, every shot missed him by a meter. I just wanted to drive my point home as I chased him down the front stairs."

Jung made a note. *And now the coup de grace:* "But you did hate him."

Hitler held up a hand in denial and put on his voice of reason. "Nein, nein. I am not a hating person. I am forceful, when I need to be, but not given to hatred."

A deliberate, substantial lie. Now to drop the other shoe. "Then what did you do to him?"

"Nothing." Hitler's face became like stone, devoid of feeling.

What? "You didn't fire him?"

"Of course I fired him! For Geli's sake! That was only to be expected!"

Jung nodded and offered a lie of his own to calm Hitler. "Yes, of course. It was only reasonable." *Except for shooting at him.*

Hitler nodded back.

Jung thought, *he feels he's scored a point. That is good, but I must keep him a little off balance.* He flipped back several pages in the pad and read an earlier note. "You counted Geli among your greatest losses. I believe she killed herself, is that so?"

Hitler's face contorted for a moment, then froze. "Ja. That is what happened."

Interesting way to put it. But is that what happened? "Could you tell me about it?"

"Nein."

"Does this make you sad?"

Hitler nodded.

He's on the edge of breaking down. I must get him to reveal his feelings about this incident. It will be dangerous, but it might help him. And Dulles, too. "Yes, it is very sad. A young girl, so pretty and so close to you, someone you'd known and loved for a long time . . . " Jung gestured at the bust on the shelf.

Hitler leaned forward and covered his face, weeping silently.

" . . . Someone you miss," Jung continued.

Hitler began convulsing with suppressed sobs.

Success, Jung thought. "Take your time. Just stay with your feelings."

Hitler jumped from his chair and walked from corner to corner of the room, wiping his eyes while facing away from Jung. "It was . . . it could have been an accident . . . She . . ." He took a long breath. "I cannot go on."

I may have taken Hitler a bit too far. I hate to back away from this issue, but maybe I can return to it an opportune time. And maybe not. Jung said, "Perhaps we should take a break."

Hitler headed straight for the box of chocolates. He picked it up and held it out to Jung, who stood, hesitated, then took one piece. Hitler grabbed several more.

Chapter 33
Löwensburg

The break had turned into lunch, which was a relief for Jung. The therapy had worn him out. Though there was little physical activity in therapy, the necessity of listening and processing every single word the client said was draining. At several points during the morning, Jung felt it had become a *sitzkrieg*—trying to get more reactions from Hitler, while Hitler wandered off into irrelevant anecdotes or rationalizations. Often, Hitler would say less and less, standing and trudging the room's diagonal and pausing beside the candy box to dig out a piece or two.

Hitler excused himself as soon as they'd eaten, to "take care of some urgent business." Jung tried to take advantage of the Führer's absence to rest, but found himself going through his notes from the morning session, his mind racing.

Hitler's evasiveness continued after lunch, and Jung filled only one more notebook page in a half hour, a few terse notes not related to anything vital. He decided to return to the previous tack. "Can you provide some details of what happened the day Geli died?"

Hitler dismissed this with a casual hand gesture. "That was all a long time ago."

"It's only eleven years."

"It seems like a hundred . . . " Hitler looked off into space.

"You claimed to have a good memory for details. Why not on that day?"

Hitler stared at him. "I was devastated."

He's avoiding the question. I can't let him get away with playing the grieving uncle, Jung thought. "Obviously, at some level, you still are. But am I correct that you didn't kill her?"

Hitler sat up straighter, clenched both fists, and retorted, "Kill her? Of course not. That is unthinkable." He pounded on the arms of the chair.

Jung, expecting this reaction, stayed calm. He nodded and gestured with an open hand. "All right, we both know you are innocent. What possible reason can you have for not answering my questions?" Jung held his breath, waiting for the response. Or to be shot right then and there. *I hope he's a good shot.*

Hitler sat back and stared at the wall behind Jung. Finally, apparently resigned, he said, "It was a Friday." He put his hands up to his chin, covering his mouth. "I was leaving town for a Party meeting the next day. My valet, Georg Winter, came upstairs to—"

"Excuse me, I can't hear you with your hands like that."

Hitler frowned and grasped the arms of his chair. "My valet helped me get ready. I had a little argument with Geli after lunch, then—"

"An argument?"

Hitler nodded. "Ja. She wanted to visit some friend or other in Vienna while I was away. I told her she could not go, and that was the end of it, or so I thought." Hitler paused, then continued: "I gave Georg and the others the rest of the day off. I went downstairs—"

"A moment, Herr Hitler. You say, you *thought* that was the end of the argument? There was more?"

Hitler shrugged. "Not really. I was at the car, in front of the apartment, ready to go. At the last minute, Geli came out on the balcony and pleaded with me again. I . . . I am afraid I was rather firm with her. Then we drove away, the three of us; Schreck, Hoffmann, and I."

"How firm were you?"

"I said something like, 'For the last time, nein!'"

"You yelled this at her?"

"Ja, but I had to. We were out on the noisy street. It was near Oktoberfest, so people were already celebrating."

"Please continue."

"The three of us reached Nuremberg a little after two in the afternoon. I stepped out on our balcony at the hotel an hour later and greeted a crowd of supporters. It was about then that our housemaid in Munich, Frau Reichert, heard a gunshot upstairs."

"How do you know this?"

"There was a full inquiry. Her statement is in the police report."

"This Frau Reichert was in the apartment building?"

"Ja. She was in her room on the floor below. I believe she said she heard, 'a loud noise.' She had no idea at the time that it was a gunshot."

"How large was the gun?"

"Big enough." Hitler tightened his jaw and shifted in his chair. "It was a .25 caliber Walther. But I am becoming most uncomfortable discussing this. Is it relevant to my condition?"

"I believe it very well may be. But let's try get through this part quickly, then. Please continue." Jung motioned with his pen.

"They found Geli the next morning." Hitler's voice broke slightly.

"In her room?"

"Ja. She . . . she had locked herself in. Georg broke in and found her."

"Where did the gun come from?"

"From my nightstand, down the hall."

"Did you feel responsible for her death when you learned this?"

"I could not have known she would kill herself over such a little quarrel." Hitler unclenched a fist.

Jung observed the gesture and frowned. "No, you couldn't. What happened when you were notified?"

Hitler sighed. "We went back to Munich at twice the speed limit. I . . . I broke down on the way." He wiped his now damp eyes with a handkerchief.

Jung turned a page, scrutinizing Hitler over his reading glasses. "Do you remember anything else?"

"I remember visiting the cemetery, a week later. That is all."

"How do you feel right now?"

"As if I am fading farther and farther away from you." Hitler slowly drew back both hands. Then he reached over and ate the last piece of candy. He looked towards the empty box and stood. "Let me show you my den."

Chapter 34
Hitler's Den, Löwensburg

The carpet was red, except for an Oriental rug beneath an ornate desk. Beside the latter, Jung saw a wall switch labeled, "Tunnel Lichter." *What was it Olbricht said? 'The lights have been known to fail.' Hitler turned off the lights on me from here! The bastard must pull that childish stunt on many visitors. A good thing Olbricht warned me to have the flashlight ready.*" Jung looked away from the switch, to keep Hitler from seeing his interest in it.

Hitler walked to another box of candy on a table. He unwrapped it, took a piece, and offered the box to Jung. Jung declined and had just seated himself when a dachshund entered the room and trotted straight to Hitler, wagging with enthusiasm.

"Leona!" Hitler greeted the dog. He looked up at Jung. "She belongs to my secretary, but she likes me best. You do not mind, do you?"

Jung smiled. "No, I have one of those at home."

Hitler sat and pulled Leona up onto his lap. He petted her feebly, supporting his head on his other hand. "Dogs are so non-judgmental. Unlike some people."

"Unlike most people."

"Where were we?"

"Grief. Over the loss of Geli. That is significant progress." Jung took the pad and uncapped his pen.

Hitler held up a hand. "I am weary. Could we stop?"

Just as we're finally getting somewhere! We must not stop now. Jung looked at his watch and said, "Perhaps just a little longer?" He waited a moment, then asked, "Would you rather discuss more about your childhood? Or about Geli?"

"My childhood."

"Very well. Why were you so frightened of your aunt?"

"I was uneasy around her."

"What were you afraid she would do?" Jung looked at Hitler over his spectacles.

"I do not know!" Hitler yelled. "Strike me with her canes or something. She was just an obnoxious, old woman, and I refuse to talk about her any longer." Hitler folded his arms, reminding Jung of a petulant child.

Jung made another notation. "If you'd prefer, we could go back to Geli . . . "

"I said we would talk of my childhood, and that is settled."

"Very well. One moment . . . "

Jung opened the red folder, took off his spectacles and pulled out his magnifying glass.

Hitler tightened his lips. "Do you intend to examine me with that like some sort of . . . ?"

There was a two-second pause. *Some sort of what?* Jung wondered.

" . . . Insect?" Hitler finished.

Jung felt a chill. *What was that hesitation about? Is this poor self-image, a feeling he can't measure up to scrutiny?* "No," Jung said, "I'm afraid my eyes aren't up to reading Dr. Sauerbrach's tiny handwriting."

Jung silently scanned a document from the folder with the aid of the magnifying glass, then made a note in his steno pad: *insect?*

Hitler tapped a foot and frowned.

"According to Dr. Sauerbrach," Jung continued, "your x-rays show a childhood spiral fracture of the radius in your right arm. Was your father the one responsible?"

"I fell."

He fell? Jung thought. *That is more likely to break an ulna. Did he really fall? Or was that a story made up by a parent, trying to cover up abuse?*

Hitler tapped his fingers and fixed his steel blue eyes on Jung, unsmiling. The dachshund looked up at Hitler, then jumped out of his lap and ran from the room.

Jung sensed he should stop, but was anxious to learn how the injury happened. "You fell?" he asked.

"I said so, did I not? Do you think I invented that story?"

Jung gestured, palm upward. "I only want to verify that this fall is something you actually remember, rather than —"

"My memory has something wrong with it? Is that what you are saying?" Hitler jumped up and approached Jung, waving his index finger. "You are nothing but a fucking spy!"

Jung drew back in his chair. "I am not a spy. I am a doctor, and I came here to help you."

"You were sent here to undermine my authority," Hitler growled.

Jung stood, letting the notepad fall to the floor. "And how the devil would I do that?"

Hitler clenched his fists, put them on his hips and leaned forward. "My High Command want you to say that I have lost my mind." He shook a finger at Jung's face.

"My report will state that your complexes do not equate to pathological abnormality."

"Complexes? What complexes?" Hitler shouted.

Jung shot back, "Forget complexes. The bottom line is

that you are not mad. You're responsible for your actions."

"Responsible? You say that as if it were a bad thing. Ja, I am responsible. Responsible for returning Germany to its former glory and strength. Responsible for reuniting the Reich. Responsible for demolishing the Treaty of Versailles!" Hitler's voice grated and he quivered as he spoke. He clenched his jaws and turned white in the face.

Jung sensed that pressing Hitler further could likely be fatal. Yet backing down could also be dangerous and would give Hitler mastery of the situation; all progress would stop. *I can't go forward safely and I can't go back safely. I can only try to deflect him.* "I agree," Jung said, "You have been responsible for all those things. But at a cost, Herr Hitler."

Hitler clawed the air with both hands "The cost is mine to judge, not yours. Who are you to judge me? Have you lived my life?" Hitler's voice lowered an octave and rasped as he shouted. "Have you had all your friends torn to bloody shreds in the blink of an eye, in a filthy trench? Have you applied caustic chemicals to your mother's cancerous breast, and watched her die slowly and painfully?" Hitler stared at Jung from eyes without depth, without warmth, frightening Jung to the depths of his being.

This is the Hitler I remember from Berlin, the robot with no humanity. This will end badly if I can't calm him down, "I have not, of course," Jung said. "'Responsible' was not intended as a condemnation. I apologize for any appearance that it was. I sincerely want to assist you."

Hitler reeled. "Assist me? You are being paid by the High Command. Why should I believe you?"

Jung "I give you my word as a professional therapist —"

"Your word as a dead man would be more reliable." Hitler pulled the gun from his pocket, held it aloft, and shook it. "Why should I not just kill you right now?" He cocked the pistol and pointed it at Jung.

If I die, the mission is lost. He'll put Mary in a camp, and she'll die, too. The war will go on, Switzerland will be invaded. My family, my grandchildren, and all the others, will live under the Nazi boot. I must keep going until he listens to logic, or kills me. "If you shoot me, Herr Hitler, that would remove all doubt in the minds of the High Command, do you not think?"

Hitler pointed the weapon at the floor. "I could simply make you disappear."

He waved the pistol around, making Jung want to cringe. Instead, Jung shrugged, though it took an effort to keep his hands from shaking. "Everyone knows what disappearing in Germany means, Herr Hitler."

Hitler decocked the gun and put it away, then grasped his head with both hands. "Get out! Get out of my sight! Leave here at once."

Jung wished to do just that, and turned to prepare to leave, but he forced himself to remain in the moment, and not give in to his fear. *Think!* He glanced back at his chair. An index card lay on the seat, dislodged from his pocket when he'd taken out his magnifying glass. Even from where he stood, he could read, "OSS Agent #488." *I am an old fool! I forgot to burn the information Dulles gave me!*

Jung looked away from the card quickly, lest he draw attention to it. Escaping now was not an option. He had to recover that index card, no matter what.

He turned back to Hitler. "Please, one more thing before I go. It is most important. When did you sleep last, Herr Hitler?"

Hitler slumped. "Three nights ago."

"I apologize. I have asked too much of you in your exhausted condition. Before I leave, I would like to at least help you sleep. May I try to accomplish that much?"

"More dumb questions? More pills?"

"No more questions and no pills. I'll try light hypnosis

to let you sleep for up to eight hours."

Hitler raised his voice again. "Why should I trust you? How do I know you will not try to make me bark like a dog or piss in a wastebasket?"

Has Hitler been hypnotized before? Could those things have happened to him? Jung quashed both mental images and said, "If you like, you may have someone observe and intervene if they think I overstep."

"I must sleep. I . . . must."

"Then get ready for bed, Herr Hitler, and we'll start whenever you're ready."

Hitler motioned for Jung to wait, then faltered into an adjacent bedroom, pushing the door almost closed behind him. A buzzer sounded.

Jung leapt back to his chair and retrieved the notepad and the incriminating card. What to do with it? He folded it and stuffed it with trembling hands back into his pocket. *I have no time for anything more. Or do I?*

Jung picked up his briefcase and took out Mary's mandala before stepping quietly to the bedroom door. He risked a quick peek through the opening. His eyes widened and he whispered, "*Mein Gott!*"

To Jung's relief, Hitler was facing away from the door. His back bore a random pattern of thin, white scars from his pajama bottoms to his shoulders.

"We are not supposed to witness that," a low voice said behind Jung, startling him, He turned to see a handsome SS bodyguard right next to him. "His father did that," the guard said, "with a dog whip. The scars go down his thighs. His father beat him senseless once, too."

Jung's mind raced. *Where did this man come from?* Nearby, an open door, concealed seamlessly in the wainscoting, gave the answer: a secret passage in the wall. Jung realized now that he and Hitler had never been alone. Someone had always been within three meters of the Führer. And no one had intervened when Hitler drew his weapon.

"Have you been told why I am here?" Jung asked the guard.

"Everyone knows. You are a doctor, come to help him sleep. It is hoped that you can."

Hitler called out, "Come."

Jung and the guard entered into the room. Hitler, now wearing pajamas, reclined in the bed, looking exhausted. The bodyguard went to a sturdy chair in a corner near a rondel window. Jung sat in a matching chair beside the bed and held up the mandala where Hitler could see it.

Jung said, "Now rest your mind and focus on this painting—"

"Mandala."

"Yes. As an artist, you would, of course, recognize what it is. Now, try to grasp all its colors at once. Nothing else needs your attention, just the mandala. You are perfectly safe here. Feel yourself relaxing, becoming calmer and calmer . . . "

Within a minute, Jung saw Hitler sink into a deep slumber. Eyes closed, the Führer now snored softly. As Jung exited the room, holding the mandala, the SS bodyguard saluted him with a relaxed hand, then leaned back in his chair to watch over his Führer while he slept.

Jung was still trembling as he located another guard. In as calm a voice as he could manage, he requested a ride to Bludenz. Jung left Löwensburg via the tunnel, accompanied by an SS driver.

Chapter 35
Gasthaus, Bludenz
7:00 PM, June 30, 1942

Mary waited for Jung on the stairs outside the gasthaus. She grew increasingly nervous as she watched the sun sink towards the mountaintops to the west. It was still bright daylight when she saw a black Mercedes speed towards her down the main street. *That's got to be him,* she thought. When the car pulled up to the curb and the SS driver opened the back door, Mary saw Jung stagger as he stepped out. She rushed down the steps to steady him, then helped him inside to the elevator.

"Are you all right?" she asked, as the elevator car creaked and lurched its way up its cage to the top floor. She watched Jung sway along with the car and gripped his arm. "You look tired."

"I am exhausted; I need sleep."

"I'll order something sent up from the kitchen. Then you can hit the hay." *After you tell me what happened.*

Mary went downstairs and ordered a light supper sent up. When she returned, Carl was on his bed, fast asleep. She didn't have it in her to wake him, so she sat in a chair and ruminated about about her affair with Allen Dulles.

A loud knock at the door awakened Mary from a Gestapo-filled nightmare. *"Zimmerdienst!"* a man announced, then rapped again. Still partway in the dream, she imagined he'd said, *"Sicherheitsdienst."* She bounded out of her chair in a panic, then realized room service had arrived, not Himmler's Security Service.

Now fully awake, Mary saw Carl was sitting up, reading *Mein Kampf* on the bed. "You should have got me up when you woke," she said as she opened the door for the waiter.

After they'd eaten, Mary shoved her plate away and asked, "Are you done with the evaluation?"

Jung leaned towards her and whispered, "Do you think it is safe . . . ?"

Mary stood. "Maybe we should go outside. Are you up to an after-dinner walk?"

"Yes. I have had a nice nap. A walk would be fine." He looked out the window. "We have an hour before sunset."

They ambled along the well-kept streets of Bludenz, pretending to look in the shop windows. Mary checked behind them from time to time. When there was no one near, she put her head closer to Jung's and asked, "So tell me, what was he like?"

Staring at the sidewalk, Jung said, "At times, he was not the monster I took him for in Berlin. He can simulate complete normality, but it comes and goes."

She put her arm around Jung's waist. "What's he like when it goes?"

Jung looked at her. "Self-will run amok. He lies constantly."

"No surprises there." Mary grimaced.

"No surprises here, either. I grew tired, and I carelessly called him 'responsible.' Hitler took that in a far worse sense of the word than I intended—consciously, at least—and he became mad as a rabid fox."

"Holy cow, Carl! Did you get anything out of him after that?"

"I was more concerned with survival. He pulled a gun on me."

Jumping Jehoshaphat! "A gun? A loaded gun?"

"I don't know; he didn't pull the trigger."

Mary felt her stomach lurch. "You could have been killed!" She stopped and leaned against a lamppost. "What did you do?"

"Whatever I could to restore accord. As a last resort, I hypnotized him, using your mandala to put him under."

"He actually slept?"

"Like a woodchuck."

Mary saw a soldier approaching. "We should keep moving." As they walked on, Mary said, "So Hitler is crazy?"

"Not necessarily. I had provoked him with my judgmentalism." They passed a pawn shop window, and Jung pointed in at a display of clocks. "Look at these, Mary. Do you notice anything?"

She stopped and pressed her face to the glass. "They're all different kinds . . . "

"Yes, and . . . "

"They all have the same time."

"Exactly. They are in good repair. But a faulty clock is hard to predict."

"Unless it's completely broken."

"That is the problem. Hitler is not completely broken, so it isn't as simple as sane or insane. It is a matter of degrees and kinds. To predict Hitler's actions, I must examine his clockworks and answer completely Dulles's question: 'What makes Hitler tick?'"

Jung started to walk away, but Mary stepped back and read the gold lettering on the storefront glass:

Armbanduhren	Uhren	Zeitmesser
Chronometer	Stowa™	IWC™
Montblanc™	Rolex™	Glashütte™
Reparaturen	Mühle™	Schlosser

"Look, Carl." She pointed at the IWC insignia. "Isn't that Emmy's company?"

"One of them, yes." He looked at her. "In case you're wondering, they're are also sold in England and America."

Mary checked the street in both directions before asking, "Any idea what makes him tick, so far?"

"He was abused as a child, whipped and battered. If he is typical of such children, he will have certain traits: grandiosity, control issues—"

"Yeah, that's Hitler."

"—Feelings of abandonment, poor self-image, and so on. All those could make him more predictable; the question is, how much? As of now, I can only guess. I hope to mesh the gears together with what I learn tomorrow." Jung interlaced his fingers to illustrate.

Mary thought, *Carl already almost got shot; he may be pushing Hitler too far.* "Don't take chances," she told him. "Maybe you should just tell him he's fine and get out of there."

"No, I must continue. If he has slept well and feels refreshed, there are areas I would like to explore . . . assuming I don't get myself killed, first."

"What sort of areas?"

"I am almost certain he killed Geli Raubal."

Mary turned to face Jung. "Really? Why do you think that?"

"It has been eleven years since Geli's death, and Hitler still has a huge reservoir of grief associated with her. It is as if she died yesterday. A guilt complex could explain that."

Mary wrinkled her brow. "But why would he kill her?"

"She once had an affair with his chauffeur right under Hitler's nose; she might have started another. Hitler's abandonment issues would guarantee a violent reaction if he thought Geli were leaving him for another man. I have no proof, of course, and I can't imagine how Hitler got away with it. I must find out."

"Suppose you do. Can you keep him from sensing that you know?" *And shooting you.*

Mary saw Jung's jaw tighten at the thought. "I will have to be more careful," he said with a sigh.

On the way back to the gasthaus near twilight, Jung said, "What about you, Mary? I don't for a minute imagine you behaved yourself today."

"*I* found a soldier who trained at Döllersheim."

"You did?" Jung stopped walking. "That was most fortuitous."

"Fortuitous, hell, Carl; Döllersheim is the biggest training camp in Germany; everybody from southern Germany trains there."

"Did this soldier have any idea why Hitler emptied the town?"

Mary shrugged. "Not really. They used it for artillery practice, blasted the hell out of the place."

"That is odd. I wonder . . . " Jung continued towards the gasthaus.

"Wonder what?" Mary hurried to keep up with him.

Jung held up a finger. "Did they blow up the church? And the church records?"

"He didn't say, but I'll ask him tomorrow."

Jung waved the idea away. "Forget it. Too many questions would be risky."

"Look who's talking."

Jung yawned. Mary got him back to his room, helped him into bed, and turned out his light.

Chapter 36
Terzendorf Concentration Camp
8:00 AM, July 1, 1942

Early the next morning, Olbricht drove his grey Opel up a graveled road to the barbed wire double gate at the camp. Guards snapped to attention, saluted, and swung open one side of the gate to admit him. *Now to get this over with and go back to Bludenz,* he thought. He parked in front of the administration building, beneath the shade of one of the camp's two trees, and looked around. Dirt, everywhere, not a blade of grass. Olbricht left his driving gloves on.

He got out of the Opel and stalked into the building, carrying a small, black valise. He swung the latter up onto the bare wood counter.

The camp Commandant entered the front room from an adjacent cubicle. "Welcome, Herr General." He glanced at the valise.

"You received my message, ja?"

The Commandant held up a hand. "Ja, but—"

"Good." Olbricht put a sheaf of official papers on top of the valise. "I have come for Rosenberg, Dr. Marcus Rosenberg, psychiatrist, as arranged."

"We should discuss—"

"Some other time." *He wants more money. He will not get it.* Olbricht tapped the valise. "Here is the money, as we agreed. Bring me Dr. Rosenberg, please. Without further talk."

"If you insist." The Commandant pressed a button on the counter, and a few seconds later, an obese guard with a low forehead, his overcoat and boots covered with dust, entered and saluted.

"Ja, Herr Commandant?" the man said, before noticing Olbricht. Mouth agape, he stared at the General.

The Commandant opened a ledger and ran his finger down a list. "Bring me Number three-two-four eight-seven-seven. Be quick. Do not keep the General waiting."

The guard saluted and hurried outside. Olbricht strode the length of the office repeatedly until the man reappeared and obsequiously sat a plain cardboard shoebox down on the counter. Fine grey dust spewed from under the lid. The guard bowed awkwardly, stepped back, and said, "Three-two-four eight-seven-seven, Herr General."

"What is this?" Olbricht demanded.

The Commandant pointed. "That is Rosenberg, three-two-four eight-seven-seven, as I attempted to tell you."

"I wanted him alive." Aghast, Olbricht pointed at the papers. "This is an order for his release, signed by the Führer a week ago."

The Commandant held up a paper. "And this is an order for his execution, signed by Reichsführer Himmler two days ago." He placed the order on the counter neatly beside the shoebox.

Olbricht read the document. *Signed by Himmler, as stated. Someone at the OKW has turned informer! This could have serious consequences for our other plans. I must tell General Halder as soon as I can.* "There has been a terrible mistake," Olbricht said.

"I regret if there has, Herr General, but I only did exactly as I was ordered." The Commandant indicated the box.

He obeyed orders. I am guilty of saying the same thing to Jung a few days ago. Olbricht closed his eyes and took a deep breath. When he opened them, the Commandant was staring at the valise. "Any payment is now out of the question, of course," Olbricht told him.

The Commandant shoved the box of ashes towards Olbricht, who took the valise instead and stalked out of the office. He was almost back to the Opel before he heard the guard racing after him.

"Herr General! Herr General! One moment, please."

Olbricht stopped and faced the guard, who gestured towards the barracks. "Herr General, we have another Dr. Rosenberg here. A younger one. Will he do?"

"Is he related to Marcus Rosenberg?"

"Jawohl, Herr General. He is the son."

"He might do. Where is he?"

"He is in a punishment cell."

"Show me." Olbricht motioned for the guard to precede him.

The guard led the General to a small shed and, taking a key from his pocket, unlocked a padlock and removed it from the hasp. Someone within cried out. The guard swung the door open, revealing an unshaven man in prison-striped garb, blinking in the light. The guard stood aside and said, "Sigmund Rosenberg. Dr. Rosenberg, the younger."

Sigmund lay on a filthy pile of straw. He was barefoot, his face covered with dirt, dried tears, blood, and bruises. He looked up at Olbricht, then tried to crawl away, but there was no place for him to go. He sat up and wiped his eyes with a ragged sleeve.

Olbricht entered the cell, and a stomach-turning odor met his nostrils. "*Donnerwetter!*" he exclaimed, covering his nose and mouth.

The guard shrugged. "I am sorry, Herr General, I did not know he was anybody important."

Olbricht wanted to slap the guard, but placed a gloved hand on his shoulder instead, and looked him in the eyes. "Assist me, would you?"

"Most certainly, Herr General."

Olbricht and the guard helped Sigmund to his feet, and he stumbled outside, supported between them.

Within the hour, Olbricht led Sigmund to the Opel. He had been cleaned up, shaved, and provided with fresh civilian clothes, as well as a shabby overcoat. The guard followed, coatless, carrying the box containing Marcus's ashes.

When they headed for the car, instead of back into the camp, Sigmund looked at Olbricht and asked, "Please, may I ask what are you going to do with me?"

"Dr. Carl Jung sent me. I am taking you to him, and then you will be going to Switzerland."

Sigmund, his mouth agape, stared at Olbricht. His knees started to give way, but Olbricht steadied him.

The guard held the box in his outstretched hands and gave a slight bow towards Sigmund. "This is yours, Herr Doktor."

"What is it?" Sigmund reached for the box.

Olbricht stepped forward and took it. "Never mind about this, now. Get in the car. Up front with me." While Sigmund climbed into the Opel, Olbricht stowed the ashes on the floor of the back seat. He got in and drove out of the camp, dust flying from the car's wheels.

Once the Opel turned off the camp's gravel road and onto the tree-lined, macadam main road, Olbricht took out a sheaf of documents about as big as a passport. Holding them up, he told Sigmund, "These are your traveling papers. If we are stopped, which I doubt will happen . . . " He indicated the OKW flags on the front fenders. " . . . you are not Dr. Sigmund Rosenberg; you are Dr. Marcus

Rosenberg. These papers were made out your father's name. Do not lose them." He gave the packet to Sigmund.

Sig looked at the papers. "You intended to free my father?"

Olbricht felt his face burn. Sigmund clearly didn't know his father was dead. "Ja. I had those exit papers signed by Hitler personally."

"But where is my father? Why are you taking me, instead of—" Sigmund broke off and his eyes widened. "The box! He is in that box!" He groaned and swayed in his seat, clutching his head between his hands. "He is dead!"

Olbricht stamped on the brakes and pulled to the side of the road. Sigmund cried for a long time, reeling, moaning. Finally, he leaned back and covered his eyes with one arm, his breath ragged as he tried to contain his sobs.

At last, Sigmund grew quiet. Olbricht put a hand on his shoulder. "We have a long way to go today, Herr Doktor. When you are up to it, we can talk. In the meantime, I must drive without distractions. Do you understand?"

Sigmund nodded and wiped his eyes on his sleeve.

"Good." Olbricht put the car in gear and pulled out onto the road. Sigmund slept.

An hour later, they reached the inn where the General had stayed the night before. He parked the car, hesitating before gently waking his slumbering passenger.

Chapter 37
Bludenz to Löwensburg
9:00 AM, July 1, 1942

Jung didn't sleep well. Images of Nazis goose-stepping into his homeland flickered through his mind like a newsreel, keeping him from dozing off. In the morning, bleary-eyed, he yawned as he arose, dressed, and walked downstairs to wait for the SS driver. As the sun warmed him, he thought how nice it would be to just go right back to Zurich and forget about Germany and its obnoxious Führer. But those jackbooted images from the night had reminded him of the importance of completing his mission.

The driver arrived punctually, greeted him as "Herr Lang," and took him swiftly to Löwensburg. Jung trudged down the tunnel, his briefcase in one hand, his flashlight, with fresh batteries, ready in the other. But the lights didn't "fail," this time.

Upon emerging from the elevator, Jung was escorted to the red-carpeted den, where Hitler now walked on a diagonal, as before, head down. He looked up as Jung entered.

"Did you sleep?" Jung asked, already knowing the answer from Hitler's more energetic step.

Hitler nodded. "I did. Nine hours, thank you much."

"Then we've had some success. Do you wish to continue for a while?"

"I leave for Berlin later today, but we may talk until lunchtime."

Relieved at getting a chance to dig further, at the same time, Jung feared making another misstep as he had the previous day. *Carefully, carefully*, he told himself.

They sat in the den, in the same chairs as before. *So much to explore,* Jung thought, *but so little time. I had better focus on the most important items and leave Löwensburg as quickly as possible.* He sighed quietly before continuing, torn between duty and fear. "Please tell me, Herr Hitler: you have dreams at night?"

"Ja. Always." Hitler crossed his legs and gripped one knee with both hands. "Often they are quite disturbing, and they awaken me. Then I have difficulty getting back to sleep."

"Do these dreams seem real?"

"Perfectly."

"I'd like to know more about them."

Hitler crossed his arms and pursed his lips. "With all due respect, Herr Doktor Jung, I do not intend to let you that far into my mind."

Another dead-end. Well, at least he warned me before I stepped in something. "That is regrettable. Could you, perhaps, give me examples of some of the repeating elements in your worst dreams?"

Hitler shook his head, but waved a hand and said, "You know: skeletons, blood, all the sort of thing you might expect in a nightmare."

Jung gave a barely perceptible nod. *Death images. Very significant, not at all the sort of thing I would expect in most people's dreams. But pressing for more details might uncover something best avoided. To let sleeping Führers lie may be the best policy.* He said, "I shall respect your wishes, then. We shall keep your dreams private."

"Good." Hitler uncrossed his arms.

Jung open his briefcase and took out a familiar sheet of paper containing four columns of words. "There's one last technique we should try."

Hitler pointed at the paper. "Word association."

Hitler has done his homework. "Yes. You know how this works?"

"Ja. You say a word, and I shoot back at you the first word I think of. My words are clues to what's on my mind."

I wish Hitler hadn't said, 'I shoot back at you,' Jung thought, but he said, "As you must also have read, the time it takes for a response is as important as the response itself." *That should stop him from over-thinking his replies. This could be the key to Hitler's mind.* "Shall we try a few words and see where that takes us?"

Hitler frowned, clearly not enthused.

He wants to shut down. "But you seem doubtful, Herr Hitler."

"I'm not sure this is of value for my condition."

"You are afraid I will judge your responses?"

"Based on yesterday's experience, ja."

Jung thought for a moment, then replied, "This is not a diagnostic test, in itself, so you shouldn't worry about the results. But since you have reservations, I'm going to provide you an option that I don't normally suggest. If I say a word that is very uncomfortable for you, just say 'pass,' and we'll go on to the next word."

"That is acceptable."

"I may sometimes deviate from my list and reflect your response, repeating the word you have just said. Again, continue with the first thing that comes to mind."

"Very well, I understand."

Jung rearranged his chair at a ninety degree angle so he could observe Hitler without being easily seen. More important, Jung didn't want Hitler to see which responses resulted in notes being made on the notepad. "This is a standard hundred word list, a fourth of them verbs. Nothing in it is aimed at you, personally. It's the same for every client."

"Ja, ja. I know all this. Go ahead."

He's getting impatient. Jung started reading the words, pausing for Hitler's response after each one. *"Head . . . "*

Hitler replied, "Foot."

"Green . . . "

"Grass."

"Water . . . "

"Glass."

"Sing . . . "

"Dance."

"Dead . . . "

A slight pause from Hitler, then, "M . . . mother."

Jung underlined 'dead' as he reflected Hitler's response, saying, *"Mother . . . "*

A longer pause before Hitler replied, "Sad."

"Long . . . "

"Short."

"Ship . . . "

"Gangplank."

"Pay . . . "

"Back."

A circle around 'pay,' then, *"Bread . . . "*

"Beer."

"Rich . . . "

Hitler paused and then said, "Jew!" He looked at Jung and smirked.

Jung barely managed to suppress a frown. Underlining 'rich,' he skipped to, *"Stab . . . "*

From Hitler came a long pause, then "Pass."

Jung circled 'stab' and said, *"Swim . . . "*

"Pool."

"Mountain . . . "

Hitler hesitated. "Elevation."

Jung noted the pause and repeated, *"Elevation . . . "*

"Above."

Jung thought of this high place, this Löwensburg, where Hitler could look down on the mere mortals of his Reich. He underlined 'mountain' twice. *"Book . . . "*

"Mein Kampf."

Jung grimaced. *Didn't see that coming.* *"Ask . . . "*

"Order."

"Box . . . "

"Munitions."

Jung wrote 'Munitions' in the margin, saying, *"Brother . . . "*

"Edmund."

Jung glanced up to observe Hitler's face, now a blank mask. *He's holding himself in check. Or so he thinks. We'll see how long he can keep that up.* *"False . . . "*

"True."

"Woman . . . "

"Mother."

"Home . . . "

"Happy."

"Father . . . "

A long pause followed before Hitler said the logical, if evasive, "Parent."

Noted. *"Aunt . . . "*

"Uncle."

"Bird . . . "

"Nest."

The next inducer word was 'fall,' but Jung had a sudden inspiration to say, *"Butterfly . . . "*

"Incest."

Quickly: *"Insect . . . "*

"Wasp."

"Flower . . . "

"Bee."

"Tree . . . "

"Grass."

The test continued to the end of all the words. Hitler had declined to respond to only a handful. While they took a short break, Jung looked over the list and his marks. *No sign of schizophrenia. A few strange answers, but only one response that is important. And now I'm ready to get home . . . if Hitler will let me.*

Jung was tired from the strain, but quite pleased with himself, until a stray thought crossed his mind: *What if I, in a careless moment of exhaustion at the crucial point, had reflected the wrong word? I'd be lying on this red carpet, dead, right now. I need to stay focused if I'm going to get home without being murdered . . . .*

Chapter 38
Biergarten, Bludenz
9:00 AM, July 1, 1942

After Jung had left Bludenz that morning, Mary watched through the lipstick telescope and soon saw Albert and Heinz coming down the street and entering the biergarten. She hurried downstairs and up the street to join them there. The two were already drinking breakfast when Mary greeted them with a coy grin and "Hallo, meine Freunde!"

"Maria!" Albert sprang up and pulled out a chair for her. "Heinz, a glass for Maria."

After a few minutes of conversation, Corporal Albert said, "Private Heinz, did you not have some postcards to write?"

"Nein," Heinz said.

"Ja," Albert insisted. "You said you must write to your mother today. Have you forgotten?"

"What?" Heinz looked puzzled, then suddenly twitched in his chair. "Ouch!" He rubbed his shin and said, "Ach, ja! My mother!" He grimaced, drained his stein, and left.

Mary moved her chair closer to Albert, sitting with him thigh-to-thigh. "I hoped I'd run into you again," she said, smiling at him.

"I, too." Albert met her eyes.

She put her hand on his arm. "I'd like to talk more about Döllersheim."

"I am not sure we should."

"It's all right. We're alone, now." Mary beamed at him.

"I . . . *we* could get in trouble. Döllersheim is not supposed to be discussed."

Mary let her hair fall across her eyes and said, "There's nothing left of the town. What harm could it do to talk about it?" She swept her hair to one side and looked at him, pouting.

"I do not know . . . "

"I won't tell anybody. I promise." She moved her hand down to his thigh.

Albert looked around the room before leaning towards her and saying, "There is not much to say. We shelled the town, then others came and practiced house-to-house combat in the ruins."

"But why did Hitler order it destroyed?"

He shrugged, raising his eyebrows. "No one knows."

And now for what Carl wanted to know: "What about the church?"

"They had taken away the altar and the statues and stained glass windows, of course, but the roof was demolished by shrapnel, and the rest was badly damaged." Albert shook his head. "It was a creepy place."

"Creepy in what way?"

Albert hesitated. "Macabre." He fell silent.

Mary noted that Albert had turned a bit grey. *Something is amiss. I need to follow up on this.* "What's the matter?"

He put down the stein and looked at her. "I do not want to say any more . . . "

"I'm sorry." She tried to look very disappointed. "I was just wondering if you have any photos . . . "

He put his hand on her arm. "We should not talk here, Maria. But, yes, I do have some photos. Do you want to see them?"

"Yes."

He looked down at the table. "They are back at my room." He paused, gave Mary a bashful little glance, then added, "It is only a short walk from here. Do you mind?"

"Not a bit. Let's go."

Chapter 39
On the Road to Innsbruck
09:00 AM, July 1, 1942

Olbricht awakened Sigmund and said, "We are at an inn. Do you want something to eat?"

Sigmund rubbed his eyes, then stared at him. "Ja, very much, Herr General, but do they serve Jews, here?"

"They will serve anyone I say to." Olbricht left his gloves on the Opel's steering wheel and went around to open the passenger door. "Come." He took Sigmund's hand and helped him to his feet, then led the way into the inn, checking to make sure his passenger was able to keep up.

When they entered the inn's busy restaurant, silence descended as all the diners stared at Olbricht. He suspected they didn't see a lot of Wehrmacht officers eating there, and probably never a General. He decided to abandon his usual low profile and play the Prussian *Junker*. *The more attention they pay to me, the less they'll notice Dr. Rosenberg.*

Sigmund wasn't wearing a yellow *Jude* insignia, so the General considered passing him off as *Wehrmachtsgefolge,* a civilian auxiliary employee. *No, he'd have a badge or armband. I'll just pretend he's my nephew, if anyone asks.*

"*Herr Oberkellner!*" Olbricht called out. "A table, please!"

The headwaiter scurried to the front of the restaurant. "Right away, Herr General! There are two of you?"

"Ja. We will be discussing important business, so a table away from the others."

"This way, Herr General." The headwaiter didn't even look at Sigmund.

After they were seated in a quiet corner, Olbricht noticed that Rosenberg was trembling. "Relax," he said.

"I will try, Herr General, but it is difficult. I think you understand, under the circumstances."

"Call me 'Uncle.' What did they call you at home?"

Sigmund's eyes widened with surprise. "Siggy," he said, and his eyes began to fill with tears.

Olbricht, fearing he might break down completely, put a hand on his arm. "Steady, Siggy! You need some food in you. You may cry all you want later. Let's get you fed."

"All right." Siggy wiped his eyes with a napkin, then added, "Uncle."

The waiter appeared and took their order, collecting the necessary ration stamps. Once the food was brought, Olbricht ate his potatoes, then shoved his plate toward Sigmund. "I'll eat later. If you're still hungry, finish my breakfast. I need to call my superior. All right?"

Sigmund, his mouth full, merely nodded.

Olbricht used the desk phone in the lobby to put in a call to General Halder, then waited in a small telephone alcove for the call to go through. He turned to check on Sigmund from time to time. The telephone rang, and he picked up the receiver. "Olbricht."

"This is Halder. How goes it?"

The connection to Berlin was clear, with no static. Olbricht hoped this was a sign that the call wasn't being monitored. "There has been a snag, here, General Halder."

"What sort?"

"To get Jung's cooperation, we promised we would release Dr. Rosenberg."

"Ja, I heard it was all arranged."

"Rosenberg has been executed. By Himmler's order."

Halder exhaled heavily into the phone. "That is most unfortunate."

"Rosenberg's son was in the same camp. I took him, instead, hoping that will satisfy our part of the bargain with Jung."

"That is the least of our considerations, Olbricht. Someone must have informed Himmler of Jung's visit. This could jeopardize our entire . . . enterprise." There was a long pause, then Halder added, "You must return to Berlin immediately."

"I guaranteed Dr. Jung he would not be detained."

"I realize that, but I am ordering you to stand aside. With Himmler involved, anything could happen. The less we attract his attention, the better. We can make cautious inquiries from here."

Olbricht frowned. "What about the son?"

Halder hesitated, then said, "Drop him at any Gestapo office. They will . . . take care of him."

Olbricht hung up the phone and looked at Sigmund, who was still enjoying his first decent meal in many months, unaware his life was now in as much danger as before.

Olbricht placed a call to the gasthaus in Bludenz. It only took a minute to go through, but the desk clerk told him that Maria Rufenacht was not in her room nor in the restaurant; she had apparently gone out.

Verdammt! I told her to stay in the fucking gasthaus! "Very well, let me leave a message." *What to say?* "Tell her that Friedrich has been called to Berlin. Dr. Arberg has passed away from complications. The schoolmaster is coming from Berlin to console Herr Wolff. Friedrich will see what allows itself to be done from Berlin, but advises you to return home immediately until all these matters have resolved themselves. My deepest condolences."

After the clerk repeated the message, Olbricht promised him twenty Reichsmarks if he gave Frau Rufenacht the message as soon as she returned. He ended the call and swore. *Scheisse! Maria was an idiot to leave the gasthaus. But maybe she can pick up Jung and get a ride back to Mauren with one of Hitler's men. Or they might get caught between Hitler and Himmler. I would help, but I have my orders.*

Chapter 40
Albert's Room, Bludenz
9:15 AM, July 1, 1942

Albert's furlough quarters in Bludenz consisted of a small, dreary room in his mother's house, barely enough space for his bed, a bedside cabinet, a chest of drawers, a table beside a mirror, and two chairs. Everything reeked of camphor, a sign that he was seldom there. No one else was home.

Mary sat at the table, and Albert, already well lubricated with beer, poured schnapps into small glasses and sat close beside her. After a few swigs, he took her hand and said, "We were not supposed to take pictures. We were not even supposed to have a camera, but I did, anyway."

"That was brave of you, Albert. Did you get photos before and after?" She gripped his hand and looked into his eyes.

Albert downed another shot of schnapps and stood. "Some. They are in my rucksack." He poured more liquor into Mary's glass, then staggered toward his bed.

He returned with a stack of photographs and clumsily organized them before passing them to Mary one at a time. "This is how the shops looked when we got there . . . "

The first photograph showed an orderly row of quaint little stores, a hodge-podge of different styles, most of them two story, with Alpine half-hip roofs, colorful murals and flower boxes, and a few with half-timbered walls.

"And the houses . . . " Albert showed Mary a street lined with rustic Austrian homes, similar to the shops.

Mary feared this photo tour could take a long time. "Nice," she said. "What about the church?"

Albert didn't answer her question, but handed her two more snapshots. " . . . And here is how they all look now."

The little homes and shops, once so pretty, were now knee-high rubble.

Mary gasped at the destruction. "Shh . . . " She caught herself at the last split second. *Jeez, I almost said 'shit.' Allen was right. I'm not ready for this. And I've had way too much to drink.*

"*What did you say?*" Albert mumbled, trying to focus his eyes on her.

Mary swigged at her schnapps to give herself a little time to think. She took too much, choked, coughed, and finally managed to wheeze, "Scheisse. Total *abgeflacht.*" She pointed at the photograph.

"Yes, all flattened." Albert shrugged.

Damn, Mary thought. *That was a close call. No more schnapps for me.*

Albert had other ideas. He splashed a generous quantity of the liquor in and around her glass, then passed her another snapshot. "This is the church, Saints Peter and Paul, before." He paused and looked at the next photos. "But perhaps I should not show you these." His brow furrowed and he put the rest of the photographs down.

Mary wanted to grab them up. *I have to see these photographs*, she thought. She began to flirt with Albert in earnest, grabbing his arm and leaning her head against him. "Oh, you can show them to me!"

"You will not tell anyone, will you?"

"Of course not." She gave him a soft kiss on the cheek.

Albert rapidly laid out ten more pictures in front of her.

Mary looked at them, and her eyes widened. *These are the worst of all! How did Carl know to ask about the church?*

After a few more minutes of conversation and drinking, Albert lay snoring on the bed. Mary quietly moved the lamp from his bedside cabinet to the table. She lit the lamp. Taking her lipstick camera, she removed the cap and dropped it in her lap. *I sure hope Albert's down for the count; if he sees me with this spy camera, he'll turn me in to the Security Service.* She began taking microfilm copies of Albert's snapshots.

But as she took the first photo, she felt a familiar tickle in her nose. *Scheisse!* she thought, *not now!* The tickle grew worse. *I'm . . . going . . . .to sneeze.* She fought the impulse, pressing her wrist to her nose, but it was no use. *I'm going to sneeze my brains out!* She put down the camera and held both hands over her nose and mouth to stifle the noise.

Atchoooompf! Atchoooompf! Atchoooompf! Atchoooompf!

Thank God that's over! Mary picked up the camera and sighted on the next photograph. A final sneeze erupted, unsmothered. AAAA-TCHOOO! It seemed to echo in the tiny room. She glanced at Albert, but he hadn't moved, and she went on shooting photographs as quickly as she could.

Without warning, Albert embraced her from behind. *He caught me!* she thought, before realizing he was merely amorously inclined. Very inclined, judging from the nudge between her shoulder blades.

"Oh, Maria! My heart is beating so fast with love, you must make it beat slower, or I shall die." He saw the tiny camera in her hand. He squinted. "What is that?"

"I'm just making myself beautiful for you." Mary put the little cylinder in her lap, jammed the cap back on, twisted, and took the cap off again. When she raised it to her mouth, only lipstick showed. She looked in the mirror and dabbed some on, then fluffed her hair and smiled.

"If you were any more beautiful, I'd be lying dead at your feet," Albert said, as he reached for her breasts and leaned his head against her.

Uh, oh. Nathan Hale, what would you say in this situation?

Chapter 41
Fireside Room, Löwensburg
10:00 AM, July 1, 1942

Jung grew weary after a long series of questions that Hitler answered with useless platitudes or trivial anecdotes. "I believe," Jung said, "a break would be beneficial."

Hitler agreed. He led Jung from the den and outside onto a balcony overlooking the mountains. They paused there, and Jung admired the view as Hitler showed off by naming the various peaks on the horizon. *He's on his good behavior, today*, Jung thought. *I suppose I could leave now. No, it's still early; I may learn something vital.*

After a fifteen minute pause, they walked the length of the balcony and downstairs into a smaller, cozier room with a wood smoke aroma and rustic furniture. As they entered, they passed a fireplace with a mantel holding personal trinkets and four high-quality portrait photographs. "Are those family pictures?" Jung asked, lingering.

"Just this one." Hitler handed Jung the first image, a large, tinted portrait of a seated woman about forty, in a black dress. With a slight tremor in his voice, Hitler intoned, "My mother. Klara Hitler."

Jung examined the picture, trying to grasp what this

woman had been like in real life. The family resemblance was clear, the same ears, the same steel blue eyes. *What secrets did those eyes hold?* Jung wondered. *Is this the doting mother of a Muttersöhnchen? Or something else? The photograph is almost a religious icon to Hitler.* Jung nodded and said, "Very motherly," before returning the portrait with both hands.

Hitler positioned it back on the mantel and started to take a seat, but Jung lingered, looking at the other portraits. "And who are these fellows?"

Hitler turned to him again and waved a hand. "Only some old friends. No one important."

If Hitler says they're not important, they possibly are. Jung pointed at the second photo, a studio photo of a tallish, darkly suave young man in black SS uniform. "A handsome chap, this one."

Hitler walked back to the mantel. "Ja. That is Emil Maurice, SS Member Number 2."

This is the man that had an affair with Geli. What is his photo doing here? "Emil Maurice? That was Geli's . . . " *What should I call him? "* . . . Admirer?"

Hitler nodded. "Ja, ja, that is the one. He drove for me."

Until you emptied your gun at him and fired him, Jung thought. "I'm surprised you have a picture on your mantle of this man who was so close to Geli."

The Führer spread his hands. "We soon made up. We were old friends. He was in prison with me at Landsberg in twenty-four."

"So you felt no resentment about his liaison with Geli?"

"Nein. In fact, he was the trouble-maker. Do you know what that bastard did?" Hitler grinned, astonishing Jung.

"I can't imagine."

"After I fired him, he sued me for wrongful discharge!"

Jung suppressed a smile. "Did he win?"

"Ja. Then he used my money to open a watchmaker's shop around the corner from us."

What nerve! "Did Emil live at the shop?"

"Ja, it had living quarters above it."

"So there was further trouble?"

Hitler leaned toward Jung and flourished a finger. "There might have been, but I outmaneuvered him."

"And how did you accomplish that?"

"I made him my security chief! That way, he went wherever I went. Whenever I left Geli alone overnight, he was right next to me. One less man to worry about." Hitler grinned and gave a little snicker of amusement.

Jung inclined his head. "Clever, Herr Hitler." He turned to the next picture. "And this other chap?"

The third photograph showed Hitler sitting in a Mercedes convertible beside a clean-shaven, heavy-featured SS man his own size. Both men stared straight ahead with stern expressions.

"That is another of my drivers, Julius Schreck, SS Member Number 5. He replaced Emil." Hitler hesitated, then added, "Julius passed away six years ago."

Jung couldn't bring himself to offer condolences. One less SS man was not something he felt sorry for.

The last subject, a jowly man with a penetrating stare and dark, curly hair, posed grandly, surrounded by a camera, tripod, flash powder tray, makeup case, and other equipment. Jung pointed. "Your photographer, obviously."

"Yes. That is Heinrich Hoffmann. He is very famous. He took these photos of Emil and Julius."

"Very nice work. Who took his photo?"

"His assistant, Eva Braun."

A box of chocolates sat on the mantel. Hitler opened it and said, "Would you like a truffle?"

Jung held up a hand. "Thank you, but I think it best to wait until we're done." His back tired from sitting, Jung stretched.

Hitler chose a piece of candy and bit into it deliberately.

Chapter 42
Munich-Innsbruck Road
10:00 AM July 1, 1942

Olbricht slowed as he approached a crossroads in Austria. Sigmund slept in the back seat, covered by a blanket. The sign ahead of them read "Berlin" to the left, "Innsbruck," to the right. The Innsbruck road led to Bludenz. Olbricht hesitated. *Which way do I go? Going to Berlin, as ordered, would be death for Sigmund Rosenberg, but safest for me. That safety will not last forever, though. Does Fortune not favor the brave?*

Olbricht's hands tightened on the wheel. He stepped on the accelerator and cranked the steering wheel to the right, taking the road towards Innsbruck, in direct violation of Halder's order. His *Soldatenwort* to Jung was more important to him than Halder or Rosenberg or anything else at this point, including his oath of loyalty to Hitler. Including orders.

Sigmund awoke. "Where are we?"
"Just leaving Innsbruck. Do you need to stop?"
"No."
A long silence followed. The General spoke first.

"Look, Herr Doktor, I regret what happened to your father. That was not my fault." *Or was it, in some convoluted way?*

Sigmund didn't answer.

Olbricht became irritated. "This is a time of war. War is like a truck going downhill with no brakes. We can steer, but still people get hit. Things just happen." He glanced at Sigmund, who sat with his arms folded, staring straight ahead, his jaw clenched. "Say something."

Sigmund cleared his throat and spoke softly. "Maybe . . . maybe we should not have gotten into the truck in the first place." He met Olbricht's eyes.

Absolutely right, Olbricht thought, and looked away. Constrained by his loyalty to the Führer, he could only say, "I cannot respond to that, much as I would like to. Right now, believe me, there are larger issues at stake than you or your father, and I need your full cooperation. Understood?"

"Ja," Sigmund said, then added, "Do not think I am ungrateful. I am not."

"Let us get you to Zurich. Once you are there, you may arrange for a proper burial of your father's ashes."

Sigmund said solemnly, "In our tradition, there is no such thing as proper burial of a human reduced to ashes."

Olbricht wrinkled his brow, but couldn't think of a good response. He drove west out of Innsbruck, headed for Bludenz and, beyond that, Löwensburg. He maintained a fast clip, hoping to arrive in time to save Maria Rufenacht and Dr. Jung, if that were possible. As he skidded the Opel around a turn, Olbricht saw armored vehicles parked across the road ahead. *Scheisse! What the hell is going on there? Waffen-SS.* He jammed on the brakes.

Sigmund sat up straight. "What is this?"

"Roadblock." Olbricht considered running the blockade, but the SS vehicles were well-placed, leaving no gaps that he could swerve around. He also noted that the soldiers carried MP40 submachine guns. "Do not panic. I

159

can talk our way past this."

Sigmund fumbled for the door handle.

"No!! Do not try to run; they will cut you down in two seconds. Sit there as if you are my civilian aide. It is your only chance to survive."

Olbricht rolled to a stop well short of the blockade, and an SS Captain approached the car. The General cranked down his window. "Ja? What is it, Captain?" he said in a steady voice.

"You are Herr General Olbricht?"

"Ja, of course I am." Olbricht indicated the OKW flags on the Opel's fenders.

"Your papers, please, Herr General." The officer bent down and peered across Olbricht at Sigmund. "And his as well."

Olbricht stacked Sigmund's papers beneath his own, lowering the chance that the Captain would examine them closely and see they were for a Jew named Marcus Rosenberg. Faint hope, but . . .

The officer skimmed Olbricht's identity papers before handing them to a man standing behind him in a black SS uniform.

"Guten tag, Herr General," the second official said, his voice shrill. "You're a long way from Berlin today, Olbricht, not so?" The speaker stepped forward.

Himmler.

Chapter 43
Bludenz
10:20 AM, July 1, 1942

Mary returned to the gasthaus a while later, sore, tired, and unsteady on her feet, thinking of nothing but a bath and a long nap to prepare for the return trip. The desk clerk came out to meet her, saying, "Frau Rufenacht? There is an urgent message for you at the desk."

What now? she thought. *I sure hope it's from Carl. If he finished early, we can get out of here.*

Inside, the clerk took a folded piece of hotel stationery from the room's message slot and gave it to her. A quick glance told Mary it was from Olbricht. *Uh-oh.* She took it into the small lobby and sat down. The hand-written note was legible, but cryptic. She skimmed it:

"Friedrich . . . called to Berlin . . . "

Damn it! Why would he go to Berlin. This is not good.

"Dr. Arberg . . . "

Who the hell is Dr. Arberg? Oh, wait. Dr. R-berg. Rosenberg.

" . . . passed away . . . complications . . . "

Rosenberg is dead. We've been had. What does he mean by 'complications?'

" . . . Schoolmaster coming from Berlin . . . console Herr Wolff."

'Schoolmaster?' From Berlin, so that must mean Nazi brass. Going to 'console Herr Wolff?' Herr Wolff is Hitler, so Olbricht means: Nazi brass is coming from Berlin to see Hitler. Himmler! It's got to be Himmler! He's the complication.

" . . . Friedrich will see what may be done from Berlin . . . "

Oh, that's a frigging big help! Thanks a bunch, Friedrich, you Nazi S.O.B!

" . . . Advises . . . return home immediately . . . Deepest condolences."

Left us in the lurch, damn it. Screw his condolences!

Mary's mind raced. *I can't leave without Carl. I'd better warn him there's trouble coming, if I can. Maybe he can stop the therapy and leave, if we can find a car. If, if, if.*

Mary hurried back to the front desk and asked the clerk to place a phone call to Löwensburg. His eyebrows rose, but he directed her to wait in the tiny phone booth beside the lobby while he made the call.

A minute later, the extension in the little telephone cubicle jangled. Mary grabbed the receiver and put it to her ear. "Hello . . . ?" she said. There was only static on the line at first, then Mary heard someone on the other end pick up and exclaim, "Shit!"

What the hell? Mary thought, before realizing he'd said, "Schmidt!"

She spoke loudly over the static. "Herr Schmidt, this is Frau Maria Rufenacht. I'm trying to reach . . . " She almost said Dr. Jung, but caught herself in time. " . . . To reach Herr Lang."

"There is no Herr Lang here. You have the wrong number."

Oh, Schmidt! "He's meeting with Herr Wolff today. I am Herr Lang's secretary, and I must talk to him right away."

"I shall make inquiries. Please hold."

Mary heard a *clunk* as Schmidt set the receiver down, followed by a faint conversation. Her hand shook. *I must get out of here. Himmler may be in Bludenz already.* She felt like dropping the phone and running.

Schmidt picked up again and said. "Herr Lang is with Herr Wolff. They cannot be disturbed under any circumstances. You may leave a message with me, however, and I shall see that Herr Lang gets it."

Mary was certain any message would be relayed to Hitler before Jung had a look at it. "Tell him . . . " *Should I just repeat Olbricht's message? No, it might fool a hotel clerk, but it won't fool Hitler. Screw it.* "Tell him Reichsführer Himmler is on his way there."

"Thank you. I shall let them know immediately." Schmidt ended the call.

Them. Mary hung up the receiver. *It's out of my hands, now.* She took the stairs to her room two at a time, washed, changed into her uniform, and threw her overnight gear into the shoulder bag. As she closed it, she heard a vehicle outside. *Crap! That must be Himmler. He's come for us already!*

She looked out the window. A courier and his passenger parked their side-car equipped motorcycle beside the biergarten. Mary watched them go inside, thinking, *If they're Himmler's men, they wouldn't be going for beer. I still have time.* She put on her chauffeur's cap and raced outside and down the street to the motorcycle.

As Mary approached, she heard the motorcycle's engine crackling and popping. *Still hot, no need to use the choke.* She looked at the bike. *The key's in the ignition!* She hopped on, adjusted the engine settings, twisted the throttle, turned the key, then put her foot on the starter lever, trying not to think what would happen if the bike didn't start. She kicked once . . . and twice . . . and *bam!* The engine turned over, ran raggedly for a few seconds, then smoothed out. "Halleluia!"

Mary thundered away from the curb. Behind her, over the noise, she heard someone yelling. She glanced in the mirror and saw the courier standing outside the biergarten, shaking his fist and swearing.

Mary roared along the road uphill out of Bludenz on the stolen motorcycle, making her way up multiple switchbacks toward Löwensburg, leaning into the left-hand turns, going as fast as she dared. She didn't know what kind of reception she'd receive at the top, but she had to get Jung out of Löwensburg before Himmler arrived. *Whatever happens, I'll be with Carl.*

Chapter 44
Innsbruck-Bludenz Road
10:55 AM, July 1, 1942

Olbricht leaned out the Opel's window. "Ja, Reichsführer Himmler. I am conducting some urgent business for the Führer. I trust you do not intend to interfere?"

"Not at all." Himmler smirked, his basilisk eyes slits behind his spectacles. "I would like to speak with you for a few minutes, if you do not mind."

Olbricht did mind, but knew better than to say so. "Whatever you say, Reichsführer."

"Get out, and we will talk."

Olbricht signaled for Sigmund to remain in his seat and climbed out of the Opel. But Himmler noticed that the General was not alone. "Who is that man?" He pointed at Sigmund.

Olbricht knew the safest approach was to tell Himmler the truth and pray that Sigmund would not attempt to escape. "This is Herr Doktor Rosenberg."

"Ha!" Himmler gave a short, sharp laugh, almost a bark. Olbricht had seldom seen Himmler laugh. "Another Dr. Rosenberg? I had no idea there were two of him." He turned to his adjutant. "Vogel? Did you know of this?"

Vogel shook his head.

Rosenberg clutched at the door handle beside him. Himmler waved a finger, and Vogel stepped up and blocked the door with his leg, holding up a hand. Sigmund slumped back in his seat.

"Let him out and bring him!" Himmler ordered. "Come, General, we will speak away from the others." He turned and walked away.

Olbricht followed Himmler. Sigmund came close behind, now carrying the box of ashes, accompanied by Vogel. Himmler led them to a Mercedes parked well away from the other vehicles.

"What is in that box?" Himmler asked Sigmund before they got into the vehicle.

"My father's ashes."

"Get rid of those," Himmler ordered Vogel, who snatched the box away from Sigmund, pulled off the lid, and dumped the contents in the nearest ditch, sending up a cloud of fine, grey dust. Vogel dusted his gloved hands and smirked at Sigmund, who cried out in protest.

Olbricht looked at Vogel and muttered, *"Arschloch!"*

Himmler addressed the General and Sigmund. "Get in." He gestured toward the back seat as he got into the front. Vogel closed the rear door and stepped away from the vehicle.

Himmler asked, "Now, what is all this business with Carl Jung?"

Olbricht said, "The Führer has medical concerns that I am not permitted to speak of. You have no need to know, Reichsführer, with all due respect. Herr Doktor Jung is a neutral Swiss, a leading practitioner who has agreed to come to Germany in return for the release of Dr. Rosenberg's father, now deceased by your order. But you must know all this, Reichsführer. Why are you getting involved?"

"A question whose answer you have no need to know,

Olbricht." Himmler turned to Rosenberg. "I take it you are standing in for your late father."

Sigmund, cowering in the back seat of the Mercedes, croaked his answer, "Yes."

Himmler examined Rosenberg's papers, then returned them. "You may come in handy. You will come with me." He turned to Olbricht. "You, on the other hand, are done here. You may return to Berlin. As Halder ordered, not so?"

"I have given my *soldatenwort* that Dr. Jung will be allowed to leave Germany safely. The arrangement with the Führer also included the release of the elder Dr. Rosenberg. Since he is no longer alive, I took the son, instead, hoping that would be acceptable to Dr. Jung. I cannot allow you remove Sigmund from my custody."

"He will be perfectly safe with me, Herr General. But let us not quarrel over a Jew. If you must, you may accompany us in your car . . . " Himmler cast a critical eye in the direction of the battle-scarred, field-grey Opel. " . . . Assuming that it continues to run. We shall rendezvous at Bludenz and see what may be arranged for Herr Doktor Jung. That is where you were going, not so?"

Olbricht nodded stiffly. *Is there anything that Himmler does not know?*

Chapter 45
Löwensburg Entrance
11:10 AM, July 1, 1942

The road leveled off, and Mary slowed the motorcycle as soon as she saw the huge Nazi eagle above the tunnel entrance. She clutched the handlebars tighter at the sight of it. *Will the guards remember me from yesterday? Or has the courier reported that I stole his motorcycle? Will they shoot me on sight?*

As Mary reached the parking area, she pulled off her leather cap to let her hair blow freely. She saw the guards looking at her, alert but not alarmed by her presence. She motored slowly to the entrance and parked nearby, then pulled out her papers and walked over to the guards.

"I am Frau Rufenacht, here to pick up Herr Lang. Please, could you tell him I have come?"

One guard took a cursory look at her papers and handed them back. Another asked, "Is Herr Lang the elderly gentleman you dropped off yesterday?"

"Yes. He was visiting Herr Wolff."

The first guard opened a small metal enclosure beside the doorway and took out a telephone receiver. He dialed a number and handed the phone to Mary. "You are connected to Herr Wolff's adjutant, *Leutnant* Schmidt. Go ahead."

Mary said, "Herr *Leutnant* Schmidt, I have arrived to pick up Herr Lang."

"I did not know you were coming, Is this Frau Rufenacht?"

"Yes. I thought it best to take my employer home, since Herr Wolff is expecting company."

"Wait there at the entrance, please, and I will let them know you are here."

"Thanks." *I hope this doesn't take long. I want to get us out of here before Himmler turns up.*

Chapter 46
Dining Room, Löwensburg
11:15 AM, July 1, 1942

Jung sat across from Hitler in the dining room again, talking about operas they'd enjoyed. Outside, clouds scudded across the mountains. Their table was set with a vase full of fresh hyacinths, coffee cups, and remnants of strudel on fine china. In front of Hitler sat the ever-present box of chocolates; Jung had his notebook and the red medical record folder close at hand. A bodyguard passed through the room, silently handing Hitler a message on his way. Without reading it, Hitler met Jung's eyes. "So, Dr. Jung? Where does that leave us?"

Jung considered how to answer the question. *I got what I came for. From here on, it is mostly risk, with little to gain. I must give Hitler no reason to toss me in a camp. Above all, I must not judge him.* Jung picked up his notepad and spoke cautiously. "I believe we made progress on the insomnia."

Nodding in agreement, Hitler took a stem of blossoms from the vase beside him.

Jung wondered what that signified, but he paged through his notes and continued reassuringly, "I have seen no signs at all of schizophrenia or psychosis." *Yet.* "Some unresolved grief is evident, probably a result of the losses we discussed."

"Ja, there is grief." Hitler spun the flower stem in his fingers. "That is certain. Anything else?"

The less Hitler thinks I know, the better. "Not a lot. If you had allowed me to analyze your dreams, I might have more insight." *Now the risky part.* Jung tapped the notepad with a finger. "You have read about mother complexes?"

"Ja, of course," Hitler didn't look pleased with this topic, frowning, even though he'd admitted that he had been close to his mother.

Jung hurried to say, "A mother complex is not at all unusual. In fact, it is a potential component of everyone's psyche, and may often be beneficial."

Hitler plucked a blossom from the stem. "Beneficial? In what way?"

Now I must flatter him. "It can promote the formation of lasting friendships, and result in strong will-power, well-defined goals, exceptional ambition, and a revolutionary spirit."

Jung saw a hint of a smile cross Hitler's lips.

That's all true, Jung thought, *but if I had listed the negative aspects of a mother complex, Hitler would not be smiling; he would be throwing me off his balcony.*

"Ja, ja, I have read your books." Hitler shrugged and pulled off another blossom, then looked at Jung. "Do you still imagine I have a guilt complex?"

Torn between his mission, his survival, and his duty as a physician, Jung tried to avoid the issue. "I am not sure," he lied.

Hitler stared at him with narrowed, deep blue eyes, then rapidly tore several more blossoms off the stem. "Is that so?"

He knows I'm lying, Jung realized with a twinge. *I am in real trouble and must quickly muddy the waters with truth.* He said, "It could be very serious, if you have one."

"But I do not!" Hitler snarled. "As I have already told you, my conscience is perfectly clear, "

Mine surely isn't. I have just lied to a client and, worse yet, got caught. I need to regain Hitler's confidence. I must face the issue honestly, whatever the risk. Jung trembled as he said, "A guilt complex can sap your energy. If you suffer further from exhaustion or insomnia, you should consider therapy based on that possibility." *Now I must change the subject immediately. But to what?*

Jung saw the box of candy beside Hitler and pointed at it, saying, "I also suggest you eat fewer chocolates." He attempted a friendly smile.

Hitler tightened his lips and looked at the candy with his brow furrowed.

Clearly, that isn't going to happen, but Hitler has taken the bait. I can continue moving the conversation away from guilt complexes. Jung put a hand on the red folder and said, "Also, I see in your medical report that Dr. Morrell is giving you injections containing amphetamines. If you can't cut out the candy, I would suggest tapering off those injections. They can interfere with sleep."

"I trust Herr Doktor Morrell implicitly!" Hitler insisted. "He made me much better when other doctors were of no help at all . . . " The Führer continued to say what a fine fellow Morrell was, all the while ripping blooms off the hyacinth.

Jung grew uneasy and felt sweat bead up on his forehead. *Morrell is a quack, but this is a safer topic than Hitler's guilt due to murdering Geli. But I had better not even think of the murder; if Hitler senses I know he killed her, I will be shot. And probably Mary, as well.*

Then Jung recalled three clients he'd treated after the First World War. *Maybe I can convince Hitler he does have a guilt complex, if I make it appear unrelated to Geli. That could help get me out of here alive.*

"You know," Jung said, "In the 20's, I treated several former soldiers who suffered from a certain amount of guilt just for surviving. You mentioned losing friends. We should consider the possibility that you have some unconscious regrets for living, when they did not."

Hitler was silent for several moments and put down the flower before saying with a little shrug, "I was greatly saddened at the time, but I never felt guilt for surviving. After all, that was everyone's objective."

"You wouldn't necessarily be aware of those feelings," Jung persisted. "It is an unconscious thing, as the books say. Perhaps it would help to tell me more about the incident."

Hitler nodded and began his story, one Jung could sense he'd told many times. "In 1914, we were in the trenches near Ypres. My friends and I were eating dinner together one night, as we always did. Despite the rough conditions, we were very jolly. Without warning, a Voice in my mind said to me, 'Get up and go over there.' It was so emphatic that I obeyed as if ordered, without thinking."

Jung scrutinized Hitler as he spoke, looking for signs of lying. There were none. *Of course, with a tale so old, there might not be a sign. But the longer he talks, the safer I'll feel.*

Hitler continued. "I walked about twenty meters down the trench, carrying my dinner in its tin pail. My friends seemed puzzled when I left them, but I sat down in the new spot and resumed eating. Within seconds, there came a flash and an explosion."

Hitler slumped, his unfocused gaze directed down at the table, his face emotionless, his hands limp on the arms of the chair. "A stray shell had burst over where I had been sitting before. Everyone there was killed. Some of those men, I knew well." Hitler looked up at Jung. "So you may be right. I should have warned them."

"You couldn't have known how to warn them, could

you?"

Hitler shook his head and took a deep breath. "I have, ever since, relied on that Voice implicitly, again and again. It may take time, but once it speaks, it never fails me." Hitler stared into Jung's eyes. "Do you think I am a *Verrückter*, someone who hears voices?"

"Not at all, Herr Hitler. My mother also heard voices." Jung left out the fact that his mother had once been placed in an institution. "Anyway, give it some thought. As I said, if the sleeplessness resumes, you can see another psychiatrist to explore your buried feelings regarding the loss of your comrades. For now, I think we have done all we can."

"Good."

Good, he says! I have escaped from the trap I fell into! Elated, Jung had a sudden inspiration. "I have a present for you." He reached down beside his chair and took Mary's mandala from his briefcase. "Perhaps this will help you to sleep another time."

"I thank you very much, Herr Doktor Jung. You really are most kind, but I must also have my medical records back . . ."

"Certainly." Jung handed him the red folder along with the mandala.

Hitler narrowed his eyes and pointed into the briefcase. ". . . And all your notes."

Jung was caught by surprise, but after a moment realized Hitler was right. *I've finished the evaluation; I no longer need the notes.* Though Jung wanted to keep them for his psychological profile of Hitler, any delay might hint that he had other uses in mind for them. Jung took the pad with both hands and slid it towards Hitler, wondering, *How much of that will I be able to reconstruct later?*

Hitler took the mandala and the documents. Standing, he said, "Well, you may be on your way, then, Herr Doktor Jung. Thank you for coming. Your visit has been most interesting. And helpful."

Hitler held out his hand. Jung took it quickly, thinking, *We'll be home in a few hours, and I can wash my hand.*

Hitler pointed at the note on the table. "Frau Rufenacht is waiting for you at the tunnel entrance." He turned and strode out of the room, motioning to one of the guards to see Jung out.

Why didn't Hitler tell me right away that Mary was waiting? Another of his games? But I have what I came for! And more! Jung felt a great sense of relief and a thrill of triumph. *Now we just have to rendezvous with Olbricht and Marcus and drive back to Mauren. We are almost home.*

The tunnel's outer door was open, so Jung saw daylight far ahead as he exited from the elevator. He looked overhead at the electric lights. *No more Hitler-games with the tunnel lights today?* he thought. *Did he really turn them off yesterday? I wonder if he has other little jokes to play on us before we leave Germany. I certainly hope not.*

When Jung was halfway down the tunnel, he saw someone silhouetted in the distant doorway. *It's Mary!* he thought, and walked faster.

At the portal, Jung strode out into a grey day, the sunshine dimmed by scattered clouds. There stood Mary, and the guards. And a grey camouflaged motorcycle with a sidecar. No run-down, war-torn Opel. No Olbricht. And, most upsetting, no Marcus Rosenberg.

Chapter 47
Löwensburg Entrance
11:30 AM, July 1, 1942

When Mary saw Jung come out of the tunnel, she rushed forward and embraced him. "I'm *so* glad to see you," she said.

"Where is Marcus?" he asked. "Where is General Olbricht?"

Mary took Jung's arm and led him towards the motorbike without speaking further. As soon as they were beyond earshot of the guards, she said, "Olbricht called and said to get out of Germany as soon as possible. Himmler's on his way here. Get in."

He looked at the vehicle and wrinkled his brow. "I don't know if I am up to riding in that contraption all the way home."

"Olbricht has the car. This was all I could find." Mary took Jung's briefcase from him and tossed it into the sidecar.

"Find?" Jung's eyebrows lifted. "You didn't steal it, did you?"

"Sure, I did. But there's more bad news. Marcus is dead. Himmler's orders, I'm guessing."

"Damn Himmler! Poor Marcus. He . . . he was one of my best—"

The clouds began to sprinkle rain, spattering Mary and Carl with drops.

"No time for that now. Let's go." She looked up at the darkening sky. *Crud. I hate riding on wet pavement.* She handed Jung her cap. "Here. Wear this."

He put on the cap and got in. "It has been forty years since I rode in one of these things."

"It's only thirty kilometers to Mauren. Once we're there, we'll have the Auburn, and you can rest. You'll be okay." *I hope.*

A guard beside the tunnel door closed a cabinet, turned, and held up a hand. "Halt!"

Mary's heart skipped a beat. *Now what?* She gunned the accelerator, preparing to make a fast departure.

The guard ran toward them. "Herr Lang, you must not forget your pipe," he said, handing a clasp envelope to Jung.

Jung thanked him and stuffed the pipe and tobacco into his pockets.

They'd have come after us if they looked inside! Mary thought, pulling away slowly.

She followed the road downhill to the main road and then northwest, away from Bludenz. The traffic in their direction was mostly slow-moving empty produce trucks on their way back to Liechtenstein and Switzerland. *How much will this delay us?* Mary wondered, riding cautiously over the wet macadam.

At first, she passed the trucks one or two at a time, trying not to frighten Jung or tire him. *Where the hell is Himmler?* she wondered. *He could be anywhere between here and Innsbruck. But his car will have to get around every truck I pass. The more I pass, the better.* She checked the road behind them, then pulled out and, taking the motorbike to over a hundred kph, passed eight trucks during a gap in oncoming traffic. *Open road ahead, at last!*

Mary glanced at Jung, who was holding on tight. He let go with one hand, waved it at her, then gripped the sidecar again. *He looks tired. And wet.* She slowed a little.

Soon the road narrowed as it passed over a stone bridge. Far ahead, Mary noticed a huge structure on a mountainside. *We're nearing Feldkirch.* She let up on the throttle and coasted, peering in the rain-speckled handlebar mirror. *Nobody in pursuit. Looks like we're going to make it!*

An armored troop carrier passed by, going the other way. *Uh-oh! Waffen SS insignia. Did they see us?* Several hundred meters behind the troop carrier was another. It slowed, swerved, and stopped dead, blocking the road in front of Mary. Drainage ditches full of ferns on both sides prevented maneuvering around the vehicle. She braked hard. More black-uniformed SS men than she could count were piling out of the vehicle. *Damn! Himmler phoned ahead.*

"Trouble, Carl," she yelled loud enough for Jung to hear.

"I see them. Can you turn around?" he shouted.

Mary looked back and saw the same thing there: SS troops from the first vehicle were closing off the road behind her. "Too late," she shouted, down-shifting and bringing the motorcycle to a full stop just short of an SS man standing steadfast in the roadway, his hand upraised.

He jabbed a finger at Mary, and, without speaking, pointed at a spot beside the road. Mary pulled the motorbike into it, and an officer carrying an MP40 motioned for her to cut the engine. She shut it down properly. Silence.

The officer walked around the motorcycle and looked down at Jung in the sidecar. "You are Herr Doktor Carl Jung?"

"Yes."

"Your papers," he demanded.

Mary and Carl surrendered their passports and visas to him. He examined the documents closely, then said, "You two, come with me. Leave the motorcycle where it is." He stared at the latter. "That is a military dispatch rider's motorcycle. The penalty for stealing one is death."

Mary said quickly, "I'm the one who borrowed it. Dr. Jung wasn't there when I took it."

The SS officer turned away from her. "That is not important now. Walk this way," he ordered, striding past the troop carrier towards a Volkswagen cabriolet parked beside the road.

As he struggled to keep up, Jung asked, "Where are you taking us?"

The officer pointed at the ancient fortress on the mountain above them. "There. Schattenburg." He thrust them into the back seat of the car, where he handcuffed them to an iron ring attached to the floorboard. Then he sped towards Schattenburg via a long series of switchbacks.

Mary gripped Carl's hand. It was wet and cold. She went round and round in her head, thinking, *I should have gone faster. I should have demanded a car and driver from Hitler. I should have waited until dark . . . .*

At the top of the mountain, the SS officer released them and took them inside, where two guards escorted them down several flights of stone stairs and into a shadowy room full of torture engines and implements, deep in the bowels of Schattenburg castle. There, they shoved Mary and Jung into a small, iron-barred cage, slammed the door, locked it, and went away.

"Hell and damnation!" Mary said. *I've got to get out of here! I can't let Carl die like this!*

Jung took off Mary's leather helmet and gave it to her. "I think we're in deep trouble."

A long silence followed. The minutes ticked by slowly. *This may be the end,* Mary thought. *Why did I talk Carl into this? This isn't his fight; he's a neutral. The worst part is, the only helpful thing I've done for him is giving him a damned cyanide vial. If he didn't lose it.*

She leaned close to Carl and whispered, "You still have your ampule?"

"Yes. You?" He shivered.

She nodded and put her arm around him. "I do, but we don't know what Himmler wants, yet."

"By the time we find out, we may be strapped onto one of those." Jung pointed at the nearby torture devices. "I think I'll put it where I can use it quickly."

"Put it in your cheek, but don't forget it's there!" Mary whispered.

Jung took the little container out of the tobacco pouch and put the glass vial inside it between a cheek and his upper teeth. Mary did the same with hers, thinking, *We probably will be dead in less than an hour.*

Chapter 48
Schattenburg
12:05 PM, July 1, 1942

An eternity passed before a guard returned and opened the cell door. "Come out," he ordered. "The restroom is there, beside our spiked chair."

The toilet facility had no door. Jung turned his back and let Mary use it first. While they relieved themselves, the guard turned on the torture chamber lights.

Jung tried not to look at the contents of the chamber. *I wish he'd left the lights off. I'd rather not be reminded what these devilish things are designed to do.*

The guard sat on the nearest torture engine, a three meter long table, very sturdy, with ankle straps at one end and a horizontal capstan at the other. "You may sit." He indicated a similar rack opposite him. "We will wait here. Reichsführer Himmler will arrive shortly." He smirked and waved a hand at the room's hideous furnishings. "If you have any questions about how these work, please ask."

"What the hell have I gotten you into?" Mary muttered after a minute of silence.

Jung hissed his reply. "We must get out of here. Whatever it takes. I have what Dulles wants."

The SS man stirred. "No talking."

"May we smoke?" Jung asked him. *I wonder if I can cock the gun and shoot him before he realizes it's not a pipe.*

Mary jabbed an elbow into Jung's side.

"No," the SS man said.

Jung stared at the floor, his eyes avoiding the fiendish devices surrounding them. He then stared up at the ceiling, which was a mistake. It was festooned with hooks and pulleys, both small and large, whose purposes he couldn't stop imagining. He looked at Mary and tried to smile, but failed.

A commotion in the hallway outside the chamber roused Jung. Jackbooted feet sounded on the stone stairs. "He's here," Jung said, standing up.

Mary stood beside him, took his hand and squeezed it. Seconds later, Himmler entered, his eyes sparkling behind his spectacles as he approached Jung, accompanied by an aide. "So you are the famous mind-doctor. I am Heinrich Himmler, Reichsführer SS."

"We know who you are," Mary said.

Himmler pointed at her. "Vogel, shut the bitch up."

Himmler's aide grinned and swung an open hand at Mary's face. She fell back against the rack, twisting away from Vogel to avoid the slap by a mere centimeter.

Jung looked on in horror. *If Vogel connects, Mary's ampule might be crushed. She could die.* "Stop!" he yelled.

"Enough," Himmler told Vogel. "Why have you come to Germany, Herr Doktor Jung?"

"A professional matter," Jung replied, relieved that Himmler had called off his aide.

"Concerning the Führer, not so?"

Betraying Hitler to the Allies is one thing; giving information to Himmler is another. I can't just tell him everything. "Professional secrecy forbids me to answer that question."

Himmler frowned. "I doubt you would be visiting Germany as a tourist. There's only one thing that could draw the famous Dr. Jung here, and that would be a patient of the greatest importance. So, you see, I already know the answer to my question."

"Then why did you ask it?"

"Just to get our conversation moving in a friendly manner. To start."

"If it seems to be moving, that is an illusion. I have nothing to say to you."

"Since you are not eager to answer questions, nor I to ask them, I will just tell you what I think." Himmler strode back and forth in the aisle between the two racks, gesticulating with one hand. "The OKW have requested that you interview the Führer and determine whether he is of sound mind. You have completed your examination and are supposed to give General Olbricht your results, at which point you will receive payment for your services." He turned back to Jung. "Not so?"

"I'm not being paid; I was guaranteed that Herr Hitler would release Dr. Marcus Rosenberg from a concentration camp and let us leave Germany unhindered. That was to be my only payment."

"How noble. Now tell me your . . . diagnosis, would you call it?"

I shouldn't tell him anything, unless I really must, Jung thought. "Why do you not simply call Hitler and ask his permission to receive a copy of my report?"

Himmler waved away that idea. "A copy might be of value. But a copy he doesn't know I have would be of greater value." The Reichsführer SS sidled close to Mary, making her cringe. He ignored her and gave the nearest capstan an inquisitive spin. This seemed to amuse him.

That's a threat, Jung noted. "Then ask General Olbricht for a copy, and let us go back to Switzerland, as we were promised."

"Only you and Dr. Rosenberg were to be given safe passage." Himmler gripped Mary's arm and glared at Jung. "I do not believe this woman is covered by Führer's guarantee of leaving Germany safely. "

"Yes, she is!" Jung's voice rose. He quickly composed himself and added, "She accompanied me here; it's understood she leaves with me."

"Do you have that in writing?"

"I took General Olbricht's word as a German officer for our arrangement." Jung asked himself, *Why didn't I get this written down? It seems so stupid of me, now.* "My visa includes her."

Himmler pulled their papers from an inside pocket and held them up. "Frau Rufenacht is not named on these documents."

He's going to force me to cooperate by using Mary, Jung thought. "Those cover me and my driver. Frau Rufenacht is my driver."

Himmler gazed around the room, looking at all the torture devices. "Do you know what all these things are, Herr Doktor Jung?"

"I believe I do." Jung felt sweat running down his forehead.

The Reichsführer stalked the room. "Thumbscrews . . . an iron boot . . . strappado . . . spiked press . . . . He paused before an oversize iron statue of a woman in a dress. "This is our Iron Maiden. She has been in this room for over three hundred years. Vogel, show Doktor Jung some of her finer points." Himmler smirked.

Vogel took a long crowbar off the wall and levered the contraption open, revealing a forest of strategically placed spikes. He silently indicated on his own body where each spike went, making grotesque faces.

"Oh, just tell him, Carl!" Mary hissed. "Client secrets aren't worth risking our lives."

Jung felt a wave of nausea and looked away from the Iron Maiden. "Close it up, I'll give you the information you want."

The Reichsführer shook his head. "First tell me: is the Führer sane? Or insane?"

Jung hesitated. *If I say he's insane, Germany will get a new Führer who can defeat the Allies. If I say he's sane, Hitler will stay in power, his evil intentions unrestrained. If I delay another second, Mary may bite her cyanide vial. I have to give in.*

"He is sane," Jung said. "His narcissism, his psycho-neuroses, and his complexes fall short of what we call insanity. That is my assessment." Jung felt more relief than guilt at telling Himmler this. He also saw Mary relax and lean on the rack beside them.

Himmler turned on his heel and started up the stone stairs. "Bring them to the yellow room," he ordered Vogel.

Whatever the yellow room is, it can't be worse than this, Jung thought. *Or can it?*

Vogel and the guard took Jung and Mary up the stairs and down a corridor to a high-ceilinged Baroque room with pale yellow walls. Besides the double door entry from the corridor, two ornate doors at either end, one gold-embellished, one silver, gave access from adjoining rooms. No instruments of terror, just fine rugs and antique furnishings. Jung felt his heartbeat return to near-normal.

Himmler had not yet arrived. Jung and Mary and the guards waited by a window, perched on delicate chairs—*probably worth a hundred Reichsmarks each,* Jung noted.

An ormolu clock ticked away the seconds on a marble-and-ebony sideboard. Jung looked at a guard, who looked back at him and shrugged. *All in a day's work to him.*

Himmler surprised Jung by entering through the gold door, closing it behind him. "Vogel, you and the guards wait in the foyer downstairs." When they were gone, Himmler indicated a desk and chair beside the gold door.

"Doktor Jung, sit there. There is paper in the drawer. Write your assessment of the Führer, and date it yesterday, but do not sign it." He took out an expensive-looking blue pen from an inside jacket pocket and handed it to Jung.

Jung uncapped the pen and took a piece of paper from the desk. He felt reluctant to do this, but found it far easier than spending another minute in the torture chamber downstairs. He wrote:

Feldkirch, Ostmark, June 30, 1942. I, Carl Gustav Jung, MD, doctor of psychiatry, find the client, Adolf Hitler, of sound mind, with no impediment to performing his necessary tasks.

He blotted the wet ink so it wouldn't smear. "Does that suffice?" he asked Himmler.

The Reichsführer read it, then placed the blotter so that it covered the text. He went out by the gold door and returned with two sturdy civilians. Jung signed the statement, followed by the two witnesses, who were each sworn to secrecy, and given a five Reichsmark coin. After blotting their signatures, Himmler escorted them out into the corridor and could be heard giving them directions to the exit.

He returned, folded up the diagnosis and put it in his inside pocket. Mary, much to Jung's horror, took out her lipstick and dabbed some on her lips. She asked, "May we leave, now, Reichsführer?"

"No. Herr Doktor Jung, take out, please, another piece of paper."

What now? Jung sat back in his chair, unnerved. He thought once more of the torture engines downstairs and the cyanide capsule in his mouth, and prayed that he and Mary would depart from Schattenburg soon. Taking more paper from the drawer, he asked, "What am I supposed to write?"

Himmler clucked. "You are so straight-forward, Doktor Jung! Of course, I want you to write there a statement that

Hitler is crazy as a loon."

"What?"

"Oh, you do not have to phrase it quite that rudely. Use your favorite professional euphemism that means, as the English say, 'barmy in the crumpet.'"

I don't understand—"

"You are not required to understand. But let us say, I believe in keeping all my options open. Write. And date it today, please." He waved a commanding finger at the paper.

Jung wrote:

Feldkirch, Ostmark, July 1, 1942. I, Carl Gustav Jung, MD, doctor of psychiatry, find the client, Adolf Hitler, of unsound mind, with significant impediments to performing his necessary tasks.

Again, Himmler covered the text with the blotter and brought in a new pair of witnesses by the silver door. These, too, signed below Jung, were sworn to secrecy, and given five Reichsmarks before being taken out into the corridor by Himmler.

The instant he left the room, Mary ran to the desk, moved the blotter, and photographed the document. Jung was caught by surprise, but managed to shove the blotter back in place while Mary made it back to her chair by the window just before Himmler returned.

Himmler stood at the desk, looking down, frowning.

Fear gripped Jung. *Something is wrong. Does Himmler know Mary photographed the document? How can he tell? Did I put the blotter back in the wrong place?*

But Himmler just put the second diagnosis in his pocket with the first, patted them several times, as if to make sure they were there, then rubbed his hands together and said, "And now, Herr Doktor Jung, I must decide what to do with you."

Jung said, "We've given you what you wanted. Why not let us return to Switzerland?"

Himmler folded his arms. "And why would I do that? You are of no further use to me, but you could possibly be a threat."

Jung replied in as steady a voice as he could manage, "Once again, my agreement with Hitler was that he would let us leave Germany after my visit. I helped him to sleep and have submitted my accurate evaluation, as agreed."

Mary stood. "If you don't release us, Hitler will make trouble for you."

Himmler shook his head. "If the Führer objects to my killing you, I will simply hand over Dr. Jung's first evaluation. Once he has proof of his sanity, he, too, has no further need of you." Himmler smiled and swept a hand through the air in front of him.

Jung insisted, "My safety was also guaranteed by General Olbricht. How do you think he will react to your violation of his *soldatenwort*?"

"He can do nothing! If necessary, I will have him tossed in a camp."

"If you do that, you'll provoke the entire OKW!" Jung said.

"They have all sworn oaths of loyalty to Hitler. He will keep them in line. In accordance with the Führer principle, they will obey as long as he lives."

"But what if you and Hitler have a falling out?" Jung asked, hoping to find himself and Mary an escape.

"For that, I have the second evaluation." Himmler laughed, a high-pitched cackle. "He will continue to see things my way, lest that assessment somehow fall into the wrong hands."

We're in deep trouble, but I mustn't panic. Think of something, he reprimanded himself. He said, "My Swiss and Swedish colleagues think highly of me. If I don't return, they will apply pressure that could affect Germany's supply of ball bearings and precision manufacturing instruments."

Himmler removed his spectacles and began cleaning them with his handkerchief. "We can win the war without those things."

"Baloney!" Mary said. "You're not winning the war *with* them."

Himmler scoffed. "We could simply invade Switzerland and force you to produce such goods at the point of a gun." He tried to put his glasses back on, but caught one ear piece in his left eye.

We're getting to him, Jung thought. *Keep the pressure on.* "We've mined all the Alpine passes. If German forces invade Switzerland, we'll just blow up the passes on top of them. And the factories along with them."

Mary added, "And the Swiss numbered bank accounts, too."

Himmler's face fell. "We . . . we'll seize the bullion."

Touché! Himmler has Swiss bank accounts, the snake! Jung realized.

"Not if you can't find it, Herr Himmler," Mary replied. "You could look for a thousand years and not find a pfennig."

Jung stepped in again. "Your Führer has attacked Russia. Remember how that ended for Napoleon! Maybe you should worry what will happen when you lose."

"Nonsense." Himmler wiped his brow with the handkerchief. "It is summertime, and we are only a few weeks from total victory in Russia."

"Fine," Jung said. "If you are that sure of victory, what difference will it make if we go back to Switzerland? You gain nothing by imprisoning us and have much to lose. Why take the risk? What are you afraid of?"

"That you will talk about your visit here to treat the Führer. The German people could draw the wrong conclusion."

Jung said, "Yes, and the Swiss people could draw the wrong conclusion, too. I'd be forever known as 'that therapist who treated Hitler.' It would mean the death of my professional career."

After a second, Himmler said, "You might send Olbricht another diagnosis. That would complicate things."

"I'll give you my word that I won't do that," Jung replied.

Himmler paused again, then smirked and said, "I have a much better idea." He looked at Mary.

"What are you going to do?" she asked, her voice unsteady.

"I have kept my options open." Himmler turned away and motioned. "Follow me outside and see."

Chapter 49
Outside Schattenburg
12:35 PM, July 1, 1942

Himmler escorted Jung and Mary to the fortress entrance. Jung saw it had stopped raining. The next thing he noticed was Friedrich Olbricht, leaning against his convertible, smoking. *A friendly face at last!*

Mary exclaimed, "General! You came back!"

He smiled and walked towards them. "I was delayed. I came as soon as I could." Turning to Mary, he asked, "You understood the message I sent you at the gasthaus?"

"Yes." She pointed silently at Himmler.

Himmler interrupted. "General, Herr Doktor Jung will ride back to Mauren with my adjutant. I cannot let you accompany him, lest you discuss his evaluation of the Führer. That is *verboten*. The matter is fully in my hands."

Olbricht's jaw clenched. He hurled his cigarette to the pavement and crushed it beneath his boot.

Himmler turned to Jung and Mary. "General Olbricht is leaving for Berlin. Say goodbye and nothing else."

Mary shook the General's hand and said, "Auf Wiedersehen, Herr General!"

"Auf Wiedersehen, Maria. It has been a pleasure

meeting you." He turned and put out his hand to Jung. "I suspect we shall not see each other again, Dr. Jung. Goodbye."

Jung grasped his hand. "Goodbye, General. I wish you good fortune."

Himmler said, "Leave us now, General! Heil Hitler!"

Olbricht returned Himmler's salute, then pivoted and strode away without looking back.

"We are done here," Himmler said.

"I assume you'll trust me not to send Olbricht a letter?" Jung asked.

Himmler nodded. "If you will give me your word as a professional. And of course, nothing would prevent me from intercepting such a letter. But more importantly, I have insurance."

"Insurance?"

"Come." Himmler led them to where the cars of his cortège were parked. He motioned to Vogel, who dragged a man by an arm out of the biggest Mercedes and brought him forward. The man, tear streaks down his face, reached out his arms to Jung. "Dr. Jung! Help me!"

I don't recognize this man. Turning to Himmler, Jung asked, "Who is this?"

"This is your friend from Vienna, Sigmund Rosenberg."

"Sigmund!" Jung embraced his friend. *He's been in a concentration camp so long, he no longer looks like the man I knew!*

Sigmund wept. "Dr. Jung, they killed my father. Reduced him to ashes, then put him in a shoebox."

Jung's own eyes filled with tears. He couldn't bear to look at Sigmund's anguish. "I heard Marcus has been killed. I'm sorry, Sigmund. I'll appeal to Hitler and try to get you released."

"No, you won't!" Himmler said.

Sigmund sobbed and laid his head against Jung's shoulder.

Himmler's face bore a slightly amused air. "I intend to keep this Jew in a safe place to ensure your sensible behavior, Doktor Jung: You must agree not to contact Hitler or anyone at the OKW, not to publish your diagnosis—nothing at all about Hitler—including articles like 'This is the Führer's Brain' in *Time Magazine*."

"Very well, I promise not to contact the OKW or Hitler, or publish anything more about Hitler's mind." *If Himmler only knew what I really plan to do!*

"Or mine, either, come to think of it," Himmler added.

"I agree. May I ask where Rosenberg will be kept?"

"I have a place for him in Munich."

Jung wondered if Sigmund would end up in another concentration camp. "What about after the war?"

"After Germany is victorious?" Himmler shrugged. "He can probably remain in Munich, if you cooperate, as agreed."

"What if Germany loses the war?"

Himmler frowned. "Do not try my patience with more ridiculous notions, Doktor Jung." He took out Carl and Mary's papers and handed them to his adjutant. "Captain Vogel will drive you and Frau Rufenacht to the Mauren border-crossing." Himmler turned to Sigmund and said, "Jew, you will ride with me to Munich."

Sigmund stood back and looked at the ground between him and Himmler, shoulders slumped, saying nothing, visibly hoping for nothing. As Himmler led him away, Jung watched Sigmund through tear-filled eyes. *If I never see him again,* Jung thought, *I'll always remember him like this.*

Later, Jung rode towards Mauren in the back of a small Mercedes Benz with Vogel at the wheel. Mary sat next to Vogel, who persisted in trying to get her to make small talk, with little success.

Chapter 50
Mauren
1:10 PM, July 1, 1942

At the Mauren border-crossing, Vogel stopped the Mercedes beside the guard shelter and went inside with Jung and Mary's papers. They watched anxiously from the car. "Do you think we're safe?" Jung asked Mary.

"Yeah, pretty sure. Vogel has his orders. Nazis are great believers in following orders." Mary looked at the barbed wire gate, twenty meters ahead of them. *But Himmler still could phone here with new orders,* she thought. *We won't be safe until we're on the other side of that border."*

"I hope you're right," Jung said, "the longer I have this suicide ampule in my mouth, the more afraid I am I'll accidentally swallow it."

"Just don't bite it. Only another few minutes, Carl."

They both exhaled loudly as Vogel came out. He jerked their doors open, saying, "Out." He returned their documents and escorted them to where the Auburn was parked. "Auf wiedersehen, Herr Doktor Jung, Frau Rufenacht." Vogel clicked his heels. "I will see you both when the Wehrmacht comes to visit Switzerland! It will not be long." He smirked and turned away.

"Arschloch!" Mary said under her breath, as she watched him stride towards his car. She opened the Auburn and started it while Jung got into the back. After Olbricht's cigarette-smoke-and-exhaust redolent Opel, the Auburn smelled almost heavenly to Mary. *Just twenty meters to safety!* she thought as she warmed up the engine.

Jung rolled down the chauffeur's partition and leaned back in his seat, yawning. They crossed slowly into Liechtenstein as Vogel stood watching and waving. Mary and Jung paid no attention to him.

Chapter 51
Liechtenstein
1:15 PM, July 1, 1942

Once they had reached the main part of Mauren, Mary stopped the car. "Let's get rid of the cyanide," she said. She removed the suicide ampule from her mouth.

Carl took out his tobacco pouch and spat his ampule into it, then passed it to Mary for hers, and stashed it in the secret compartment beside him.

As the armrest snapped closed, Mary felt a wave of relief pass over her, remembering how close Vogel had come to breaking her ampule in the torture chamber. She looked in the rear-view mirror, then accelerated towards Vaduz. Passing the last of Mauren's buildings, she made the Auburn's tires squeal as she took a narrow macadam road leading off to the left. "Shortcut," she said.

"Where are we going?" Carl asked.

"Back roads, mostly rural. I'm leery about returning through Vaduz, after seeing that carload of Hitler's finest thugs there yesterday. We can take this road as far south as Balzers, then cross into Switzerland at the border station there. You can sleep."

Carl leaned forward, resting his arms on the front seat.

"How much longer will this route take? "

"Not much. Fifteen minutes or so. Almost home, thank God." Mary watched Carl in the mirror. "Did you find out what makes Hitler tick?"

"Yes," he said wearily. "Primarily a guilt complex due to murdering Geli Raubal."

"He did kill her, then?"

"He most certainly did."

Mary checked the road behind them in the mirror. No one there. "What about the locked room? And Hitler's alibi for the day Geli died?"

"According to him, there were three people in his car when they left Munich after lunch: Hitler himself, photographer Heinrich Hoffmann, and the driver, Julius Schreck."

"Are you saying there was a fourth man?"

"Hitler's security chief, Emil Maurice, lived above his watchmaker's shop just around the corner. He went wherever Hitler went, and would have ridden along to Nuremberg with the others to save expenses."

"Interesting. You want a cigar, Carl?"

"Yes, after I finish my story."

Mary opened another hidden drawer below the dashboard. As she reached into it, she thought she saw something flash in the mirror, but when she looked up, nothing was there except trees along the curve in the road behind them. She took a cigar from the compartment, keeping an eye on the mirror, and said, "Okay, Emil Maurice is in the car. What difference does that make?"

"A lot, as I'll explain later. Geli was shot with Hitler's gun, so he must have gone back."

"He could have just left the gun behind." Mary reached forward and pushed the cigarette lighter down into its socket.

Carl shook his head. "No. Hitler told me he always kept it with him."

"Hey, people forget things."

"Not someone as obsessive as Hitler! And Hitler had a valet, Georg Winter, to lay out his traveling clothes. They both wouldn't have forgotten the gun."

Mary grimaced. "Okay. I'll give you that. But why did he go back?" The lighter popped out and she lit her cigar.

"Geli had been begging Hitler all morning to go to Vienna. Knowing him, the farther he got from Munich, the more his distrust would grow. He admitted to me he'd had his eye on other women. If he had been honest, probably more than just his eye! He would have projected his own unfaithfulness on Geli, and sooner or later, he'd have ordered Schreck to turn the car around and go back to Munich."

Mary took the cigar from her mouth and blew smoke. "Okay, you've got Hitler and his gun and his three stooges back at the apartment. Then what?"

"They'd be running late, so his friends would have waited in the car while Hitler went inside. He probably caught Geli packing her suitcase, getting ready to sneak off to Vienna. An altercation ensued, and he shot her."

"Do you think she was going to see another man?" Mary asked around the cigar.

"Don't get ahead of me. When Hitler didn't come back right away, the others would have become concerned. They'd have gone inside and found Geli dead in a pool of blood and Hitler grief-stricken at what he'd done."

"Wouldn't someone have heard the shot?"

Carl waved a finger. "Nobody did. According to Hitler, the police report said no one heard anything until after three. He also told me he gave his staff the afternoon off when he left. If your boss gave you the rest of the day off on a Friday during Oktoberfest, what would you do?"

"I'd go to the nearest biergarten and practice my stein-hoisting, sing silly songs, then come home and sleep it off."

"Even if they stayed in the servant's quarters, there

might have been too much noise on the street in the early afternoon to hear the shot. But more likely they all went out as soon as Hitler drove off. That would mean there was no one around until they trickled back home later in the afternoon."

"So what did Hitler's friends do when they ran up to the apartment?"

"They would undoubtedly have wiped his fingerprints from the gun and put it in or near Geli's hand. Then they would have arranged for a loud noise later that afternoon, when Hitler was far away in Nuremberg."

Mary checked the rear view mirror. All clear; nothing but farmland and dairy barns. She looked back at Carl. "How would they manage that?"

"A watchmaker like Maurice would know a dozen clever ways, but Hoffmann would have fulminate of mercury percussion caps among his flash equipment. My favorite hypothesis is that Maurice forced a cap onto the striker of Geli's alarm clock and set it for after three o'clock."

"But Allen said Geli was locked in her room with the key on the inside."

"That was not at all difficult. Look at this." Carl took out his pocket watch and held it over the front seat beside Mary. "Emmy's grandfather's company, IWC, made this timepiece."

"Bully for him. So?"

"Her grandfather began his career as an apprentice locksmith. Virtually every German and Swiss watchmaker did the same thing. Emil Maurice would have learned locksmithing, too, and had all the skills and tools necessary to lock Geli's door from the outside."

Mary glanced at Carl. "Jeez." She focused on avoiding a series of potholes in the road, then said, "So Geli was already dead when all those witnesses saw Hitler in Nuremberg?"

"Yes, but Hitler would have been prostrate with remorse, unable to greet the crowd."

"So why did dozens of witnesses say they'd seen him on the balcony?"

"It wasn't Hitler. It was Schreck, the driver. There's a photograph of him in the fireside room at Löwensburg. He had heavy features and was Hitler's exact height. Hoffmann, the photographer, would have brought his full makeup kit along. Up on a balcony, with minimal makeup and a false mustache from Hoffmann's kit, Schreck could easily have passed for Hitler. At three p.m., while Schreck impersonated Hitler on the balcony, Maurice or Hoffmann could have helped the anguished Hitler up the back way to a room. And about then, Maurice's noise-maker would have gone off back in Geli's room."

"Holy cow, Carl." Mary slowed for a tightly winding section of road, dividing her attention between Carl and the road ahead. "But why did Hitler kill Geli? Jealousy?"

"I have a theory—"

Splat! A bullet hole appeared in the back window, sending Carl diving to the floor. Mary looked back and saw a black Citroen full of men right behind them. "Ohhhh, shit! Gestapo!"

More holes pierced the window, and Mary heard lead spattering the bullet-proof bodywork. She accelerated in the middle of a turn, sending the Auburn slewing from side to side as she tried to regain control. "I thought we had a guarantee!"

Carl yelled from the floor behind her, "They promised we'd leave Germany safely. We did. Now Hitler can have us killed in Liechtenstein."

Mary held the accelerator pedal down and used the entire width of the road, the Auburn's tires squealing at every bend. A second Citroen appeared in her rear view mirror right in back of the first. As they entered a long straight, Mary saw a third, far behind the second. "Jeesh!"

she muttered, her knuckles whitening on the steering wheel. *I'm glad Carl can't see these guys. I won't tell him we have three carloads of Gestapo after us.*

Leaning against her door to avoid shots coming through the rear window, Mary floored the accelerator and watched their pursuers fall back. She kept her foot down until the speedometer read 105 mph. Despite its greater weight, the three hundred horsepower V-12 soon left the Citroens behind, out of sight.

"Yee-haa!" she yelled.

Carl, his head still below the rear window, called out, "I'm glad someone is amused by this."

Mary chuckled, but she maintained full speed. In her mirror, she saw Carl sit up and look back, then kneel on the floor, again. When the road entered a forest and wound among the trees, Mary backed off on the throttle. As they rounded a curve, they encountered a tree fallen across the road. Mary stopped the Auburn just in time to avoid hitting it. "This looks fishy," she said, mostly to herself.

"Shall I get out and move it?" Carl asked.

Mary doubted Carl could budge the tree by himself. "I don't see anybody around," she said. "You sit tight." Leaving her door open, she jumped out and hoisted the leafy end to one shoulder, struggling to shift it out of their path. Before she could swing it completely clear, she heard a shot, and a bullet struck the tree beside her head.

Mary dropped the tree and ran back to the car. "Sniper! Stay down!" Another shot. A man emerged from the forest on Carl's side of the car, carrying a bolt action rifle with telescopic sights. Mary dove to her knees beside the driver's seat and fumbled with the seat lever. She heard the sniper yell, "We want you alive. Come out with hands high."

Another gunman loped out of the trees behind the first, similarly armed. "Give up!" he said. "We will not shoot. We know you are not armed."

"They want to kill us and make it look like an accident," Carl called out.

Mary swung another compartment from beneath her seat and pulled out a 10 gauge, sawed-off shotgun. She half stood and saw the second sniper only a few meters away from the car, his rifle pointed directly at Carl, who ducked just as the sniper blew a hole through the window above him.

"Stay down!" Mary told Carl, but she saw him rise up again and stick the stem of his pipe pistol through the bullet hole. She aimed the shotgun over the top of the car and pressed the trigger. A huge *boom* followed, and the second assassin's head exploded. She immediately fired the other barrel, splattering the first sniper in his tracks as he raised his rifle.

Mary looked into the back seat. Carl was sitting there, staring at the pipe pistol, a tiny wisp of gunsmoke rising from its muzzle. Hands shaking, his eyebrows raised, Carl commented, "It makes a hell of a noise, for something so small!"

"Nice shot, Carl. Now let's get the hell out of here." Mary threw the 10-gauge on the front seat and kicked the compartment closed as she got behind the wheel. She drove around the tree, going partway off the asphalt, tires crunching, and gravel flying up in back of them.

As they rocketed off down the road, Mary looked in her mirror in time to see the first two Citroens arrive, coming into the turn at high speed. The first hit the tree and blew a tire, stopping dead in the middle of the road. The second crashed into it, demolishing both vehicles. Mary smiled as she saw a column of dense, black smoke billow from the wreckage.

Chapter 52
Approaching Switzerland
1:30 PM, July 1, 1942

"I think we lost them," Mary said, checking the mirror as the Auburn swayed along a winding country road. She perspired heavily, steering at high speed, trying to avoid potholes on the bad road, and hoping they didn't blow a tire. "I need to ask Allen for a raise."

Carl, watching the rough road, looked grey with fright. "I need to tinkle."

Mary pointed at the hole in the window beside Carl. He gave her a sour look to let her know he was not amused.

"We should be at the border soon," she said. "You can pee there."

At last they saw the Swiss border ahead of them. Mary screeched to a halt at the Liechtensteiner station and held their documents out to be checked and stamped. She looked back and saw a car approaching. *The last Citroen!* "Hurry, please," she urged the guards.

The Liechtensteiners, oblivious to Jung and Mary's plight, continued to stamp, handed back the papers, and ever so slowly raised the barrier.

Mary looked in her rear view mirror again. The Gestapo

car was very close, its engine whining, four men leaning out its windows, firing pistols. The Swiss border guards, seeing what was happening, raised their barrier and urged Mary through. She jammed her foot down on the pedal and crossed into Switzerland, rear tires squealing.

The Swiss swung the steel arm down and sent the concrete barrier trundling across the road as soon as the Auburn passed through.

Mary heard the Citroen's brakes squeal. She watched in her mirror as it skidded across the border, broke the steel arm, and smashed into the concrete barricade. The Citroen rocked back and forth on its springs for a moment before Swiss .50 caliber machine guns chewed it into scrap metal.

An hour later, Swiss soldiers had cleaned up the border station, and Mary and Carl had taken time to rest and recover. They waved at the guards and drove away slowly. As the Auburn motored along, Mary saw Jung lean in whatever direction the car swayed. *Carl's worn out,* she thought.

Jung asked, "Do you suppose we are safe, now?"

"Hitler can't reach this far." *Probably.*

"What about Himmler?"

Mary wasn't sure. "He got what he wanted; he probably won't bother us." *I hope.*

"Then wake me when I'm home," Jung said, sitting back and closing his eyes.

"I called Allen from the border station. He wants to see you in Bern right away," Mary said. In her mirror, she saw Carl's eyes open.

"I want to see Emmy, first. Allen will have to wait till tomorrow," Carl replied.

"Ten thousand more people will die between now and then."

Carl sighed. "Then wake me when we get to Bern."

Chapter 53
OSS Station, Bern
4:00 PM, July 1, 1942

"We're back," Mary said, bringing the Auburn to a gentle stop.

Jung woke from his slumber in the back seat and sat up straight, trying to get his bearings. *I never thought we'd make it!* He saw they were parked behind the OSS building, beside a driveway where Jaffe stood in old trousers and an undershirt, washing a car. Mary leaned out and said, "Hey, Jaffe, before you can wash this, there are bullet holes in the windows to patch." Jaffe just frowned at her.

Jung clambered out of the car, yawning. When Mary got out, Jaffe grinned and turned the hose on her. "You almost got me canned, you little witch!"

Mary screamed when the cold water hit her and ran away. Jung held out his hand toward Jaffe and motioned for the hose. He took it, bent forward, and ran water over his own head. Then he straightened and offered Jaffe the hose. When the chauffeur reached for it, Jung squirted him in the face.

Inside the building, his hair still damp, Jung placed a

call to Emmy at Küsnacht.

"Jung," she answered.

Jubilant, Jung smiled at the sound of her voice. "Emmy, it's Carl. I'm in Bern."

"I'm glad you are back, Carl . . . I was worried. Is everything all right?"

"It went very well. I can't say anything more. I'll be home tomorrow."

They said their goodbyes, and Jung went to shower and dry his hair.

In the briefing room, an hour later, Dulles walked rapidly back and forth. Mary, wearing a spare uniform borrowed from Jaffe, poured coffee from a carafe into cups on the gun table. Jung, now in clean, dry clothes, was recapping for Dulles the cover-up after Geli's murder. " . . . For the Munich police, it was an open and shut suicide. Hitler actually got away with murder."

Mary asked, "But why did he kill her? What possible —"

Jaffe knocked and entered the room in a sombre mood. "Here are your prints," he whispered to Mary. He put the spy camera and a stack of photographs on the desk beside her, then left.

Dulles waved away Mary's question and turned to Jung. "How'd you crack him, Dr. Jung?"

"First, I had to accept the fact that Hitler considers himself a savior, destined by Wotan or some elemental god to restore Germany to greatness. He feels no guilt for the war or for his crimes against the Jews—not the least bit."

Mary covered the photographs with a file folder. "If his treatment of the Jews doesn't make him feel guilty, what on earth would?"

Jung held up a hand. "We'll look at that later, too. Second, Hitler made a wonderful Freudian slip during our word-association test. When I gave him *schmetterling,* the

German for *butterfly*, he meant to say *insekt*, but he responded with *inzest*, instead."

"Incest. Holy Hell!" Mary said.

"Yes," Jung said. "Hitler was so anxious to respond quickly, he unconsciously revealed what he most wanted to hide. Valuing my life, I covered his slip by replying *insect*, as if reflecting the word I had heard. I don't think he noticed what had happened, until possibly after I had already left."

Mary looked at Jung. "Hey, wait. *Butterfly* is not on the test."

Jung shrugged. "My instinct told me I should say *butterfly*."

Dulles said, "Incest—the relationship with his niece."

"More than that." Jung took a pencil from the table and went to the family tree on the wall. "On Saturday, you showed me that Hitler's mother and father were first cousins, another incestuous pairing." He traced the link on the chart.

"Which we already knew," Dulles said.

"Then there is the fact that Hitler's father died when Adolf was fourteen, an adolescent. The mother was only forty-three at that time, and, according to Hitler, they were 'very close,' just the two of them. I leave the rest to your imagination." Jung spread his hands.

"A classic Oedipal situation," Mary said.

Jung nodded. "That is mere speculation, of course."

"Of course," Dulles said.

"But given the recurring theme of incest in Hitler's background, I have a new thought. Mary, you asked me to discover the identity of Hitler's unknown grandfather." Jung indicated the box with the question mark on the genealogical diagram.

"That was a joke," Mary said.

"Regardless, I have come back with a candidate."

"Other than the step-father, Hiedler?"

"Yes. This fellow right here." Jung circled Johannes Schicklgruber and drew an arrow down into the box beside Maria.

Mary stood. "Jeezum, Dr. Jung! Maria's own father?"

Jung shrugged. "It has been known to happen. Even with an old goat, which he would have been at the time."

Dulles jumped in. "What could that do genetically?"

"Nothing good." Jung put down the pencil. "Hitler probably knew the full family history, including who his actual grandfather was, and more."

Dulles raised his eyebrows. "There's *more*?"

"Much more. As a child, Hitler was particularly afraid of an aunt. When I asked why, he got very upset, and I had to drop the subject. Later, I brought it up again, and as he tried to dismiss the matter, he mentioned 'her canes,' plural. My guess is that the aunt had a genetic deformity, one serious enough to require two canes."

"Hunchback," Dulles said, nodding.

"So-called, yes." Jung turned to Mary. "Now show us your photographs."

Mary took the pictures from Döllersheim to the bulletin board. Jung and Dulles looked over her shoulder while she pinned up the first, a church with the windows boarded up. "This is Saints Peter and Paul before it was used for artillery practice . . . and this is after." The next image showed the church, roofless, windowless, the walls pockmarked by shrapnel, craters all around it.

"Why did they do this?" Dulles asked, looking at the church.

Mary ignored him. "And this is the churchyard." She put up the third photograph, a moonscape of shell craters cluttered with bones and shattered coffins. "According to my soldier friend, the graves had been emptied before the shelling, but apparently there was another layer of older, forgotten graves beneath them."

The next three photographs displayed more human

remains: the partial skeleton of a hunchback, and close-ups of disjointed hands and feet with six digits each. Mary pinned the rest of the snapshots on the bulletin board: dwarf skeletons, intertwined rib cages of Siamese twins, a hydrocephalic, and the complete skeleton of a two-headed baby, perfect except for mutual distortion where their skulls abutted.

Dulles examined them and shuddered. *"Dans Macabre."*

Jung pointed at the pictures. "Döllersheim itself and its cemetery symbolize to Hitler his incestuous roots. Destroying them was his first method of eradicating his origins, but not his last, unfortunately."

"I need a drink." Dulles went to a cabinet and took out a burgundy, uncorked it, and poured them each a glassful. "I guess we know why Hitler is single."

Jung took a small sip of wine. "Saying he's 'married to Germany' is just an evasion. Anyone with his genetic background would hesitate to marry."

"Okay, this is interesting, but let's get down to cases." Mary looked down at the blood-red wine in her glass, then back at Jung. "Why did he kill Geli? Did he think she was going to run off with another man?"

Jung held his glass up to the light, admiring the deep, red color. "When Hitler went back to Munich to check on Geli, I'm fairly certain it went something like this: He entered the apartment and found her with her suitcase packed, ready to depart for Vienna. Accusations of infidelity flew from both sides. He accused her of leaving for a tryst, probably with a Jew. Ultimately, she told him the truth."

"Which was?" Dulles said.

Jung put his glass down on the workbench. "She was going to Vienna to see her doctor."

"Uh-oh . . . " Mary said.

"Yes, she was most probably pregnant, and Hitler's

209

greatest fear was fathering a child like those in Döllersheim." Jung pointed at the photographs. "He had to kill Geli before she could get her baby to Vienna, beyond his reach."

Allen shook his head in disgust. "Cold-blooded murder."

"A double murder," Mary said. "But would we expect any less from Hitler?"

"We wouldn't now, certainly, but remember, this was in 1931, early in his career, before the Night of the Long Knives. This was Hitler's first murder. I can't say it was entirely premeditated. He may have shot her within two or three seconds of being told the baby was his." Jung knocked the ash out of his pipe. "Faster than that, if he was waving his pistol about, which he was known to do. "

"The irony of it!" Mary said.

"And the shame!" Allen said.

Jung nodded. "Yes, think of it: the Führer of the Master Race fathering a defective child. It would have ruined him. But the relevant thing is neither the irony nor the shame." Jung walked back to the bulletin board and passed a hand across the photographs. "These represent a window into Hitler's soul. His blood really is tainted, and it is this genuine and most profound stigma that he projects upon the Jews."

After a brief silence, Jung turned to Dulles. "Having recognized this, we can say without any doubt that Hitler will try to kill all the Jews in order to negate his own imperfection."

"He's already started." Grim-faced, Dulles took down #404's message from a bulletin board and handed it to Jung. "This is an eye-witness account of Jews massacred just two weeks ago near Terzendorf. We have unconfirmed reports of a dozen more mass executions all across occupied Europe."

Jung read the message and looked up at Dulles. "It's

probably too late to save them," he said, his throat tightening.

Dulles shook his head. "We may save some. Russia, mostly."

"Which reminds me of another subject you asked me to look into: why Hitler invaded Russia. It's obvious, now."

Allen slammed his hand down on the table. "That's where the last free Jews in Europe were. Oh, my Lord. Is that what this war is all about?"

Mary said, "Not *Lebensraum*?"

"Not Lebensraum. *Totensraum.*" Jung put away his pipe. "I'm beyond exhausted. I think that's all I can do today."

Mary said, "You've been very brave, Carl. I'm proud of you." She embraced him and gave him a big kiss on his lips.

Carl saw Dulles, who was standing behind Mary, roll his eyes at the affectionate kiss. Dulles met Jung's eyes and smiled.

"I don't feel particularly brave," Jung told him. "I'm still afraid of what Himmler might do."

"Not Hitler?" Dulles asked.

"Himmler is the more dangerous of the two, and I worry that he may send his Gestapo here."

Dulles shook his head. "Don't worry, Dr. Jung. You'll have bodyguards 'round the clock. First thing tomorrow."

"Thank you, Allen. And now I must go shower again until I have washed away the contamination of Nazi Germany, and then sleep for a hundred years."

Chapter 54
Jung's Home, Küsnacht
8:00 PM, July 1942

Jung's study, like much of the house, was decorated in what might be called "Swiss Provincial." A fine collection of comfortable furnishings and oriental rugs, both old and new, crammed the room. Jung sat there, reading a mystery novel, when Emmy entered that evening. "Were you expecting visitors?" she asked. "Mary Rufenacht just arrived with some men."

He put the book down on his desk. "Yes, I am." He stood and looked around the room. "I think we would be most comfortable in here. Please send them in."

Emmy left and returned with Mary and Allen Dulles and three others. Emmy stood there, waiting uneasily to be introduced, but no one said a word. "Will you want coffee?" she asked, finally, frowning.

"No, no," Carl said. "Please don't bother yourself. We will be fine."

Emmy turned to leave, but Mary told her, "Actually, Mrs. Jung, I believe we will need coffee, please. I'll come with you and bring it back." The two of them went out.

All the men wore civilian clothes. Dulles pointed at a

sturdy, grey-haired man, about 5-foot-8, with an Irish face. "Dr. Jung, this is my boss, Major General William Donovan from OSS Headquarters in Washington. Next to him is Colonel David Bruce of our London station . . . " Bruce was a wiry, dignified American in a custom-made suit. " . . . And John Collins of the British SIS." Collins wore thick, horn-rimmed glasses and a tiny mustache. Dulles concluded the introductions with, "Gentlemen, Dr. Carl Jung."

Jung shook hands with the visitors, then invited them to sit in sturdy chairs arranged around his desk.

Donovan said, "I've already been briefed, but Allen Dulles will fill you London people in on the latest development. It's extremely important that what you hear tonight not be repeated outside this room." He nodded at Dulles.

Dulles continued, "Recently, the Bern OSS station acquired a reliable source of ongoing intelligence about Adolf Hitler's decisions."

Colonel Bruce asked, "Can you reveal the source?"

"Hitler, himself," Donovan replied.

Collins said, "What did you do, fit him with a microphone up his bum?"

Dulles said, "Dr. Jung, as you may be aware, is an internationally famous psychiatrist. This summer he did a face-to-face assessment of Adolf Hitler's mental state, obtaining key information to construct our most accurate profile of Hitler to date, one that will let us predict fairly well both his strategies and his responses to our actions."

Collins stared at Jung, frowning. "Face-to-face? You actually sat down and chatted with Hitler?"

"Yes, I did," Jung said, putting his hand into his pocket and grasping his pipe pistol souvenir.

"How did you arrange that?" Bruce asked.

Jung took out the pistol and looked down at it. From force of habit, he slid the stem back to make sure there wasn't a bullet in it. "It was at the request of the German High Command, who were growing nervous about Der Führer's mental state."

Collins smirked. "As well they should. So tell me, Dr. Jung, is Hitler crazy?"

"As Mr. Dulles said, I went into Germany and asked Hitler dozens of personal questions, in a building full of Nazis, yes?"

"Yes." Collins nodded, clearly puzzled.

Jung said, "Then to get to the point, Hitler is sane; I am the crazy one."

The others laughed, except for Collins, who said, "For someone who is sane, as you allege, Mr. Hitler seems to have a most unusual propensity for evil. How can that be, Dr. Jung? Surely he must be a madman."

There was a knock at the rustic, round-top door. Allen Dulles let Emmy Jung and Mary into the room, accompanied by a bodyguard bearing coffee and *kuchen*. Emmy didn't linger. As soon as the tray was set down, she smiled at Mary, then left immediately with the guard. Carl helped Mary dole out the refreshments.

Once the coffee was served, Jung sat again and said, "Before I answer that last question, I would like to mention that it was Mary Bancroft, here, who accompanied me on my sortie into Germany. If it weren't for her, I would be pushing up edelweiss somewhere in occupied Austria or Liechtenstein."

All eyes turned towards Mary, who acknowledged their attention with a wave and a nod, then sat beside Jung.

"Regarding Hitler's sanity, Mr. Collins, I stand by my analysis," Jung said. "Hitler is not out of touch with reality. He knows it is wrong to kill, but he believes that he serves a higher purpose. Also, he operates under the impression that the end justifies the means. Put those two beliefs together, and there is no limit to the evil you can do, and still be essentially sane."

Collins said, "But surely, believing that he serves a higher purpose is delusional."

Jung waved the pipe. "We all have beliefs. Did you ever attend church?"

"Er . . . yes," Collins said. "A long time ago. When I was young. Quite young."

"You did that based on your faith. That is quite the subjective thing." Jung gestured with each hand, to the right and the left. "You believed there were benefits of attending church. Hitler believes he's saving the German people. The fact that you were likely right and Hitler is likely wrong doesn't make you sane and him the opposite." Jung looked around the room. "Did you have another question, General Donovan?"

"Based on your meeting Hitler, what can you tell us about him as a person?" Donovan asked.

Jung loaded the little suicide pipe with tobacco as he spoke. "Hitler was severely abused by his alcoholic father as a child. I observed, among other things, a tendency for him to pace a room on the diagonal, a clue that he may have been confined in a small space as a child, and has retained a desire to make rooms seem as spacious as possible. From that and other forms of abuse, would typically follow perfectionism, hypervigilance, and an extremely poor self-image—"

Collins snorted at the notion of Hitler having low self-esteem.

Jung turned to him. "No, Hitler's pretentiousness is not a sign of confidence, but of quite the opposite. His *Parteitag* extravagances reflect an abysmally low regard for himself. His allusions in *Mein Kampf* to being 'stabbed in the back,' his envisioning the Jews as oppressors, those things all reflect an underlying victim mentality."

Donovan prompted Jung: "But you were talking about his childhood. Is there more?"

"Yes. Hitler contracted measles when he was about

eleven. His brother was ill at the same time and died of measles encephalitis. From Hitler's slow gait and his tremors, I deduce Parkinson's Disease, a common aftereffect of encephalitis."

Jung lit the pipe, then continued. "That could also account for his poor impulse control, as shown by his frequent rages. The rages may also indicate adrenaline addiction, as could his histrionic speeches."

Donovan stood and flexed his back, saying, "I think what we would like to know, Doctor, is how your observations of Hitler can help predict his military actions."

Jung drew on the pipe before saying, "In any given tactical situation, I can predict his response with, roughly speaking, eighty percent accuracy, based on his known traits. For example, as the child of an alcoholic, he will tend towards grandiose gestures, such as massive attacks coordinated across a wide front. His perfectionism will manifest itself as delayed decisions. With the proper use of misinformation, we can help him imagine reasons for even more delay. His inflexibility will not let him adjust his tactics to match new situations; he will continue to do the same thing he's already done, even if it's a disaster."

Jung put down the pipe to free his hands. "One particularly helpful quirk is Hitler's "Voice." He has an inner voice that warns him of danger." Jung looked at the SIS representative. "Don't laugh! It has saved his life on several occasions. We may turn this Voice to our advantage. He believes that it is infallible. Fool his Voice, and he must obey it."

Dulles raised a hand. "In more practical terms, please, Doctor?"

Jung picked up a large sketch pad and a black crayon from his desk. "Name a place in Axis territory, please, Allen."

"Sicily."

Jung held the pad where the others could see and drew

a rough map of Sicily. "Let's say you want to attack here." He put an X on the island. "You prepare by appearing to accidentally leak secret information, a little at a time. All this data must point at somewhere else, say, Sardinia." Jung drew an irregular shape northwest of the first island. "Later, when you strike Sicily, Hitler's Voice will tell him it's a feint, an attempt to draw forces away from Sardinia. He will sit tight, waiting for the 'real' attack. By the time he acts, it will be too late." Jung drew a little British flag over Sicily.

Collins had his arms folded across his chest. "Can you give an example of how you would make him think Sardinia is the target?"

Mary answered the question without waiting for Jung. "It's easy. You have the British Army order maps of Sardinia, hundreds of 'em."

Jung nodded and said, "Hitler's agents will pass such information on to him. A dozen or so little deceptions like that and Hitler's Voice will be absolutely certain you intend to invade Sardinia."

Collins frowned and peered at Jung, "This fooling his Voice business, you believe it will really work?"

Jung waved the pipe. "He has a mammoth guilt complex resulting from murdering his girlfriend. That, in combination with his other complexes, renders him so inflexible, you could pull that same trick over and over, and deceive him every time."

Colonel Bruce asked, "How would you characterize Hitler overall, as a person?"

Jung looked at the crayon in his hand and thought for several seconds. "He's an actor, an actor in a tragic role far bigger than he is; he is Charlie Chaplin's evil twin, playing Bismarck."

Collins got the last word. "I still think he's barmy in the crumpet."

Jung smiled.

Chapter 55
Küsnacht
10:00 PM October 30, 1942

The moon was rising over the Alps. It had been a warm day for October, and twilight fog wafted up from the lake as Carl Jung, his driver, and a second bodyguard arrived at his blackout-shrouded home. The driver pulled into the drive and stopped a short distance from the house, idling the ex-OSS Auburn with its lights off. The bodyguard went ahead, his machine pistol drawn, to check the path and let the house guards know they were coming.

Fog swirled around the car as Jung sat there in the moon shadows. The night was cool, but he was bundled up in his trench coat and, beneath it, a bullet-proof vest. He sighed, wondering at himself.

It had been a long day. He had reopened his practice and treated eight clients, a full load, then delivered an hour-long lecture at the university. He closed his eyes, anticipating a glass of wine and a chat with Emmy before bedtime.

A noise startled him. Jung swiveled and looked through the rear window.

Two men in trench coats and fedoras came out of the

wisps of fog, lit by the moon.

Jung gripped the driver's arm. "Men are coming. Behind us. Gestapo, I think."

"I see them. Get down." The driver blinked the headlights to signal the guards at the house.

Jung ducked below the windows and fumbled in his pocket for the pipe pistol. He twisted the bowl, cocking it, thinking, *If they try to take me back to Germany, I won't be joining them.*

Jung watched as the driver opened his door a crack, poked his Mauser pistol out, and aimed it, shouting, "Don't move. Show your hands and identify yourselves.

One of the men said in English, "We are refugees from Austria. We are looking for—"

"Shut up! Keep your hands in the air!"

Jung sat up to see what was happening. Guards came running from the house, surrounded the men, and frisked them before standing back. Nothing.

"Papers!" the driver ordered, getting out of the car. He collected the men's passports, looked at them under his flashlight, and took them to Jung in the car. "Anybody you know?"

Jung examined the passports. Both were German, with new covers stamped "Jude" in large *fraktur* letters. *Probably not Gestapo, then,* he thought. He opened the first and saw the photo of a plump, swarthy, man named Heymann. *Nobody I know.* He flipped open the second passport. The photograph therein showed a rather gaunt Dr. Sigmund Rosenberg.

"Sigmund!" Jung yelled. He slid out of the car and ran to embrace his friend. "You made it! Himmler let you go!"

Sigmund smiled a broad grin. "Ja. He did. He called it 'being expelled,' though. I was staying with Himmler's cousin in Munich when it was bombed on the nineteenth. His home burned to the ground, and we all had to leave."

"What? I thought you were taken to another camp! But

Himmler's cousin?"

"Yes, this is he." Sigmund indicated the short, chubby man beside him.

"Oh." *Himmler's cousin is a Jew? This is a shock.* "But how did you get out? That passport would get you thrown in a camp."

"Himmler arranged for visas and the necessary bribes."

"I didn't think he had that much compassion," Jung said.

Heymann interrupted. "Compassion, he has none of. The man is a sadist. Any tiny bit of compassion is his wife's. I am an embarrassment to the Reichsführer, so, in kind, I would like it understood that I am a cousin by marriage only. I am no direct relation to Heinrich Himmler. None whatsoever. He is a devious snake. More devious than Hitler, say some who know both," Heymann spat.

Jung shook his hand. "Welcome to Switzerland, Herr Heymann."

Heymann grinned. "The snake said to say hello to you and that he trusts you to keep your promise."

"I have not forgotten. But I am more than a bit surprised he released Sigmund and is relying on my promise alone."

"That is not the situation," Heymann said. "Tell him, Siggy."

"Tell me what?"

Sigmund cleared his throat. "Dr. Jung, he still has my father."

Jung had a momentary, bizarre vision of Marcus's ashes in a neat pile on Himmler's desk. "Your father? But you said he was dead. The shoebox. The . . . "

"The ashes? Someone else's; they had plenty." Sigmund grimaced. "Himmler had kidnapped my father to sabotage your trip. One day, there was a knock at Heymann's door. I opened, expecting Gestapo, and there was my father, alive. I couldn't believe it. He lived with us until the bombing.

Himmler has held him back in case you do . . . something involving *Time Magazine*. Do you know what he meant?"

An article I must not write titled 'This is Heinrich Himmler's Brain.' "Yes. I suppose this was his idea of keeping all his options open. Do you think he will let your father go after the war is over?"

Sigmund shrugged. "Himmler seems to believe a few good deeds will save him from the hangman, so I am hopeful."

"Let us hold that thought in our hearts," Jung said. "Now let us get out of the fog and celebrate. I have a bottle of sherry I have been saving for when the war ends. We shall open it now. Come!"

Chapter 56
East Prussia
9:00 AM, July 9, 1943

On July 9th, 1943, American and English forces struck Sicily before dawn. Word soon reached the Wolf's Lair, and the on-duty radio operator relayed the report to General Zeitzler, who arranged to have Hitler awakened by his SS bodyguard.

This may be the beginning of the end, Zeitzler thought. He, along with Generals Krebs and Heusinger, stood waiting, grim-faced and arms folded, beside a large Mediterranean map on the Wolf's Lair briefing room wall. As Hitler approached, all came to attention and gave him the full Nazi salute with exclamations of "Heil Hitler!"

The Führer saluted casually with his usual hand-to-shoulder gesture before speaking. "What is it?"

Zeitzler responded rapidly, picking up the pointer from beside the map. "An Allied invasion, Führer. Sicily. They have established secure positions . . . " He turned to the map and pointed at the island in two places. " . . . Here, and here."

Hitler didn't reply. Krebs filled the silence. "We plan to bring in reinforcements from Greece." He waved a hand across the map.

Heusinger added, "We have alerted additional units in Sardinia to be ready to mobilize, if needed."

Hitler leaned towards Krebs, fists clenched, "Nein! Leave the reinforcements where they are! This is only a feint, another example of British deception!"

Zeitzler turned paler than usual. "But Führer, the Allies have attacked in significant numbers. On two beaches. It is quite evident that they intend to use Sicily as a jumping off point for their attack on Italy."

"Nein!" Hitler shouted. "I have fully analyzed this situation, and it is only a feint. The real Allied objectives are Greece and Sardinia." He snatched the pointer from Zeitzler's hand and whacked the map repeatedly east and west of Sicily. "Here and here! Here and here!"

Zeitzler, mortified, felt his face redden. The other generals remained silent.

Hitler turned away and stalked out of the room.

During the days that followed, Zeitzler stood by helplessly as Hitler refused the High Command's repeated requests for reinforcements for Sicily. On July 19th, two weeks after the invasion, Hitler finally gave permission for the transport of additional Wehrmacht units to Sicily. *Too late*, Zeitzler thought. *By now, the Allies have a secure foothold on the island, and there is nothing we can do to dislodge them.*

Chapter 57
Berchtesgaden
5:10 AM, June 6, 1944

On June 6th, 1944, German commanders looked out over the English Channel at daybreak and saw it filled with dozens upon dozens of Allied ships. They immediately notified Hitler's staff in Berchtesgaden, including General Zeitzler and the elderly Field Marshal von Witzleben. Because of the staff officers' fear of Hitler's rages, no one woke him until 9:00 a.m. By then, the first waves of Allied troops were already ashore.

About 9:25 a.m., Hitler joined Zeitzler, Field Marshal von Witzleben, and Generals Olbricht and von Rundstedt, who were gathered around his desk in the study. Zeitzler had a strong sense of *deja vu* as he unrolled a map of France on Hitler's desk and secured its corners with paperweights. *Something tells me this is going to go badly,* he thought.

"What is it this time?" Hitler demanded, clearly in a foul mood.

"Normandy, Führer." Zeitzler swept his hand along the map's beaches and surrounding areas, pointing at tactical features. "Airborne infantry dropped here, and here, in advance of the landings. Two bridges are in Allied hands, here, and here. Troop landings all along the coast line from Sante-Mere to beyond Caen. In considerable force."

Hitler dismissed all this with a gesture, calmly saying, "This is not the real invasion. It is only a feint."

Von Witzleben grimaced, then indicated the Normandy coastline. "Führer, our commanders in the field assure me that this is more than a token attack. The Allies have already attacked and possibly secured a third bridge by now."

Hitler shook his head. "Nein!" he roared into von Witzleben's face.

Von Witzleben took a step back and didn't say another word.

Zeitzler and the other generals tried to maintain a united front, remonstrating with Hitler, but he pounded his fists on the desk and told them, "The actual invasion is planned for Pas-de-Calais under Patton! Every single piece of intelligence we have points to that. Our best operatives in England have informed me that Patton is still twiddling his dick in Knutsford."

Zeitzler took a turn. "But Führer—"

"It is a feint, I tell you! They will attack here!" Hitler stabbed a finger at Pas de Calais again and again, then left, fuming.

Zeitzler, horrified, watched him go. *This is Sicily all over again. Why can Hitler not see that?* As he turned back to the others, he caught Olbricht and von Witzleben nodding at each other, eyes narrowed. *I wonder what those two are up to,* he thought. *But no, I shall not wonder. I do not want to know. I must not know.*

That afternoon, General Zeitzler began drafting his resignation from the Wehrmacht.

Chapter 58
Küsnacht
10:30 AM, December 12, 1944

One day late in 1944, the postman delivered a thick envelope to the Jung residence. The return address was in care of the Swedish Red Cross in Stockholm. Wondering what it was, Jung took it to his study and set it aside until after tea.

That afternoon, he sat by a window and opened the envelope. It held an official form, a note, and a list of prisoners recently released to Sweden by Himmler's order. One name was circled: Marcus Rosenberg, MD. Rejoicing, Carl smiled. *Marcus made it out of Germany!* The note said:

Dear Herr Dr. Jung:

I am, as is evident, alive, a miracle. Another: I am also quite well. I have not words to express my gratitude, but hope to do so in person soon for what you have done for me and Sigmund. Without your intervention, we would have joined those, now known to be in the millions, ground to dust by the German killing machine. I feel as someone who has a hundred times stepped off a railroad track just as an express train roared past, missing him by only a centimeter each time. I understand Sigmund is still in Zurich. Please give him my love and ask him to write in care of the address on this envelope. Also, if it's not too much trouble, please fill out the enclosed form and return as indicated. Kind regards

Marcus Rosenberg

Jung filled out the necessary papers, but heard nothing further until after VE Day.

Chapter 59
Berlin
April 30, 1945

In mid-afternoon, as Berlin's defenses collapsed under a Russian attack, Adolf Hitler said goodbye to members of his staff and various officials in the musty *Führerbunker*. Then he retired to his study with Eva Braun, sitting beside her on a sofa, their glass cyanide ampules on the coffee table in front of them. He talked with her for almost an hour, recalling better times, avoiding any event after 1939. There was a long silence, with nothing more left to say.

Hitler looked at Eva for a few final moments. "I think it is time," he said, then reached for his pistol and rotated the safety lever forward with his thumb. From the corner of his eye, he saw Eva pick up her capsule and place it in her mouth. He immediately put his own capsule between his teeth and held the pistol to his temple. "Now!" he ordered.

He heard Eva crush her ampule, and he bit into his fragile glass cylinder and pulled the trigger. A loud *bang* from the .30 Walther, and Hitler fell forward with his head resting on the table. Germany's Führer, leader of the Third Reich, destroyer of millions of human lives, was dead.

Chapter 60
Bern and Küsnacht
May, 1945

On VE Day, May 8th, 1945, Mary Bancroft placed a call to the Jungs' home in Küsnacht. When Jung answered, Mary said, "Hey, Carl, Allen is throwing a victory party at the Bern office this Saturday. General Donovan will be here and a bunch of other top brass from London and Washington. You and Emmy are invited. Can you make it?"

"Thank you, Mary, but I think not. I've been tired for a long time, and I'm trying to catch up on my rest."

Mary was disappointed and wondered if that were true. *He has been under a strain. I'd love to see him receive his OSS service medal at the party, but I'd better not press him.* "All right. Promise me we can get together soon, though. Run it past Emmy."

"Maybe in a few weeks." Carl hung up.

When Emmy returned her call the next day, Mary was quite surprised. Emmy told her, "Thank you for the invitation to the American party, Mrs. Rufenacht. I am sorry Dr. Jung cannot come, but we are not in the mood for celebrating, yet. I think you understand."

"Yes, I do." Mary heard of more and more discoveries

of Nazi atrocities every day. The estimated concentration camp death toll grew by leaps of a hundred thousand and up. Many of those who had learned the scope of Nazi horror didn't feel there was much to celebrate, even in victory.

"It was nice of you to invite us," Emmy continued. "But I am curious why you thought of us."

"Dr. Jung is supposed to receive a medal for his assistance to the OSS during the war."

"Aha. A medal," Emmy said. "What assistance?"

Uh-oh. "He never told you?"

"He has told me very little. I know this must have something to do with the bodyguards and Carl's visits from unidentified strangers behind closed doors, but other than that, I have been left out of things."

"I apologize, Mrs. Jung. Security on Carl's . . . Dr. Jung's work has been very tight." Mary had a sudden idea. "Maybe my bosses and I could bring Dr. Jung his medal and fill you in officially at the same time. Would that be inconvenient?"

"I am planning a farewell luncheon for Carl's bodyguards in a week or two. It will be very informal, so it would be easiest for me to just add several more to the luncheon guest list."

On the day of Emmy's luncheon, May 25th, Jaffe drove Mary Bancroft, Allen Dulles, and General Donovan from Bern to Küsnacht. When they arrived at Jung's home, Mary knocked on the ornate double door, then stood aside. She watched as Emmy Jung opened the door and stared out, wide-eyed, at the American General in full uniform.

"Come in," Emmy said after a moment. "You would be Mary Rufenacht's 'boss,' I suppose?" She offered her hand.

As Donovan shook it, he said, "We've met once before. I'm General William Donovan. These guys . . . " he indicated Mary, Dulles, and Jaffe, " . . . have to call me

'General,' but you can call me 'Bill.'"

Mary was happy to note that Emmy appeared charmed by Bill Donovan. Emmy smiled and greeted Mary and the others, and they joined the gathering in the high ceilinged dining room. Present were most of the two dozen students who had served as Carl Jung's bodyguards between June 10th, 1942, and May 8th, 1945.

While Emmy introduced General Donovan and Allen Dulles to the former bodyguards, Mary wandered around the room until she found Jung talking to two men. She greeted him rather formally, inhibited by the occasion.

"Do you remember Dr. Sigmund Rosenberg?" he asked her, indicating the man nearest him.

This was a surprise to Mary, who had last seen Sigmund being led away by Himmler's SS thugs. "Yes, I certainly do." She took Sigmund's hand and squeezed it hard. "You've put on weight."

He nodded and smiled. "God be thanked," he said. "And this is my father," he added, indicating the older man beside him, "Dr. Marcus Rosenberg, just arrived from Sweden."

A while later, General Donovan gathered Mary and Dulles and Jaffe. "Okay, let's give Dr. Jung his medal," he said.

"And let Emmy know why he's getting it," Mary added. "I'll go get them. Why don't we use Carl's study?"

Mary found Jung in the kitchen. "Carl, General Donovan wants to see you and Emmy privately, if you don't mind." She pointed at the rustic round-top door that led to the study.

Carl drew Emmy away from her guests, and they followed Mary to the Provincial-style study. Jaffe closed the door, remaining outside to ensure privacy.

Once the door was shut, General Donovan stood in front of a stained glass window and said, "Dr. Jung, we owe you more than we can repay, and more than I can say, so

I'm not even going to try. Harry Truman told me to thank you, and pardon me if I quote him verbatim: 'Thank Dr. Jung for keeping that son-of-a-bitch Hitler from taking over the world.' So thanks, Dr. Jung. Well done." Donovan shook Jung's hand.

"Hear, hear," Allen said.

Mary said, "Dr. Jung should get a parade. With ticker tape."

"The best we can do is a medal," Donovan said. He reached into a pocket and pulled out an OSS service medal. He looked at it, hefted it in his hand, then pinned it on Jung's lapel. "It's just a small token, but it expresses the gratitude of a lot of people. Millions, if they only knew."

Emmy said, "But what did you do, Carl? I think I have a right to know what you've been up to these past three years. It must have been important." She looked at Donovan and at Mary and frowned. "Important enough to give Carl three heart attacks."

Jung looked at Donovan. "Is it all right if I tell Emmy the entire story now?"

"Go ahead, Dr. Jung." The General turned to Emmy. "But you must never repeat a word of this, Mrs. Jung. You'll understand once you're told."

"All right, tell me, Carl," Emmy said.

Carl took her hand. "You remember that client I visited in '42, Herr Wolff?"

"The man near the Austrian border. I have never forgotten. I knew you were hiding something from me. That was when all the late night visitations began. And the bodyguards."

Carl nodded. "It was not on this side of the Austrian border that Herr Wolff lived, but the other side."

Emmy frowned and tilted her head, then opened her eyes wide. "You went into Germany?"

"Yes, I and Mary Bancroft." Carl pointed at Mary.

"Carl, that was terribly dangerous. You never should

have done it!"

"A member of the Oberkommando Wehrmacht visited me one night and insisted I come and treat Herr Wolff."

Emmy held up a hand. "Wait! Do not tell me . . . "

"Yes, Herr Wolff was Adolf Hitler."

Emmy brought her hand to her mouth, then took it away to say, "I am glad I did not know where you went. If I had known, I would have been petrified every second. What possessed you to go?"

Carl grimaced. "General Olbricht promised to release Marcus Rosenberg from a concentration camp if I would evaluate Hitler's mental state."

Mary interrupted. "Dr. Jung went to keep Hitler's louts out of Switzerland by stealing his deepest, darkest secrets for the Allies."

Emmy gaped. "Carl! You didn't analyze Hitler!"

"Yes, I'm afraid I did exactly that."

General Donovan told her, "Dr. Jung gave us a profile of Hitler's personality that allowed us predict his actions with high accuracy from mid-1942 on."

Emmy said, "I can't believe you did that! In fact, I am sorry you told me. It was not only dangerous, it was unprofessional and unethical. I hope no one else finds out."

Mary was disappointed by Emmy's reaction. "It was heroic!" she said.

"It was expedient." Emmy looked at the oriental rug beneath her feet, then back at Carl. "But it was very brave, and I suppose it saved a lot of lives. Well done, Carl!" She embraced him, kissed him tenderly, and said, "And now, please excuse me, I have company to attend to." She turned and left the room.

Jung shrugged. "A prophet is not without honor, except in his neighborhood."

Allen Dulles put a hand on Jung's shoulder. "If people knew what you've done, you'd get a dozen medals—Croix de Guerre, Allied Victory Medal, Hero of the Soviet

Union . . ."

Jung shook his head. "No, no. The notoriety would be most unwelcome. Besides, medals are not particularly useful. If I got a Paperweight de Guerre, or an Allied Victory Pencil Cup, I might get a little use out of it," Jung joked. "But what can you do with a medal?"

Dulles said, "Wear it. Hang it on your wall."

"That's just it, Allen," Jung said. "I cannot display it. Someone would ask what it was and what I did to get it, and I cannot tell them. Ever. Emmy is quite right; no one must know what I did. I'd become known as that psychiatrist who rats on his clients. That would be the end of my practice, and I am never going to give up working with clients."

Mary said, "I'm sure glad to hear that, Dr. Jung. I have a friend who needs therapy—"

Jung shook a finger at her. "I'm not falling for that again!"

Dulles and Donovan shook Jung's hand and rejoined the company in the other room. Mary stayed behind and hugged Carl. "You did a wonderful thing."

"I'm an old lion, but I can still bite. And it was *we* who did it, a young lion and an old one." He took hold of her hand. "I couldn't have done it if you'd stayed safely in Switzerland."

"Carl, I want to give you something to remind you that you're my hero, whenever you look at it." Mary reached in a pocket and pulled out a dark blue cylindrical object. She took it in both hands and held it out to him. "I hereby award Carl Gustav Jung the Mary Bancroft Prize for Utter Nerve." Then she kissed him on the lips.

"What is it?" he asked. "I certainly hope it's not another gun. It looks just like a pen."

"Yeah, it is. You stole Hitler's secrets; I stole Himmler's pen."

Jung framed the pen and put it on his office wall. In later years, when anyone asked what it was, he would say, "A client stole that pen from Heinrich Himmler and gave it to me as a reward for unsuccessfully treating her latent kleptomania."

Appendix A
Biographies

GENERAL FRIEDRICH OLBRICHT (October 4, 1888 - July 21, 1944)

General Olbricht had a pivotal part in "Plan Valkyrie," the plot to kill Hitler. Olbricht led the "Replacement Army," a contingency force created to restore order in the event of a rebellion. The plotters hoped to use this force to generate the rebellion it was designed to suppress.

The conspiracy failed due to incredibly bad luck. Hitler was saved when an officer shoved Stauffenberg's briefcase containing the bomb beneath the conference table, directly next to a thick wooden trestle. Of the ten men at that end of the table, the bomb killed four. Hitler was standing on the other side of the trestle, halfway down the table. He received only minor wounds, including some hearing loss. His Parkinson's Disease improved temporarily.

Stauffenberg had left the bunker after placing the bomb. Hearing the explosion, he assumed without checking that Hitler must have been killed. He reported Hitler dead, and the conspirators went ahead based on that misinformation. When it was announced Hitler was alive, the plot collapsed.

The plot depended on Hitler's death. Some believe that had the cabal pushed ahead, regardless of Hitler being alive, they would have succeeded. This is unlikely. All German officers had sworn oaths of loyalty to Der Führer. Only his death would have freed enough German high-ranking military men to act effectively against the Nazis.

According to some accounts, Hitler had been growing more suspicious of those close to him, and it's possible that his "Voice" somehow intuited the impending danger—a change in atmosphere, unusual behavior by his military staff, a look, a word, might be enough to warn his Voice.

Olbricht died first, allegedly shot by rifle fire while evading arrest on the night of July 20th. More probably, he was ordered shot by the officer in charge in an attempt to obscure the latter's part in the conspiracy. As a result of the failed assassination, the Nazis executed or imprisoned as many as 7,000 Germans, most of them innocent. The deaths of some OKW officers were protracted, filmed in color for the after-dinner amusement of Hitler and his guests. Still others died in concentration camps, along with many innocent relatives and associates.

ALLEN W. DULLES (April 7, 1893 - January 29, 1969)

Allen Dulles came from a family active in public service, including a US Secretary of State. After graduating from Princeton, he entered the diplomatic service, but continued his law studies at George Washington University.

In 1942, Dulles was appointed chief of the new Office of Strategic Services (OSS) station in Bern, Switzerland, adopting the nom de guerre, "Mr. Burns," a play on "Bern (S)," the OSS station identification. Dulles had a highly-placed contact among the July 20 conspirators, Abwehr agent Hans Bernd Gisevius.

His memoirs include *The Secret Surrender* (1966). In March, 1945, Dulles and SS General Wolff, working in secret, engineered the mass surrender in northern Italy of almost one million Axis soldiers, whom Hitler had ordered to fight on to the death. This cooperation between Dulles, Wolff, and others, saved the lives of tens of thousands of Allied and Axis troops. (General Wolff's reward for his participation was four years in an Allied POW camp.)

The OSS was the forerunner of the CIA, where Dulles was Deputy Director, 1953 to 1961.

MARY BANCROFT (October 29, 1903 - January 10, 1997)

Mary Bancroft came from a phenomenally wealthy New England family with roots going back to the early 1600's. Her father, an attorney and journalist, was at one time the publisher of the Wall Street Journal. Mary started attending Smith College in 1922, but, extremely precocious, soon gave it up as boring.

Bancroft eventually married Jean (not "Jacques") Rufenacht, a Swiss banker. This marriage was a disaster, but it brought her to Zürich in 1935, where she became a journalist and free-lance writer. That was where she met her therapist and mentor, Carl Jung, who cured her psychosomatic sneezing fits, which may have been related to the fact that her father committed suicide by inhaling a poisonous gas of his own devising.

In 1942, Mary joined Allen Dulles at the Bern OSS office, working as an analyst, translator, and interrogator. According to OSS records, her nom de guerre was "Mrs. Pestalozzi."

After the war, she divorced, returned to the United States, and lived a very active and colorful life. At seventy five, she was still charming, and a magazine article referred to her as, "one of the world's most fascinating women."

Mary Bancroft wrote a book regarding her OSS work in Switzerland during WWII, *Autobiography of a Spy* (1983). She was not a blonde, but a very Irish brunette, never to be mistaken for someone from either Danzig or the fictitious Mittelbrenn.

CARL GUSTAV JUNG (July 26, 1875 - June 6, 1961)

Carl Jung came from a family of Swiss clergy. His mother was not completely stable, heard voices, and was given to vaporous maundering. She was in a sanatorium briefly early in Jung's life, creating abandonment issues that probably influenced his psychological makeup and his career.

Jung's career was a distinguished one, working with Sigmund Freud and other pioneers in modern psychiatry. As was more common in the early days of psychiatry than now, he was attracted to and formed close relationships with several patients. The negative aspects of such friendships are now widely recognized. Later, Jung was especially close to a colleague, Toni Wolff, and worked with her for many years until his heart attack in 1944.

Jung's wife was Emma Rauschenbach, one of the most wealthy heiresses in Switzerland. Her grandfather, an industrialist, took over IWC™, a foundering watch company, and turned it into the successful horological manufacturer known today as IWC Schaffhausen™. Emma was very intelligent and became an accomplished therapist with a large practice and many publications. Unhappy with Carl Jung's attentions to other women, she tolerated his working with Toni Wolff until his health was in jeopardy after several heart attacks. At that point, Emma drew the line, not for herself, but to protect him.

Jung actually was OSS Agent Number 488. Based on his knowledge and observation of Hitler and Mussolini, he published psychological profiles of Der Führer and Il Duce in *Hearst's International Cosmopolitan* (January 1939), attracting the attention of Allen Dulles at that time. Jung predicted Hitler's actions during the war, right up to and including Der Führer's ultimate suicide. Jung lived to age eighty-six, after a long and eminent career.

Allen Dulles once said: "Nobody will probably ever know how much Professor Jung contributed to the Allied cause during the war . . . His work [must stay] highly classified for the indefinite future." [Bair]

Appendix B
Hitler's Third Front

The Holocaust may have ensured an Allied victory.

General details of the Holocaust are well known. Beneath a few "Potemkin Village" showplace camps, there were forced labor camps and death camps. An extensive network of assembly and transit camps supported the latter. Teams of police and SS units gathered Jews, and others, and put them on trucks or trains to the assembly camps.

The exact number of SS, guards, soldiers, Jew hunters, collaborators, and other workers involved in genocidal operations is hard to determine. Key records were destroyed as the Eastern Front collapsed, but estimates go as high as 500,000 [Goldhagen.] In *Mila 18*, Leon Uris mentions a range of 200,000 to 300,000, roughly ten to fifteen divisions.

As a side note, it is estimated that at the start of the war, there were 150,000 "*Mischlings*," half and quarter Jewish men, in the Wehrmacht. Hitler's decree of April 8, 1940, expelled many thousands of those half Jews from service.

It is also known that Hitler diverted not just manpower, but also trains, trucks, gasoline, and other critical resources to serve the Holocaust, especially on the Eastern Front, where his primary objective seems to have been to kill Jews, a disastrous, as well as evil, strategy.

Once the Battle of Britain was won, the outcome of the war was statistically in favor of the Allies. But in late 1944, the OSS intelligence gathering system in Europe was shut down as Allied advances left most of it behind. Just weeks later (6 December, 1944), the Battle of the Bulge began, and German troops forced the Allied lines to retreat near the Ardennes and Luxembourg. It is interesting to consider what might have happened if Germany had had another ten or twenty divisions, with matching resources, to throw into action in the Ardennes region.

Without those losses in manpower, German forces might have captured the depot at Stavelot, where three million gallons of gasoline were stored. According to Peter Caddick-Adams' *Snow and Steel,* Col. Joachim Peiper's unit penetrated within a few hundred meters of the site, the largest military depot in Europe. If Peiper had taken it, the war might have been prolonged for months, or longer.

Worse, a German victory at the Battle of the Bulge might have let them complete their atomic bomb and use it on London or New York. Depending on the relative timing of US and German bombs, the Allies might have had to seek a truce on Germany's Western Front, leaving Hitler free to deal with Russia in the East, all by itself.

But Germany lost the Battle of the Bulge. Men that might have been used there had been either expelled from the Wehrmacht as Mischlings, or diverted to rounding up, transporting, imprisoning, and, ultimately, murdering Jews and other civilians all across Europe. The Holocaust was Germany's Third European Front, a front too many, even for the Great German Reich.

Appendix C
Hitler's "Voice"

There is no doubt that Hitler's Voice was real. It saved his life during WWI and apparently guided him throughout much of his early career and WWII. But what was it? Was it demonic? Some preternatural power? Or is it explicable by known psychology?

There is a concept that may explain the Voice. The Guardienne Hypothesis says that every individual has a semi-autonomous part of the unconscious mind that, in an emergency, takes control of the body. It has a will of its own. It requires some autonomy, because in emergencies there isn't time to ask for permission from the conscious mind. The Guardienne is a necessary and powerful unconscious function of the human brain.

Constant exposure to emergencies will cause the Guardienne to take over additional parts of the brain and become stronger. It recognizes intoxication as an emergency, a state where it can become active, and it enjoys the euphoria of being in control. It can think up excuses to drink, or subtly set up situations likely to result in drinking. When a person drinks, the over-sized Guardienne becomes activated and will drink until the person is intoxicated or unconscious. Once the Guardienne has achieved a certain level of power, there's no going back, and the more powerful it is at the start, the more likely the individual is to become an alcoholic.

Hitler's story herein of how his Voice saved him in the trenches during WWI is partially from *Mein Kampf*. Can the Guardienne explain the Voice? How did Hitler know he was in danger?

Hitler's father was an alcoholic. Hitler had a good chance of inheriting a similar brain with a proclivity for drinking.

It's possible that Hitler's Guardienne heard an explosion

much further up the trenches, followed a minute later by another half as far away. Hitler may not have even been consciously aware of the sounds, but the Guardienne automatically began computing, in the manner of an idiot savant, that the next shell would hit close to him and his friends. Hitler's Voice quickly "spoke" to him, warning him to move away. Hitler obeyed and lived.

What does the Guardienne do?

Faster reflexes, enhanced speed: This is the primary mission of the Guardienne. Seated somewhere in the cerebellum, close to the brain stem, it has much faster reflexes than the frontal lobes, whose signals take a longer path. The Guardienne can help athletes, particularly in contact sports, to perform better.

Crisis strength and agility: We've all heard stories of small people moving heavy objects in an emergency. An example:

Two brothers were burning leaves on a farm and set the barn roof on fire. Minutes later, they found themselves atop the barn, ladling water out of a galvanized tub. They doused the flames and poured the rest of the water out. Then they tried to carry the empty tub back down the ladder. But the tub was too bulky to manage, and they had to toss it to the ground.

They wondered, *How did we get it up the ladder full, when we couldn't get it down the ladder empty?* Neither could remember. They had been under the control of their Guardiennes. Like sleepwalkers (below), they couldn't recall what had happened.

High dream speed: Some dreams, even long, involved ones, often take place in a matter of a few seconds. This time warp may be due to the difference in clock speeds between the conscious and unconscious minds.

Hypnic jerks: When a mechanism is switched from a slow computer to a fast one, there is a momentary upset as the system control feedback loops adjust themselves to the higher signal speed. The higher speed Guardienne may take over some body functions during sleep. As it does so, sudden muscle contractions may result. This is called a hypnic jerk. Sometimes they wake the sleeper up, and they're often accompanied by a dream of falling.

Sleep-walking or somnambulism is a well-known phenomenon. A sleep-walker's conscious mind is not functioning, but the Guardienne is able guide him, or her, around the house or even outside. It has full access to the body's locomotive, visual, and cognitive regions. The conscious self usually has no memory of sleepwalking.

Déjà vu is the sensation that one is re-experiencing an event that happened earlier. It is conceivable that, since the Guardienne operates at a faster speed than the conscious mind, under certain circumstances it stores a memory before the conscious mind can do so. When the conscious mind, lagging behind a few milliseconds, tries to store that event in memory, some part of the memory (perhaps the part that prevents storing the same record multiple times) realizes that the second input is a duplicate and sets off the alarms.

Alcoholic blackouts, where a drunk continues to talk, move, drink, fight, rage, and even drive, are similar to sleep-walking. The drunk is under full control of the Guardienne; his conscious mind has already passed out. Later, the person can remember few or none of those actions, which sometimes include mayhem or murder.

Hypnosis consists of putting the conscious self to sleep, leaving the Guardienne in charge. There are stories of marvelous feats accomplished under hypnosis. These stories may be somewhat embellished, but there are still many unexplained wonders.

Side note: Children's imaginative play involves a hypnotic state. This would also be true of so-called "play therapy." It's well established that hypnotized subjects will often say whatever they sense is desired by the therapist. "Play therapy" is no exception.

Profound feelings of power are often experienced when the Guardienne is in control, probably due to its faster reflexes. We're "in the zone." This is pleasurable, which is a primary factor in addiction, below.

Alcoholism, as explained above. The Guardienne may be related to gambling addiction and to PTSD, as well.

High alcoholism rates in some societies: In a culture involved in constant group-against-group warfare, survival will favor those with the most powerful Guardiennes. In time, evolution will ensure that the entire culture has larger Guardiennes than a peaceful one, and potentially, a higher alcoholism rate. This would seem to apply to Native American culture with a history of constant tribal warfare and alcoholism mortality rates 514 percent higher than the general population. [Source: aspeninstitute.org]

Road rage and unwarranted violence: Since the Guardienne was developed for emergencies, it is not equipped to pay attention to the long-term consequences of its actions. When activated by a near-miss in traffic, it may retain control, resulting in an angry and dangerous vehicular confrontation.

Inability to disengage: Lacking a signal that the emergency is over, the Guardienne will maintain control. A policeman in the grip of his Guardienne may continue to fire his pistol until it's empty. This is not surprising. Every gunshot is another sign of an emergency, which causes the Guardienne to pull the trigger again and again, in a stimulus and response chain reaction..

Denial: Although it's convenient to imagine the Guardienne as located in a particular area of the brain, it appears to have extensive access to other areas. Even with its limited reasoning ability, it can draw on memory and other parts of the brain, and can even intercept and block dangerous (or merely inconvenient or unpleasant) sensory, ocular, and auditory signals before the slower forebrain can receive and act on them.

Summary
The Guardienne concept can explain:
1. Faster reflexes, enhanced speed
2. Crisis strength and agility
3. High dream speed
4. Dreams of falling, hypnic jerks
5. Sleep-walking
6. Déjà vu
7. Alcoholic blackouts
8. Hypnosis
9. Profound, euphoric feelings of power
10. Alcoholism, possibly PTSD.
11. High alcoholism rates in some cultures
12. Road rage and unwarranted violence
13. Inability to disengage once triggered
14. Denial

Appendix D
Book Notes

The first point of diversion between this book and reality occurs just before September 29, 1937. It's assumed herein that it was fellow psychiatrist Mathias Goering (Hermann Goering's cousin), who obtained passes for himself and Carl Jung to attend the military parade during Mussolini's visit to Berlin on that date. It's further assumed that both psychiatrists also attended a reception for *Il Duce* that evening, and that Jung was there briefly introduced to Hitler. Neither assumption is real, as far as anyone knows.

Did Jung actually meet Hitler? Jung told H. R. Knickerbocker in 1939: "I was only a few meters away from the two men and could study them well. In comparison with Mussolini, Hitler made upon me the impression of a sort of scaffolding of wood covered with cloth, an automaton with a mask, like a robot or a mask of a robot. During the whole performance he never laughed; it was as though he were in a bad humor, sulking. He showed no human sign." [*A Life of Jung* (2002) by Ronald Hayman, p. 360.]

Jung never said he met Hitler face-to-face, but he very likely wouldn't have done so if he had. His account of the event was published in Hearst's International Cosmopolitan Magazine, January, 1939, and was what first attracted the attention of Allen Dulles to Carl Jung, in reality.

Although many of the names herein are real, the events are not. The majority of the background material is based on actuality, but, to the best of our knowledge, the major premise is total fiction: Jung never treated Hitler. And if he had, his abhorrence of revealing information gained from a client, no matter how useful to the Allied cause, would have prevented him from cooperating with the OSS. If it were revealed that Jung had ever violated professional secrecy, his career as a therapist would have been all but over.

There were, however, rumors that a Dr. Sauerbruch [not Sauerbrach], a German physician, traveled to Zurich at the behest of the OKW to seek Jung's help in declaring Der Führer insane, so the latter could be removed from office. According to the story, Hitler was deteriorating mentally and drinking heavily. (Hitler was alleged to be a teetotaler, but pie-eyed shots of the Führer taken during his meeting with Mannerheim on June 4, 1942, tell a different story.)

Jung, of course, would not have wanted his name associated with Hitler in any way, so Sauerbruch's trip, if it had happened, would probably have been in vain.

Let no one say that this book is inaccurate. It's based on so many non-facts, that 'inaccurate' hardly describes it. It is not intended as a history of Hitler or Jung or WWII. Most of it is factual, but certain things have been unabashedly altered in the interest of cinematic or literary impact or simplicity. One key simplification: The OSS was created from its predecessor, the Coordinator of Information (COI), on June 13, 1942, but the office at Herrengasse 23 wasn't rented until Dulles moved to Bern for the duration of the war in November, 1942.

The balcony at the Deutscher Hof hotel in Nuremberg wasn't added until after 1931. Hitler used to stand at a window on the second floor. [US notation]

Was Hitler insane? Not until well after 1942. The earliest evidence of insanity may be this: According to Albert Bormann, in May of 1945. Goering urgently wanted all the situation conference notes destroyed. "They must be destroyed immediately," he said, "or the German people will discover that for the last two years [i.e, after May, 1943] they have been led by a madman!" [See Schroeder's memoir as referenced in the Bibliography, herein.]

Hitler's psychological makeup was very unusual, but not in directions that could be considered insane as normally defined. According to those nearest him, he was in touch with reality to the end. His alleged ordering about of no longer extant divisions and talk of secret weapons never completed could be explained by attempts to maintain morale or by firm belief that his previous orders had been carried out. [See *I Was Hitler's Chauffeur* by Erich Kempka] It should be recalled, of course, that Hitler's staff and secretaries were treated kindly by him and never saw his worst side. If they had, they might not have survived to write their memoirs.

His genuine mental problems at the time covered by this book (mid-1942) consisted of a Guilt Complex, malignant narcissism, paraphilia, an Oedipus Complex, a Messiah Complex, amphetamine addiction, self-will run riot, and early onset Parkinson's, a common aftereffect of measles encephalitis. (His younger brother, Edmund, died of the latter, and Hitler was struck with measles at the same time, when he was eleven.) Another effect of measles encephalitis is loss of morality and ambition. After age eleven, Hitler's grades deteriorated markedly, and he was accused of molesting another child. His personality was without doubt shaped by his childhood in the home of a sadistic, alcoholic father and a coddling mother, and this illness may have been another significant factor.

Among other conditions rejected as premises for this work were bipolar disorder, schizophrenia, dissociative identity disorder, syphilis, and the aftereffects of a WWI gassing. Demonic possession has been proposed to explain Hitler's actions, but remains unproven. Some might say his "Voice" was demonic, but my belief is that it was an over-developed "Guardienne," the semi-autonomous part of the brain dedicated to response to emergencies. This would be consistent with his genetic legacy as the son of an alcoholic father, as well as growing up in a home where violence was a daily event. More on the Guardienne hypothesis is found in Appendix C.

Appendix E
Bibliography

Sources quoted or referred to in *Mouth of the Lion:*

Books:
Bair, Deirdre; *Jung: A Biography*, Back Bay Books; Reprint edition (November 9, 2004)
Bancroft, Mary; *Autobiography of a Spy*; William Morrow; 1st edition (1983)
Caddick-Adams, Peter; *Snow and Steel: The Battle of the Bulge*, 1944-45; Oxford University Press; 1st edition (November 28, 2014)
Dulles, Allen; The Secret Surrender; Harper & Row; 1st edition (January 1, 1966)
Goldhagen, Daniel; *Hitler's Willing Executioners;* Vintage (January 28, 1997)
Hanfstaengl, Putzi, and Toland, John; *Hitler: The Memoir of the Nazi Insider Who Turned Against the Führer;* Arcade Publishing; Reprint edition (August 1, 2011)
Hayman, Ronald; *A Life of Jung*; W. W. Norton & Company (2002)
Hitler, Adolf; *Mein Kampf*; Franz Eher Verlag, (1925/26)
Langer, Walter; *The Mind of Adolf Hitler: The Secret Wartime Report;* Basic Books; 1st ed. (September 1972)
 [Ypres incident, P39; via *The Surreal Reich*, J H Tyson]
McGuire, William; *C. G. Jung Speaking;* Princeton University Press, (1987)
Misch, Rochus; *Hitler's Last Witness: The Memoirs of Hitler's Bodyguard*; Frontline Books; 1st edition (September 19, 2014)
Schroeder, Christa; *He Was My Chief: The Memoirs of Adolf Hitler's Secretary;* Frontline Books, (July 1, 2009)
Uris, Leon; *Mila 18*; Bantam; Reissue (December 1, 1983)

Internet Sources: (links may not remain active)

Döllersheim and Strones:
http://www.ww2f.com/information-requests/50794-hitlers-stalins-made-up-town.html
Döllersheim:
http://www.viennareview.net/commentary/commentary-commentary/austrias-dark-spot
Donovan, Bill:
http://www.americainwwii.com/articles/cloak-and-dagger-army-the-oss/
Emil Maurice:
http://www.spartacus.schoolnet.co.uk/GERmaurice.htm
Geli Raubal:
http://www.absoluteastronomy.com/topics/Geli_Raubal
Geli Raubal's murder:
http://www.copperfieldreview.com/non_fiction/Did%20Hitler%20Kill%20Geli%20Raubal.htm
Hitler's alleged Jewish ancestry:
http://www.straightdope.com/columns/read/797/was-hitler-part-jewish
Hitler, astrology:
http://www.astro.com/astro-databank/Hitler,_Adolf
Hitler's family:
http://forum.axishistory.com/viewtopic.php?f=44&t=150325&start=120:
Hitler, Klara:
http://www.historyplace.com/worldwar2/riseofhitler/mother.htm
Hitler's Mannerheim visit:
https://www.youtube.com/watch?v=AlSb4KnxD7Q
Hitler's mind (by Rhawn Joseph, PhD):
http://brainmind.com/Hitler3.html
Hitler's Munich apartment:
http://www.thirdreichruins.com/munich.htm

Hitler's Parkinsonism:
http://medchrome.com/patient/living-with-disease/adolf-hitler-had-parkinsons-disease/
Hitler's rages:
http://century.guardian.co.uk/1940-1949/Story/0,,127827,00.html
Hitler's secretarial staff:
http://cloudworth.com/WW2-articles/hitler-secretaries.html
Hitler's speaking voice recorded in Finland:
http://requiemforaneditor.blogspot.com/2011/01/secret-recording-of-hitlers-natural.html
Hitler's youth:
http://www.life.com/gallery/26992/image/50715936/hitlers-humble-beginnings#index/7
Holocaust:
http://www.simpletoremember.com/articles/a/the_final_solution/
Holocaust:
http://www.jewishvirtuallibrary.org/jsource/holo.html
Jung and hypnotherapy:
http://www.thefreelibrary.com/Dreams%2c+Jung+and+Hypnotherapy.-a065014117
Jung on the Mother Complex:
http://www.nyaap.org/jung-lexicon/m
Jung on the Shadow:
http://www.shadowdance.com/cgjung/cgjung.html
Switzerland, wartime travel to:
https://en.wikipedia.org/wiki/BOAC_Flight_777#KLM_pilots_and_planes
Wehrmacht, Mischling Jews in service:
http://www.jewishmag.com/158mag/hitler_jewish_soldiers/hitler_jewish_soldiers.htm

Dear Reader,

I hope you've enjoyed *In the Mouth of the Lion*. If it has entertained you, I would be grateful if you would post a brief review on Goodreads, or on your bookseller's website, or other website or periodical.

Authors are thrilled by each and every review for their books. Short reviews and blurbs are very welcome! We look forward to reading about what touched you, who your favorite character was, which scenes you liked best, or what you learned.

If you have questions or have found a typo, please email me at JGuentherAuthor@gmail.com. (It helps a lot if you put "Reader Feedback" in the subject line.) My Twitter user handle is @JGuentherAuthor, so please follow me there. See our new website, MouthOfTheLion.com, as well. I look forward to hearing from you.

J Guenther